ST. PATRICK'S DAUGHTER

Also by Margaret Mulvihill

NATURAL SELECTION
LOW OVERHEADS
CHARLOTTE DESPARD (biography)

Sᴛ. Pᴀᴛʀɪᴄᴋ's Dᴀᴜɢʜᴛᴇʀ

Margaret Mulvihill

Hodder & Stoughton
LONDON SYDNEY AUCKLAND

British Library Cataloguing in Publication Data

Mulvihill, Margaret
  St. Patrick's Daughter
  I. Title
  823.914 [F]

  ISBN 0-340-57938-2

First published in Great Britain by Hodder and Stoughton Ltd 1993

Published by Hodder and Stoughton,
a division of Hodder and Stoughton Ltd,
Mill Road, Dunton Green, Sevenoaks, Kent TN13 2YA
Editorial Office: 47 Bedford Square, London WC1B 3DP

Photoset by Rowland Phototypesetting Ltd,
Bury St Edmunds, Suffolk

Printed in Great Britain by St Edmundsbury Press Ltd,
Bury St Edmunds, Suffolk

Acknowledgements

The lives of the saints are verbatim extracts from the Rev.
S. Baring-Gould's *The Lives of the Saints*, London 1877.

For the extract from St Patrick's *Confession* on page 232
I am indebted to Ludwig Bieler's translation (*The Life and
Legend of St Patrick*, Dublin 1949).

Lyrics from *She Belongs to Me* by Bob Dylan reproduced
by permission of Warner Chappell Music Ltd.

St. Patrick's Daughter

Saint Leudomar

ueen Brunehild is said by the Châlons Breviary to have sent for him one day to her palace, and finding him a tall, good-looking fellow, eyed him with kindling glances and made an observation to him full of warmth. Leudomar drew back and stared at her with icy eyes. So frozen was the glance that when Roger II, Bishop of Châlons, dug up his predecessor, after a lapse of four hundred and fifty years, though all the rest of the body of Leudomar was turned to dust, the glassy eye stared out of the dust heap, with all the cold indignation wherewith it had repulsed Queen Brunehild. The freezing glance seems to have been reserved to one eye.

1

For traitors, my mother was full of sympathy and understanding. We often talked about Delilah, how nervous she was that night as she lay there with her eyes closed, waiting for Samson to drop off. Even though the Philistines were set to pay her, more than Judas Iscariot, Delilah must have felt that shopping Samson was all in the public interest. My mother identified with her anyway. There was nothing mighty or hairy about my father, but still she thought she should have done something similar when she'd had the chance, got out of bed in the middle of the night to brand his chest with a warning for other women: 'This man will be a bitter disappointment to you.' Not that they, the other women, or she, the wife, should have needed such a warning. It was obvious, from the day she met him, that Eugene Murphy wasn't up to much.

He stole books from the shop in Dublin city where she worked as an assistant. One morning her boss, a Mr Foley, put his mug of coffee down on the till and said: 'Maria, you and I know there's a special corner in hell for bookstealers, but do you know something else?'

'No,' said Maria, and she was only being a little bit untruthful.

'Our lanky friend's going to get his reward on Earth.'

Her boss had been making plans. Next time the thief called, Mr Foley was going to challenge him, and at that challenge an already primed policeman was going to step out into the shop from his hiding place in the stock room.

11

Mr Foley was dying to see the look on the apprehended culprit's face, but Maria couldn't share in his excitement. She was inhibited by a strange sympathy for the bookstealer, strange because his thieving was her loss, directly relevant to the weight of her own wretched pay packet. Strange also because she had no sympathy for the thief as a poor lover of learning. Although she liked the smell of new books, Maria herself was generally indifferent to their contents. Surrounded by the latest offerings from every solvent publisher in the English language, she just grazed among the diet paperbacks, counting up the calories of all the foods she was ever likely to eat. In fact it was her lack of intellectuality that had impressed Mr Foley at the interview. She didn't look right for the job: people always said she could have been an air hostess. But Mr Foley reckoned that such an incongruously wholesome-looking assistant would be good for business. Glancing over at her, a Natalie Wood with a Dublin accent, his customers could reassure themselves that books did you no harm.

Having climbed out of love, it was hard for Maria to remember exactly what it was that had made her fall in. There may have been an Oedipal dimension to it: Mr Foley took such a fatherly interest in her welfare that she was almost bound to take a lover he didn't approve of. But that was only a small factor. In the final analysis she had to admit that the main impulse had been physical. Eugene Murphy was certifiably tall, dark and handsome. More crucially, there was something touchingly qualified about his maleness. He was as thinly and finely built as an antelope, and he was very pale. It was his gaunt stalk of a neck that often came into focus when Maria summoned up her first impressions. This pathetic quality was reinforced by the dark, oversized clothes that he wore then, good for the thieving of course, but also adding to the hunted, cold look. She had this urge to warm him up.

*   *   *

Maria knew that he retired to St Stephen's Green to read the stolen books because during her lunch breaks she regularly saw him there, sitting on a bench by the pond. His long legs reached out almost to the far side of the path alongside the bench, so that he often had to shift his focus in order to wind them up for other strollers. On the day of Mr Foley's confidence she went there on spec. If he was lolling in the usual place, she would warn him; if not, fate had it in for him.

Eugene was watching the coots when Maria went to seek him out, and when she sat down beside him he lifted his coat up to make more room for her. She just sat there for a time because she was suddenly gripped by the humiliating realisation that whereas he was already a preoccupation of hers, she was completely unfamiliar to him.

'Excuse me,' she said, and he turned to her with a look of cool but polite attention, 'but I work at the Pedagogues' Corner . . .'

He nodded and said that must be nice for her.

'Well, I just thought I'd let you know that Mr Foley, the owner, is on to you and he's going to have a Garda at the back of the shop on Thursday.'

'Is he now?' That was Eugene's response. There was no anxiety or repentance, let alone gratitude. She had to remark upon the weather several times before he invited her for a coffee.

The table they sat at had just been vacated by an elderly priest who had left fifty pence behind him as a tip for the waitress. Eugene pocketed it and put a ten penny piece down in its place. That was a slithery moment, in terms of Maria's slide into love. It was the waitress, in all probability another poor woman like herself, who had been robbed of the priest's generous tip by Eugene Murphy, but Maria persuaded herself that it was really the Church which had been expropriated.

What she remembered of their conversation was not very scintillating. Apparently he noticed her studying the cakes on the tiered stand in the centre of their table, so she explained that she was working out the calories in each one and told him how a buttered sticky bun is just as fattening as a cream cake. She was impressed when, in spite of the metabolic consequences, he ate two éclairs, so impressed that it was years before she decided to resent the fact that she'd ended up paying the bill. At the time she thought it was great the way he seemed to take everything she said so seriously. Another significant thing about this meeting was his way with his hands. Eugene had hard white hands, with long fingers and chiselled knuckles, the sort of hands you expect artistic, sensitive things of. When he saw that Maria was aroused by these hands, he made it easier for her to admire them by holding them out over the tablecloth, as if it were a keyboard.

On the day of the showdown Eugene Murphy slipped into the book shop in a suspiciously roomy duffel coat to spend the usual amount of time rubbing himself up against the paperbacks in the European drama section. He looked convincingly startled and nervous when Mr Foley pounced upon him, the Garda prematurely at his back, and asked if he could examine the contents of his coat. Eugene calmly removed the duffel coat. Then they all watched Mr Foley feeling through it, as if he half-hoped for a delightful surprise for himself.

Mr Foley squealed as he brought forth a copy of Lorca's *The House of Bernarda Alba*, but Eugene Murphy didn't look at all worried. He reached into the inner lining of the sports jacket he was wearing under the duffel coat, and pulled out the wallet containing a receipt for his purchase of this same book from another shop that morning.

After this defeat Mr Foley went through a personal crisis. The whole business had been a terrible blow to his confidence. But he started to believe in stories about police corruption and he took some consolation from the fact that Eugene Murphy had never insisted on an apology, which, if he were truly innocent, he would have been entitled to. In the meantime, Maria's fear of being spied by Mr Foley when she was arm-in-arm with the bookstealer added piquancy to the romance. Later, when she'd stopped working there, she used to hold on to her great egg of a belly and scurry by the book shop with her head bowed down in shame.

My father wanted to be some kind of artist. As a preliminary to this he worked behind the bar of a pub where poetry readings were held. He sometimes read the poems of the shyer writers, which was generally to the advantage of their work because he looked far more poetic than any of them.

According to my mother this pub was unusually full of wankers, bullshitters and pissartists. (For a long time I thought these were technical terms.) When she grew weary of listening to Eugene reading other men's poetry, she began to look at ways in which he might pursue his vague vocation at someone else's expense. The someone she selected was an American by the name of Jack Fennessy. He'd come to Ireland, land of his forebears, for the horses and the dogs, and at first my mother thought he was just another tweedy bullshitter groping around in the never-ending Celtic Twilight. But she soon found out that Jack Fennessy was a real film director, that very important people regularly paid him good money to exercise his cinematic fantasies and that one of these fantasies concerned Saint Patrick.

From this American's point of view, the Apostle of Ireland had an adventurous, even a sexy career. As a boy, Patricius had been snatched off the British coast by Irish pirates and sold into slavery. For six years he tended sheep for his pagan master, consoling himself on the bare mountainside by saying prayers. In due course, God told him to walk for two hundred miles to where a ship would be waiting to take him back to sense and civilisation. All this happened, but not before Patrick had been bitten by the missionary bug. After a series of setbacks, he returned to Ireland as a Christian evangelist. So many miracles and spectacular conversions later, Patrick

15

had done the trick for the whole island, incidentally ridding it of snakes.

What better way, Jack Fennessy was thinking, to honour his ancestors than to do the definitive film life of Saint Patrick. Even while he was confiding in Maria, the Ancient Order of Hibernians were putting up the money. Jack Fennessy was a feudal, seigneurial sort of film director. He didn't like messing with big stars – he'd had it up to here with them – he preferred horses, and 'unknowns'. Unknowns would swim in shit for the chance to be shouted at by Jack Fennessy and in Ireland, where so many people were unknown, whole communities were willing to act a part.

With a nudge from Maria, Jack Fennessy looked over the bar of this public house and into the paddock where the thoroughbred Eugene was pulling pints. As a gesture to his saintly future, Eugene found a nice new vowel for himself. Saint Patrick was Eugene Morphy. It was okay for my mother, and the newborn me, to stick with the second most common surname in Ireland.

A townland in Mayo became a fifth-century stockade. A boutique in Dublin supplied hundreds of furry bikinis for the females, knee-length, saffron-coloured tunics for the males. Two blacksmiths and any number of grooms mustered the horses, a French dog-handler kept a pack of wolfhounds at bay and the Chieftains composed 'pagan' music. There was a certain amount of national outrage when the set for royal Tara, where Patrick bested the druids with his miracles, was built at Pinewood Studios in London. The whole cast, minus the horses, had to migrate, and the townland in Mayo settled for permanent status as a tourist attraction.

When Tara was up, Maria Murphy packed Saint Patrick Morphy's bags. She might, though she never said, have been hoping that he'd resist, take some sort of initiative against the parting, but Eugene never once protested, not even about leaving me.

*   *   *

16

That was how Mrs Duggan came to have Saint Patrick living in her house in London. Above a mantelpiece littered with bills and recipes she displayed a curling black and white still photograph from the film. Eugene Morphy looked ever so beatific in a flowing woolly cape, leaning on a shepherd's crook and gazing wistfully out over the Irish Sea. My father was always great as a wistful man in black and white.

A week couldn't pass without Mrs Duggan lamenting the dispute between Jack Fennessy and his financiers, which had dogged *Patrick*'s production and frustrated its release. The Ancient Hibernians didn't like what they eventually got to see, a rough cut so steamy it made their eyes sting. Jack Fennessy's Saint Patrick had a thing about chests and nipples, but it wasn't a mother fixation. It derived from one reference in the real Patrick's *Confession*, the point where, on his voyage of escape, he's hard put not to suck the nipples of his saviours. The historians on the pay roll tried to be nonchalant. This incident had a routine context. Some people shake hands, some people rub noses and the ancient Celts sucked each other's tits. But Jack Fennessy ignored them. His Saint Patrick, my father, was an evangelical nuzzler of men, women, horses and dogs, great big wolfhounds.

The Ancient Hibernians said the film was dirty; Jack Fennessy said his conscience as an artist wouldn't allow him to clean it up. But while they were arguing, Eugene and the rest of the cast were paid to stay in character, to keep their hairstyles and their costumes, so that, in the event of a compromise, they could lead the Manhattan St Patrick's Day parade.

It was not to be. After a while Jack Fennessy's Georgian mansion needed a new roof and his fourth wife was wanting alimony, so he had to go back to Hollywood. Ten years later, at the untender age of sixty-eight, he fell off a horse and died on his ranch in Arizona, surrounded by his sorrowing children. The wives all stayed away.

That was the end of *Patrick* and of Mrs Duggan's plan to

17

go to America. She wanted to stand in some exalted spot along the parade route, to watch Eugene cantering by with his golden crozier and the slavering wolfhounds. But her disappointment didn't affect his status in her house. Eugene was always her favourite lodger, a political prisoner among ordinary criminals. He was allowed to keep an electric kettle in his room; his quota of baths was higher than anyone else's; he didn't have to report in for his tea every evening and I was allowed to stay in the spare room for weeks on end.

There were three principal reasons for my father's status in Mrs Duggan's house. First, of course, there was his charisma as the man who had impersonated Saint Patrick. Second, there was the fact that, just a few months before he died, Mrs Duggan's late and unlamented husband, Bill Duggan, had called Eugene Morphy a 'miserable misbegotten pansy'. Third, there was Mrs Duggan's belief that so long as a man was either useful or beautiful, he was entitled to the loving support of at least one woman. Eugene wasn't at all useful but he was certainly beautiful, and he had the loveliest of manners. Just as subsistence peasant communities are proud to support parasitic mystics and priests, so Mrs Duggan felt that it was her privilege to harbour a man like my father.

They lived in Camden Town, on a dark and dirty street where no birds sang. Mrs Duggan's sliver of Hebden Street reeked of the smells of work and thrift – beeswax, bleach and chicken stock – and the women who fancied my father resented it. Just when they were getting close, this stinking, gloomy house seemed to clap itself over him like a tumbler over a dice. In hope of meeting Eugene Morphy these women washed their hair every morning and they bought things they didn't want in shops he was known to frequent. But even when he'd smelled their hair and drunk the wine they'd chilled, he never stayed the whole night long. He went home to Mrs Duggan's.

She pretended great compassion for these importunate women and my own mother got counted as one of them. That was because I came to stay with my father in London whenever my mother in Dublin was fluttering for another man.

Far from compensating herself with more beautiful men or even useful ones, Ma made up for her deprivation by courting political men of conscience. She had her own version of what the matter with Eugene had been. She'd decided that he had no conscience. A conscience was like an organ of the body. You could be born without one, as Eugene Morphy, *née* Murphy, surely was. This lack meant that he couldn't help being amoral. Indeed he was innocent in his own depraved way.

My mother met the sort of men who moved her on Saturday afternoons at exclusive political demonstrations on global issues. Then it was off home for a roasted battery chicken and a bit of intimate class struggle. If a particularly sympathetic Saturday man showed signs of wanting to stay beyond the weekends, she would arrange for me to visit Hebden Street.

Mrs Duggan was not impressed. My mother did not have a proper scientific approach. She was a truly pathetic romantic, a sort of sexual banshee, too good for hell, too bad for heaven and condemned to wander this earth in search of a nice progressive man. But there was no need for me to be contaminated. I was young enough to be saved. Saint Patrick's landlady was even prepared to take on this great work herself.

The mission began on a cold summer morning, soon after the respectable, fully employed lodgers had left the house. My father was still getting his beauty sleep and so Mrs Duggan and I were together in her basement kitchen. Because it had rained heavily during the night each of the lodgers had been given a boiled egg for his breakfast. While she cleared away the dirty dishes I was asked to gather up the gutted eggshells. She spread newspaper on the kitchen table and the sticky shells were decanted on to it.

'Now take the rolling pin, Jacinta, and mash them up, not too finely, mind. No, stop!' She took the pin from me. 'Better just break them up with your fingers. That's a good girl.'

She sat back in her upholstered chair and watched me shredding the sticky shells. 'Tell me, Jacinta, what do you know about Hannibal Barca?'

'He took elephants over the Alps.'

'He did right enough, but do you know that when he was a little boy his daddy took him to a temple where a lamb was slaughtered and sacrificed to one of the gods of Carthage city. And then, d'you know what?'

'What?'

'That's enough shredding, leave them nice and prickly. Then Hannibal's dad got him to put his hand on the slaughtered lamb and swear never to be a friend of Rome's.' She told me this as though it had been an item on the early news. 'I suppose you're wondering what that's got to do with you?'

I was.

'It's only that I've been thinking what a pity it is that I can't be taking you off somewhere so that you could swear not to be expecting very much of men.'

Hoping that my father would soon rouse himself and come downstairs, I mumbled something to the effect that I'd never expect very much of men.

'What's that?'

'I said I don't think I'll ever be terribly interested in men.'

'That's only as well as maybe.' Mrs Duggan hoisted herself up out of the chair and peered out through the grimy kitchen window into the back yard. 'The rain's eased up now. The slugs will be out for a feast.' She turned to fix me with her boiled blue eyes. 'Put the shells in a bowl and we'll go and deal with them.'

In those days I always did as I was told. There was a lot

20

of creaking and heavy breathing as the bolts at each end of the kitchen door were pulled back.

Gutters dripped into this walled back yard, which smelled mysteriously foul. It was a yard with halitosis, about twenty square feet, just big enough for a line of washing, a desolate dog or an al fresco fit. It seemed to me that these London yards were places for demented people to rush out into screaming. Later, as even Mrs Duggan's bit of Hebden Street got gentrified, the yards were used by smokers. Except for a narrow perimeter of clay, her rhubarb bed, Mrs Duggan's yard was paved. She grew the rhubarb for jam and tarts, and it was probably her household's main source of vitamin C.

With an old toasting fork in one hand Mrs Duggan advanced towards her plants. Slowly she bent down to pull back skirts of foliage.

'Now, quickly! I don't want to be bent double any longer than I have to. Make a little wall of shells around the youngest stalks.'

On my knees, I started to build eggshell cairns around the stalks she had exposed. Then, high above me, the flat Duggan voice explained that I was making anti-slug mine-fields. For fear of lacerating themselves on the spiteful debris, slugs would keep well away from the rhubarb. I was still fingering the sticky clay, mounding up my little walls when she got on to my wretchedly optimistic mother's latest adventure.

'So what do you think of this fellah your poor mother's gone off camping with?'

I stayed on my knees. The question confused and embarrassed me.

'What's he like?'

I stood up and saw that the curtains of my father's room had been pulled back. With any luck he'd soon be down to rescue me.

'He's very nice. He can do cartwheels.'

'Is he old or young, rich or poor, dark or fair, or what?'

'Dark. He's from East Timor. Ma says he knows about crop rotation.'

'Does he indeed.' Quite suddenly, Mrs Duggan was diverted by a pair of juicy black slugs, which I had already seen and whose progress towards the eggshells I'd been hoping to observe. They might have been a couple, about to start a family. But just like her Hannibal, Mrs Duggan didn't believe in taking prisoners. She plunged the toasting fork into the ground, spearing a slug on each of its prongs. The oozing, punctured medallions of slug made no sound, and there was no blood, but Mrs Duggan was a monstrous sight as she held up her rusting trident and told me how my mother should know better.

'Isn't that just what she needs, an orphan man who misses his real mammy. I hope you won't be such a fool when you grow up. Get up on that chair now.' I scampered up on to the backless chair against one of the yard's side walls, and she passed the fork to me. 'Chuck them over the wall.'

I couldn't. The dead slugs were so well kebabed that they wouldn't flop off the fork, and I was reluctant to finger them. For a minute I let one hand, with the fork dangling from it, hang over the neighbour's wall. I wanted to turn round and push them into Mrs Duggan's big moon of a face, to tell her there was something she took no account of. Even then I knew it had to do with bodies. For all my mother's talk of morality and political conscience, these orphan men who aroused her had sex appeal. They cleared up the spotty rash she sometimes had on her chin and made her lose pounds, effortlessly.

I said nothing of this. Instead I scraped the prongs clean against the spongy brick on the far side of the wall and then I climbed down off the chair and handed back the toasting fork. My eyes were smarting and my nose was running. Mrs

Duggan had pulled a hanky from her apron pocket when my father, in a ragged silk dressing-gown, picked his way into the greasy yard.

'Ghastly morning, but I can see that you and Jassie are making the most of it.'

Mrs Duggan gave him a most unctuous smile. 'She's been helping me with the rhubarb.'

'Slaughtering slugs,' I yelped.

'Oh yes, well, nature red in tooth and claw.'

'Jacinta thinks I'm a bit hard on them.' Mrs Duggan gently touched the back of my neck but I jerked my head away. 'Come in and get some breakfast, Eugene. We're due for some elevenses anyway, aren't we, Jacinta?'

While he was tucking into a pair of best back rashers, which the other lodgers only got on Sundays, Mrs Duggan urged him to take me to the Natural History Museum.

From that day forward I was allergic to rhubarb, but I didn't keep up any other show of integrity. Treachery can be a mark of maturity. On my next visit to London I was an obliging Delilah among the Philistines, barely in Hebden Street before I was volunteering the critical information.

'He's a beery American who came over first on account of the draft. He plays flamenco guitar in an Italian restaurant in Dawson Street.'

Mrs Duggan was gratified by my obvious distaste. 'Ah, your poor mother! She'll never learn, will she? Students and trade unionists and banjo players, there's too many more where this one's come from. We can only live in hope for her.'

Mrs Duggan didn't see herself in Old Testament terms. Instead she often compared her position as the landlady of an all-male lodging house with that of those French café owners who wined and dined the Gestapo, just so they could be passing on useful information to the Resistance. On this honourably compromised, almost treacherous basis my mother owed her a hearing: 'She'd learn more about men from me in one hour than she'll find out in a year of tangos.' But since my mother wouldn't pay any attention to her, it was up to me to listen and learn.

SAINT VALENTINE

 uch difficulty is caused by the great number of relics of saints called Valentine, commemorated on the same day, but of whose acts nothing is known.

2

A certain Mr Byrne was by far the most useful of Mrs Duggan's last lodgers, but his bedroom bin was regularly filled with takeaway food cartons, which annoyed her because of the implication that he hadn't had quite enough at her table. Also, these empty cartons suggested a heartless self-sufficiency. To encourage marriage, Mrs Duggan thought there should be some strategic limitation, via coupons or whatever, on the sale of cooked food to men like Mr Byrne. She kept a particularly close watch on his comings and goings. Whereas his drooping moustache reminded more conventional people of Lech Walesa's, it only served to set her off about the sad fate of the ancient Irish elk.

This extraordinary animal, the best specimens of which have been found in Ireland, was neither exclusively Irish nor an elk, being in actual fact a giant deer, which ranged as far east as China and which lived during a warm phase between two glacial epochs. Mr Byrne's moustache was likened to the twelve-foot-wide antlers of the males, which were nothing to do with fighting or foraging. Rather, these accessories to the sex appeal of the male giant deer, which is what Mrs Duggan had been told the antlers really were, were their undoing. They got stuck in trees and mud, and they totally unbalanced their vainglorious bearers. Like the picture hats of Edwardian ladies, which required servants to hoist them on, they were a symbol of decadence, a signal for extinction.

It wasn't just Mr Byrne's moustache that got the elk treatment. Whenever he bought any new toys for himself – cars, squash rackets, camera lenses – Mrs Duggan's other ordinary lodger, the less-useful Mr Wilson, had to creep upstairs for fear of being denounced as a redundant elk. The truth was that Mrs Duggan felt guilty about being such a good landlady, keeping these men in such comfort that they had little incentive to be preoccupied by anything more than their visual dominance signals. In the world beyond Hebden Street their birthdays went unremembered and their little habits went unregarded, but Mrs Duggan made batter for Shrove Tuesday and she bought fish on Fridays and even though her household all but emptied for the day itself, she opened Christmas with a dinner which her pseudo-sons did not see the like of during the rest of that festival.

It was only when she began to contemplate her own extinction as a resident landlady that Mrs Duggan thought of doing something to save the elks. Instead of dealing in a conversational currency of births, marriages and funerals, she and her friends more usually traded in miscarriages, divorces, hysterectomies and unpeaceful deaths. But as these soulmates began dying and dispersing, Mrs Duggan decided to build her own ark. She talked of selling her emptied house and of retiring to the townland in Mayo where the sets built for Jack Fennessy's *Patrick* were a tourist attraction. However, she would not, like an irresponsible imperialist, just clear off and leave her lodgers in some post-colonial mess. It would be far more satisfactory if they each found alternative accommodation under the roof of more vigorous females. For hours on end Mrs Duggan sat in her basement kitchen, planning the perfect exodus, and that is how Saint Valentine became relevant. Although she was fond of saints, and Saint Patrick in particular, Mrs Duggan had never had much time for the patron saint of romance before. Valentine had been a very common name in the fourth century, or thereabouts, so there were far too many of them to be taken seriously.

*   *   *

She walked out one February morning and spent good money after bad on a roll of pink cardboard and a bottle of glittery stuff. Having worked out her design – a silver beachball on the outside, and the inscription 'I get a kick out of you' on the inside – she spent two hours making twenty valentine cards. That evening she urged her lodgers to choose some. It was first come first served, and Mr Wilson was the pioneer. Mrs Duggan had already decided that his expression put women off more than anything else about his person or personality which, so far as she could judge, were perfectly nondescript. Confronted by the cards laid out on her table he looked very annoyed, which usually meant that he was embarrassed.

'Sure you can always send one to your mother,' she encouraged him, 'or your sisters. You have sisters, don't you? It's a nice thing to do, and if you don't care to have yourself identified as the sender, no one will be the wiser.'

He took three and Mrs Duggan sighed because she knew he had a mother and two sisters. With Mr Byrne it was only a question of serious orientation. He did very well, too well, out of Eugene's leftover women. She was not reassured about his prospects as someone's husband when he asked for six of her cards and actually took seven. Typically, Mr Byrne complimented Mrs Duggan on her handiwork.

'I'm sure you'll be getting some yourself, Mrs Duggan, there must be gaggles of your admirers worn out with licking envelopes by now.'

He got a pursed smile. 'I'm sure I'd be a lot easier in my mind if you'd set your sights on some woman in particular, Mr Byrne. I'm not getting any younger, and neither are you.'

As for my father, there was no real point in recommending cards to him since, officially, he did have a partner, the artist called Xanthe with whom he ran a secondhand clothes shop. Even so, Mrs Duggan could never stand for waste, so she did suggest that he send one of the remaining valentines to me.

'My dear Mrs Duggan, that might backfire, you know. Apart from the fact that it won't be from who Jacinta's hoping to get one from, I'm not entirely sure that it's sound for a father to send his daughter a valentine . . .'

'Go away, Eugene,' he was the only one she called by his first name, 'go away out of that. What does it matter if she knows you sent it, it's still a sweet thing.'

He shrugged and stared more fixedly at her newspaper. When she wouldn't go away he said that he would, as always, leave everything in her capable hands. If she insisted, *she* could send one to me on his behalf. To make quite sure that I knew its unromantic source, Mrs Duggan enclosed a twenty pound note with the valentine she sent me. Then, partly because she was not satisfied with Xanthe as the spouse of Saint Patrick and partly because she often entertained the possibility that Ma wanted Eugene back, she sent one to my mother.

On the morning of 14th February Mrs Duggan was, as usual, up and about before anyone else. The household's salute from the female world lay on the bristly hall mat, and all but the one addressed to Mr Byrne were for Eugene Morphy. Mrs Duggan scratched her head and snorted. The other men under her roof were not beautiful, but neither were they disfigured or in any way beyond erotic rehabilitation, and both of them had steady jobs. Yet once again it was Eugene Morphy, the gazelle among her elks, who had burdened the postman most.

She took the cards down to her basement lair and when she'd steamed them open she found that only fifty per cent of the Morphy valentines were anonymous. However, two of the signed ones were innocuously collective, being from one of his classes and from the check-out girls at the super-market. Contrary to what she'd expected, the anonymous cards were the most chaste. This was just as well because they were destined for redistribution. Mr Wilson got the

30

most magnificent one, an upholstered pink satin heart, fragrant, and by far and away the most expensive of the bunch.

Mrs Duggan's second-class lodgers, who in times past may have resented the great pile of tributes to my father's amiability on the hall mat, were surprised that year. Mr Wilson looked extremely annoyed, a sign of great emotional turbulence, as he spirited his great valentine away in his coat, and Mr Byrne couldn't resist chuckling over his haul.

'Aren't you glad now you sent some yourself, Mr Byrne?' Mrs Duggan ventured and her spirits lifted when he asked if she minded him giving the house's phone number to a very particular female friend of his.

'Of course, of course,' she said with a new warmth, 'so long as I'm not woken at all hours answering it.'

When Eugene hadn't surfaced by twelve o'clock she gathered up his valentines and tramped to the top of the house to rouse him: 'Eugene, Eugene, wake up now, it's nearly lunchtime.'

He was sitting up in bed, with the sheet folded flat against his waist so that he looked, as he so often looked, like a newly risen Christ thinking about getting out of the tomb. He glanced with irritation at his clock, which had stopped. Mrs Duggan wrenched apart the curtains.

'There's a funny smell in here, Eugene, have you emptied your bin since last week?'

She resented the smell of his coffee beans. He sniffed loudly and said that he himself could smell nothing offensive. 'And since I'm the only person likely to suffer from any ill odour, I think I'm entitled to leave it at that.'

She changed the subject by unloading the valentines she'd left to him from the big pocket of her costermonger's apron.

'I wouldn't like to know what you've done to inspire this load of rubbish.'

While he was squinting at his haul she deadheaded the external layers of his noticeboard, pulling away some of the last year's valentines.

31

'Why is it, do you think, that women are so sentimental?' he murmured, but she didn't answer him. Instead, she marched over to the door and, holding it ajar so that the draught got him in his marble chest, she said: 'Before you go out I'd like you to take the bins round the back and then you can put a fiver on Galway Lassie for me in the two o'clock at Ascot. I'll leave the paper in the hall.'

After years of success in inventing lovers for herself my mother was left with nothing more than a messy address book. Sometimes in the evenings, after watching the soaps, we'd have feasts of consolation together, a thousand calories per head: cider, chocolate and crisps (salt and vinegar flavour for me, cheese and onion for her). Then with our salty hands we'd rifle through the address book and think aloud about all the places where there was hospitality owing to us: Kenya and East Timor, Iraq, Mexico and Philadelphia. Often, Ma would get a little bit maudlin and grab the book off me. Then clutching it to her breast she'd announce herself as a sincere person of few regrets. 'There's been precious little geography in my life, but I've surely had a lot of history.'

As I grew conscious of the permanent quilt of unpaid bills on our hall table I had a few regrets of my own. At first I tried to set her a good example: while the hairy lefties were eating us out of house and home, I was collaborating with the sons of petty capitalists. But if she took any notice, it didn't show. Then, soon after I'd sat for my school Leaving Certificate, I came down with glandular fever. Our doctor suggested to my mother that my susceptibility to the virus could have owed something to anxiety, 'about the future perhaps, Mrs Murphy?' and I was provided with a great new opportunity for emotional blackmail.

I didn't use it until I was at the stage where I could ail in style on the sitting-room sofa. As usual, Ma was on the floor with a tumbler of vintage cider and the address book between her legs.

'Be nice if you could convalesce in one of these places, wouldn't it?'

'Fat chance.'

She sighed. 'Still, no harm done, was there, Jacinta?'

'Maybe not, but not much good either. There's me to think of too, you know. I'll never get into the boorjwazee until you get an ordinary man with a nice car and a few credit cards.'

'Oh my God! Just like Saint Patrick. Salt and vinegar, how are you! No capacity for joy.' She went off up to her bath in a hump and as she lay there she noticed that several more of her pubic hairs were grey. When she heard me on the landing she called out. 'My pubic hair's going grey, Jacinta. D'you know what we're supposed to do about that?' She thought I might know something because I'd been filleting glossy magazines for the previous month, but I ignored her and so she had to let the water go cold working out how to get hold of a solvent car-owner. Next morning she had a plan worthy of Mrs Duggan or Hannibal Barca, whose greatest victories owed more to guile than they did to military might.

By the time the home-made Duggan valentines with the London postmarks had arrived, my mother could sneer with confidence.

'Meddling heifer! What does she think I'd be wanting with the samples she keeps under her rotten roof?'

Straightaway, she started a list on the back of Mrs Duggan's glittering card. My mother made her lists like other people say their prayers. She listed the things she liked, the things she needed, and the pros and cons of each endeavour. I probably began as a list. The address book was a kind of list, a retrospective catalogue of men. Now Ma was listing the virtues of a Mr Thomas Broderick, from whom, earlier on that same morning, she had received a dozen pink roses. His name and his telephone number had found their way into the address book, but these particulars, unlike those of most of the other men in it, were under 'B' for Broderick, rather than 'T' for Thomas. For the first time in her life, Ma was proceeding with caution. Without knowing it, Thomas Broderick had already sailed through a preliminary screening with flying colours. Indeed it was yet another indication of his eligibility as a chauffeur and a holiday-winner that he had been carefully unanonymous about these pricey valentine flowers.

Every weekday morning, after an epic bus ride into the city centre, Ma staggered into the medical records department of the hospital where she worked. Her old-fashioned, artisanal job gave full rein to the listing instinct. She was the RIP clerk, in charge of the files of patients who were dead or dying and therefore not worthy of inclusion in the computer records. Her office window overlooked the hospital's staff car park. The Great Plan had begun with geraniums, which she had bought and planted in a box on the outside sill of this window. Their maintenance gave her opportunities for studying the car-owners' form.

Few women could afford to drive to work and the men doing the worst-paid jobs tended to live locally, so the drivers who parked under Ma's window were the best-paid workers in the hospital. She soon noticed that Thomas Broderick brought sandwiches in for his lunch, a sign of sense and thrift, and that his car was brand new. Moreover, he arrived every morning at exactly the same time, and departed with equal punctuality. These habits appealed to the new realist in my mother. In November, when the geraniums needed to be taken in, she had leaned out the window to engage his attention with a smile. He was a chemist working in the lab, in charge of pregnancy and ante-natal tests.

'Isn't that interesting? You handle life and I'm in charge of the dead, the RIP files.'

He agreed with her and so she delayed her departures from the office so that she could emerge when he was getting into his gleaming car. It was not long before she was in that seductive car, being delivered first to a more convenient bus stop and then all the way out to our doorstep in Dundrum.

Just before Christmas, things had got to the stage where I was having to defrost my own dinner.

Whereas my father was still blessed with the hopping, rapid gait of a younger man, Thomas Broderick's outer form was as blunt as his way of talking. Fairytale suitors have to drink cellars full of wine or fight dragons, but his test was rigorously mundane. It derived from what my mother thought of as her only serious vice, a habit of buying outlandish shoes that were too small for her. I was forever pulling her out of shoe shops. She couldn't pass one without going in to see what was on offer. It took willpower not to try anything on, and superhuman self-control not to buy anything. Shoes were so beautiful before the weather and human feet got at them. They were a small way of changing your life.

As soon as she was home she was disappointed: if the shoes were not, as they usually were, too small, they were hopelessly impractical. As their curator I classified them by their potential functions: my mother's shoes were either killer-heeled weapons or flat and porous vessels. She was distraught when my feet matched hers so that there was no possibility of pawning the vessels off on me. Sometimes I went back to the shop to beg for a refund, but since the shoes were usually bought in sales and there was seldom anything intrinsically wrong with them, apart from the size, I never got cash.

One thing Eugene had been good for was cash refunds. He'd had a way of approaching shoe-shop managers with a tale of his poor wife's distraction over a purchase which the household could no longer afford, and he would walk out of the shop, to Ma waiting round the corner, clutching the money. After he left, the shoes took over the house. They were on the stairs and above the wardrobe, in boxes under beds and in sacks in the cloakroom.

In the January sales Ma selected the most improbable pair of shoes she had ever bought: yellow wet-look gladiator boots. The plan nearly backfired when Thomas Broderick expressed a great liking for these shoes – he was certainly connubial – but Ma burst into tears and said that even if he liked them, she didn't any more and she wanted the money back. Thomas Broderick was well able for this suburban grail. He picked up those shoes, leaped into his Ford Sierra and returned within half an hour with four crisp five pound notes. My estimation of him shot up when, after helping to unload Saturday shopping from his car, I saw those yellow boots nestling with the washing powder and the toilet rolls.

He had no reason to be worried about this sighting. I was hoping as much as he was that Ma's shoe thing would stop if she continued to enjoy his company during weekend retail hours. In the meantime his supposed way with shoe-shop managers earned him an introduction to my mother's Amnesty friends and after the valentine roses he got a seat on our sofa while she read aloud to him from brochures about holidays in the sun.

It remained for Ma to ascertain whether her shoe-returner snored, a habit for which Mrs Duggan would have agreed there was no cure. It was at this stage of an unusually staggered courtship that she decided it would be a good idea for me to finish the glandular convalescence under Mrs Duggan's roof.

SAINT MARTIAN

fter a lapse of six years in this solitude, one stormy day a vessel was wrecked near his islet, and a girl, who was one of the passengers, managed to save herself upon the rock of Martian. The hermit was placed in a sore predicament: he had no wish for the society of the young damsel in his place of retreat, and yet he had no power to drive her from her refuge. He therefore said to her, 'My daughter, we must not both live here together. In two months a ship will touch on this island to bring me what is needful for my support. Till then there is bread and water in my cave. Take it, and live here; when the ship arrives, tell the captain how you came here, and he will take you on board and convey you to the mainland.' Then he flung himself into the sea and swam ashore. For two years he wandered without finding a home, but at last died at Athens.

3

It was hard for me to picture my mother and father sitting
peaceably at the same table, harder still to see them having
anything like a decent row. He was inhumanly polite, never
rising to her vehemence, so she saved her sanity and money
by picking up the telephone without dialling any number and
blasting away at him. Sometimes I imagined that their incom-
patibility had made for a passionate affair, and I had fantasies
about an equally explosive reconciliation. Being my mother's
daughter, I made encouraging lists of the things they had in
common:

Dogs, pressure cookers and microwaves made them
   nervous.
They preferred old-fashioned clocks, watches and tele-
   phones.
They liked baths rather than showers.
They took the scallions out of green salads.
Neither of them could drive a car.

There wasn't much to go on. By the time of Thomas Broderick's cash refund I was the only connection between my
mother and my father, and if he had any objections to me
staying in London he didn't voice them. He said he was
pleased to see me, delighted I'm sure, and hadn't the glandular fever done wonders for my figure? I was, how could he
put it, less of a pudding and more of a cake.

However, there was the question of my upkeep. Eugene's

basket of mealtickets – recycling old clothes through the shop, modelling for the life-drawers at various local colleges and backing horses for Mrs Duggan – didn't leave much of a surplus for dependent daughters. He rose to the occasion by finding me a job in an apology of a nightclub called the Joint.

The Joint was housed within an old cinema building and it was so unfashionable, it was almost interestingly anti-fashionable. Once upon a time the patrons had necked in plush back seats, but now they were free to indulge in stand-up masturbation on a beery dancefloor. In compensation, the very strictest propriety was observed among their coats.

The ladies' and the gentlemen's cloakrooms had separate counters, enclosed by arched niches. Night after night I sat in my feminine niche, waiting and watching. Females got dayglo pink tickets in exchange for what they handed over, males dayglo yellow ones. I took the money, gave them half a ticket back and pinned the other half to their outdoor clothes. Because the Joint was popular for its 1970s nostalgia evenings, I got a fearful lot of shawls and stiff fur coats. I developed a knack for knotting the shawls around hangers, but the bullet-proof, patchouli-rancid coats fairly flattened me. Lloyd, my partner in the male niche, didn't have as many hides to shift, so he was often let out of his cloakroom to collect glasses for the bar staff. That left me alone for the fallow part of the night, when the coats were harvested and no one was interested in retrieving them. But I had a book with me. Mrs Duggan said a lady should never be without her book. Apart from recommending that lady, as such, a book might have very practical applications.

'Were you to find yourself in a situation, Jacinta, where for the want of a lift home one night you got into the back of a car with a number of young men . . .'

'Yes? Do I start reading aloud or something?'

'Now don't be impertinent. You might have to sit on one of them and in that case you could produce your book and place that between your own person and the young man's lap.'

Mrs Duggan was not meaning to be funny. Ever since she'd found out about her namesake she'd been cultivating her 'realistic', or grim and deadly, habit of mind.

By the time she was born, babies were casual events for Mrs Duggan's prolific parents. Nonchalantly they had glanced up at a liturgical calendar, noted that it was 15th May and named her Dymphna after the virgin martyr whose feast day that was. It was some consolation to me, only daughter of a casual father, that this poor Dymphna suffered martyrdom at the hands of an excessively loving one, a deranged Irish kinglet who followed her to Flanders and axed her to death. But what upset the youthful Mrs Duggan was Saint Dymphna's status as a patron of the insane in general and violent lunatics in particular.

'And do you know why that is, Jacinta?'

'I can't imagine.'

'It's because the farmers near her shrine took pilgrim lodgers in return for cheap labour in their fields and, of course, they got the most value out of the lustiest lunatics.'

'That's disgusting.' I was thinking how this story would appeal to my mother and what a shame it was that circumstances had ruled out a more direct and friendly contact between her and Mrs Duggan.

'That's not the only disgusting thing you're going to hear. But you can just imagine how I felt when I found out I'd been named after a racket for exploiting the mentally handicapped.'

Mrs Duggan got this kind of information from her *Lives of the Saints*, a volume of which she tried to lumber me with whenever I went out at night: the average modern paperback is not very useful as a chastity board. The other thing that she insisted I had about my person, in a polythene freezer bag, was a pre-worn pair of Mr Byrne's socks. His powerful feet, a source of great embarrassment to him, provided me with a very ecological weapon of self-defence. Friend or foe,

41

after one whiff of them, would shoot off like a bat out of hell.

I didn't have any heavy-duty *Lives* on me the night I met Hector, but Mrs Duggan would have been satisfied because I had another book. It was Bishop Asser's biography of Alfred the Great. I'd found it in Xanthe and Eugene's shop and it probably dated from his hope of some audition. It was only a paperback, but it had some physical value as the chunky fan behind which I could hide when I didn't want to notice people coming up to hassle me for things they'd left in their coat pockets.

When I tired of the tireless Alfred, I watched the dance-floor. To the music of Slade or, as bad, Elton John, the girls did formation cruising. They came in groups, they never stood directly under the lights and they kept moving. By contrast, the boys stuck to the same stations, as near to the bar and as far from the speakers as possible. Certain birds, robins, for example, operate like this. The male picks his territory and hangs about until females wander into it. Seriously predatory girls did a little nonchalant dancing from time to time, just enough to display the bits of their bodies they weren't disappointed by. It was obvious that the wild things, the ones who went in for hip-wiggling, hair-lacerating rites of spring under the disc jockey's box, had given up on the boys. But they looked as if they were enjoying themselves and until I became a believer I wanted to lose myself among them.

I was Saint Barbara in her tower until about two o'clock every night, at which stage I could begin to enjoy a less pathetic fantasy. When the music stopped I came into my own as the callously businesslike angel who sorts out sinners when they line up for the Last Judgement. The boys had jeans on, with plenty of pockets, so they seldom lost their tickets, but the girls, who stuffed theirs into their shoes and their underwear, were not so reliable. I stood there, stony faced, while they worked dayglo pink bits of pulp up from their feet to the tops of their tights and then I'd try to match sweaty, barely decipherable tickets with descriptions of the clothes they thought they'd arrived in. I could find a lot of the stuff by association. If a girl with a maroon fake fur had an illegible, wet ticket, at least her friend's brushed denim number would be near hers so I could locate it that way. Me and Lloyd worked together when the lights came on because we had to. People who had been strangers when they'd first arrived would collect their coats and leave in pairs.

The out and out sinners, the ones who had lost their tickets altogether, had to wait until the very end when, all going well, the cloakroom would be virtually empty. At this stage, during my second week, I ran into trouble. A man had come for his girlfriend's pink leather jacket, but he had no ticket for it because he said she'd left before him, feeling sick. I had no pink leather behind me, and he had one leg over my counter when Hector, the security manager, came to my rescue. With a matching menace, he told this man to come back the following day. If a pink leather blazer had been found on the premises by then, and if its ticket's holder collected it, that would be fine. If not, and he reckoned not he later told me, that was it. The Management were very sorry but that was all they could do.

It was when I saw Hector's face that I became a believer. He just looked over at me and said that I shouldn't hesitate to call him in the event of further difficulties. His brown-black eyes were hypnotically intimidating. It wasn't that he stared, or wore contact lenses. It was something to do with immense ocular cavities, which, unlike my father's eyes, refused to register changes of expression by becoming wider or narrower.

This Archangel Hector was not much older than me, twenty-two or so at the most, but because of his authority at the Joint he seemed older than that. As staff we were issued with large white tee-shirts emblazoned with 'THE JOINT' in big black letters, but Hector's tee-shirt was of a superior quality, whiter and thicker than anyone else's.

43

Because of these tee-shirts it was impossible for me to dance discreetly during my break. But after I'd bathed in the shaft of Hector's first half-smile the tee-shirt that made a moving target of me was no inhibition. I usually waited until, courtesy of the disc jockey's break, we got a blast of the twelve-bar blues. Then I waded out into the centre of the floor and danced as if a plate fit for the Baptist's head was being dusted behind the bar. If Hector's earliest effect could have been reduced to geometry it would have been the line between his steady eyes and my weak blue ones across that dancefloor. He often stood, with his arms folded across the lettering on his tee-shirt, right beside the speakers, and I was sure he took particular notice of me. But it's possible he didn't because I frequently imagined the eyes on me even when Hector was nowhere in the vicinity.

I was bold and shy at the same time. I developed a very rapt way of dealing with cloakroom affairs, for fear that I'd meet those eyes head-on if I looked up from my proper business. *Alfred the Great* came in very handy when no one was waving tickets at me and it provided me with the first occasion of a more personal conversation. I had just got to the wedding feast where Alfred was smitten by a terrible attack of haemorrhoids when Hector came sidling up to my niche.

'You're new? Jessica?'

'Jacinta.'

'Jacinta?' He wasn't completely convinced, but still his face made something very like a smile and he craned his neck to see the title of my book. 'You studyin'?'

'Not really, I'm just trying to learn more about the Anglo-Saxon psyche, so I thought I'd start at the beginning.'

This lie was inspired since the swarthy Hector was no Anglo-Saxon. He would appreciate my curiosity. Sure enough, he muttered something about Alfred burning the cakes and I said I'd tell him all about that some time. Then, without saying anything else, he stole away, from side to

44

side, in his white leather sneakers. Unlike my father's, Hector's manners were not at all lovely, but because he dispensed with routine hallos and goodbyes his comings and goings had a magical, apparitional effect on me. That's why I imagined him to be about when he was nowhere near. Not that there was anything traditionally spectral about him. He was a broad, dark and petulant case rather than a tall, dark and handsome one. His arms were disproportionately long and he walked on the outer rim of his soles. Such pigeon-toedness was a sign of strength, Mrs Duggan had once told me. Good footballers could be picked young on account of the natural tendency of athletic people to turn their feet in.

Hector sponsored my study of King Alfred by recommending the lost property room as a place of quiet retreat. With a dignified mateyness I thanked him for this suggestion, only to spend break after break there in a state of erotic paralysis. I imagined him opening the door, slipping inside and then locking it behind him with the key which he alone possessed. My break only lasted for twenty minutes and so far as I could tell his job didn't allow him any time off, but I was still able to see us rolling around the unclaimed coats and umbrellas. Every night, every hour, I made the same calculations. When I felt optimistic I was sure that Hector had offered to share his little hide-out with me for tantalisingly obvious reasons; when I felt pessimistic I decided that he just couldn't bear the sight of me limbering up with the Stravinsky girls on the dancefloor.

I didn't dare confide in anyone, certainly not Mrs Duggan. Give her an arm, she'd take the legs as well, and I hadn't as much as one of Hector's toenails to speculate upon. Besides, I had reasons for believing that, by telephone, she was having a dangerous little *détente* with my mother.

Reason No. 1. Mrs Duggan had started opening the prospectuses and forms which Ma was sending on to me. I couldn't sit on the toilet without being accosted by pictures of bright young people strolling across campus lawns. Mrs Duggan didn't like the Joint job any more than Ma did, but in her opinion a stint of dirty night work would open my eyes to the benefits of an education leading to clean day work.

Reason No. 2. Mrs Duggan was badmouthing poets. She didn't know my sexual curriculum vitae and Ma was in no position to throw stones, but when it came to my chastity neither of them trusted Eugene's interpretation of the *locus parentis* so they'd fudged some sort of consensus.

I'd been warned already about the elks and the orphans lying in wait for impressionable young girls, but now Ma's special villains were getting the Duggan treatment. Male poets are horridly immune to the mundane cares and anxieties of ordinary people, which, of course, is why they're so attractive to so many conscientious women in the first place. They can strike at any time or place. As I was setting off for the Joint, with a nice heavy book and a well-rotted pair of Mr Byrne's socks, Mrs Duggan rattled on about them: 'I don't know if I've told you this before, Jacinta, but a poet's the same or worse bother than an artist. All spirit and no wallet. Expects you to read the bus timetable.'

As far as I knew, Hector was no poet – in fact he was an intermittent sculpture student – so I wasn't infringing any explicit taboo when I continued to imagine how his broad chest and his flanged lips would feel against me. But I did give up on my sessions in the lost property room and I stopped dancing. Instead I made an effort to get to know the other workers and I spent my breaks reading in a cubicle in the least used ladies' lavatory. One night, as I rose to leave my cell, I found it difficult to open the cubicle door. I struggled with the latch again, but as a result of my struggles the door became even more tightly jammed. I stood on the toilet seat to see if I could climb over the top of the door, but I just couldn't do it. Ten minutes after my break was officially over I was still trapped, and because the neon light that advertised this ladies' was out of action there was little hope of rescue.

At first I couldn't believe my predicament. I laughed out loud and remembered the three old ladies who were there from Monday to Saturday. But they had each other for company. It was entirely possible that I'd stay, alone in a toilet, until the cleaners arrived the following morning. There was no point in banging or shouting. Against the bass boom-boom of the faraway dancefloor no one would hear me.

Soon I was very sorry for myself and for all the mean things I'd done recently. I thought of my mother and resolved to please her by calling the Broderick 'Tom' as she'd asked me to. It wasn't fair of me to be so contrary. I'd egged her on when she'd set her sights on him, been extra nice when he'd started ringing. 'Tom' had stuck in my craw because she only ever referred to Eugene as 'him', 'the saint', or 'Eugene Morphy'. Now she was being wifely with Thomas Broderick, pretending that she'd married someone like him, that she'd spent a few decades going to the supermarket on Saturday mornings and playing bridge on Thursday nights.

Thomas Broderick wasn't the only person I found to feel guilty about. I also thought of my father and worried about being a burden on him. It wasn't as if he was used to having responsibilities. Mrs Duggan usually looked after them for him, and thinking about her made me feel more nervous than guilty. Mrs Duggan had long-range ears as well as X-ray vision. I was wondering how much she knew about my inner life when I heard someone coming in to the ladies'.

I kept dead quiet, not so much ecstatic about the possibility of release as embarrassed. It must be like that when ship-wrecked people see their rescuers on the horizon. Instead of screaming with joy they start disentangling their hair and covering their privates. For fear that my rescuer would be frightened away by the voice from within the cubicle I stood on the seat again so that my head poked up over the top. Looking down I saw Hector and as he pulled the tab from a can of lager he said: 'We was wonderin' where you'd got to. Lloyd's doin' 'is nut downstairs.'

47

'That's very reassuring. Nice to know people have been wondering about me while I've been stuck here, saying my last prayers . . .'

''Old it.' He put his lager down and, by standing on the seat of the neighbouring toilet, got his own perspective on my difficulty.

'Maybe you should get some others to help, or a screw-driver. The door's really heavy.' I was so far removed now from the impure thoughts I'd been having about Hector that the possibility of indefinitely sharing a lavatory cubicle with him did not excite me. Nevertheless, he had that sort of congruity in mind, said it had happened before, and that he'd got some other unfortunate girl out by ramming the door from the inside.

'Thanks,' I said when I was on the right side of the cubicle door, 'I'd better relieve Lloyd now.'

'Naw, fuck Lloyd, do 'im good to do a bi'of work for a change. Just relax.'

'Relax! Just like that, relax!'

'You're in a right state, Jacinta.'

'You'd be in a state if you thought you were going to spend the rest of your life in a lavatory.'

'I can think of worse places.' He passed me his can but I spluttered after a slug from it, so that some beer dribbled on my chin. He came nearer and did me a Saint Veronica by wiping my chin with the hem of his beautiful tee-shirt. This gesture could have been meant condescendingly, but I decided to make a tender preliminary of it. I kissed him on his cheek. He put his hand up there as if I'd slapped him, but then he smiled and allowed me to kiss him again on the mouth. I put my hands upon his shoulders to steady myself for about a dozen perfectly executed, perfectly timed, per-fectly reciprocated kisses. Then, blissfully certain that he was aware of me in the same way that I was aware of him, I rolled up his tee-shirt. He kept smiling. I forgot about the signals he had ignored. I had him now. Definitely heterosexual, he was fluttering in front of me like a trapped moth.

I didn't want to let go of him, but when I felt a pound coin in his back pocket I made him use it for the contraceptive dispenser. He held the packet in the palm of his hand and smiled his slow smile. I grinned back. He said he'd see me in the lost-property room in ten minutes. I ran to the cloak-room and told Lloyd I'd been helping a girl who'd fainted in the ladies', and that I had to go and stay with her until her boyfriend got a taxi. Then I tore off to the lost-property room.

He was later than he'd said he'd be. I was in despair and almost total darkness when finally he slipped by the door. There was so little time. I rolled up his tee-shirt and buried my face in his waist. Then he raised me up and we kissed again. I think he said something nice about my breasts. Otherwise, my hands and my mouth moved more than his did. I was so singingly lost, when he entered me, that my lips were pressed lasciviously against the skin of one of my own forearms.

It was too easy, and too silent to be remembered precisely. For example, I couldn't remember what it was he'd said about my breasts. But sometimes, over the next few days, a shot of memory, of his strength and his succulence, would hit me, and then I would have to stand still for a moment, throw back my head and gloat.

After that I didn't mind who knew I was Hector's creature. When the flash of his preciously grudging smile hit me from the far side of the dancefloor, I smiled lingeringly and unmistakably back and then he'd raise his hand in a blessing salute. At work Hector's currency was a packet of mints. Instead of accepting the roll, which he offered me so that I could peel off my own, I insisted that he hand me the individual sweet, and instead of sucking on that I gobbled it up and waited for another. I received these nasty little mints like so many sacred hosts from his square-topped fingers. If I could have,

I would have eaten them from his palm. He always seemed to keep something about him for his pet: pieces of carved apple, chewing-gum pellets, chocolate.

But after a few days, or rather nights, I became less sure that he had been there. And if he had been, who was he? In his own brutish way he was friendly enough, and I was pleased to discover that we had an earthly connection – he knew Xanthe and Eugene's secondhand clothes shop and he had once trawled a jumble sale for them. But still I was frantic for another certain experience. When and where would we meet as lovers again? I was pleased when he asked me for some photographs of myself, not so pleased when he said he wanted to show them to a friend of his.

''E's interested in different types of daugh'ers.'

'Oh yeah?'

'Yeah. 'E's got a portfolio full of colonels' daugh'ers and vicars' daugh'ers. It's amazing, what you can tell, even from mugshots.'

'So where do I fit in?'

He looked embarrassed. 'Dunno 'xactly, maybe actors' daugh'ers.'

'That's not the same thing, not the same as colonels' daughters or vicars' daughters. I mean, you'd have to be more specific, have daughters of successful actors and daughters of failed actors.'

'I thought Euge done all right.'

'Euge! He hasn't had a speaking part in ten years.'

It was truly amazing how that remark shot out of me, but it was the truth. The most charitable investigator of my father's vocation would have had to agree that it was a bit of a non-runner. Like the doe-eyed girls plucked from Neapolitan slums to become starlets, Eugene Morphy got plucked out from behind the bar of a Dublin pub by an American with horse sense. Nobody, none of us anyhow, had seen Jack Fennessy's *Patrick* and since then its star had been in one television commercial.

50

But really I was brutal about Eugene because I resented Hector's interest in him. He said he'd kept one of the pictures I'd given him and that he'd stuck it up in his room. But he never invited me to see how it looked.

SAINT ABRA

hen Hilary heard, in his exile, that a marriage was contrived for his daughter, he was highly incensed. He had conceived the idea of dedicating the young girl to a virginal life. He therefore wrote her a vehement letter, urging her on no account to listen to proposals of marriage, and exalting the state of virginity as that which a Christian maiden ought to cleave to as her highest privilege.

Abra could not well refuse the determination of her father, whom she reverenced as an oracle of God. With the letter he sent her a couple of hymns he had composed, one for the morning, the other for the evening, and he begged her to sing these daily in order that she might have her father constantly in mind. The second of these hymns has been lost, but the first is preserved, and is sung by the Church of Poitiers at Lauds on the festival of Saint Hilary.

On the return of the bishop in 360, he found that the

daughter had acquiesced more or less readily in his decision. But apparently the surrender of the youth she had loved was not without a struggle which affected her health. Hilary found her docile indeed, but languid, probably heart-broken. She died painlessly in his presence shortly after his return, and was followed not long after by her mother.

4

None of the valentine cards, incoming or outgoing, took. Although Mr Byrne appeared to be very absorbed by one of his, it turned out to have been from a married woman, so Mrs Duggan couldn't be pleased. 'It's like fruit,' she confided, 'that sort of rot spreads, and if I don't get Mr Byrne off my hands, how can I be sure of Mr Wilson.'

When Mrs Duggan wasn't sure about something she found things to wash, which is what gave her kitchen the sweet, damp smell that I was rather fond of. Mr Byrne's vexing opportunism set her off on a massive washing harvest so that one morning, when I came down for my breakfast, she was barely visible within a spectacularly dense washing fog. With her back to me, Mrs Duggan moved about like Merlin in his cave, transferring white shirts and net curtains from the washing machine to the clothes horse, mounds of black socks from a plastic basket into the machine. It was a full half hour before she felt ready to tackle the ironing.

The ironing board was always erect. Mrs Duggan's authority as an ironer had earned her good money and an irresponsible husband in the days before polyester shirts. In her opinion there was an automatic connection between these two things – her lucrative prowess as an ironer and the shiftless, drink-all Bill Duggan. It was an Interesting Fact that the best ironers always get the worst husbands.

During previous ironing sessions she had told me about her campaign to empty the house in a civilised fashion. Now, with the Valentine's Day initiative in disarray, she was

55

thinking of other strategies. Already she had studied that morning's edition of the *Camden Advertiser*, a free newspaper that fed Hebden Street's everyday discourse of woe and fear with details of petty crimes that seemed all the more horrible because of their random, local nature: stories about ruthless door-to-door conmen; about schoolteachers being knocked from their bikes by muggers on Hampstead Heath; disabled people having their wheelchairs stolen; children having their pets tortured. I never read this terror sheet if I could help it, but now Mrs Duggan was insisting that I examine the classified advertisement section on the back page. Above the articles for sale there were some exceptionally lonely hearts.

'Just look at them,' she said, stabbing the air with a stout forefinger, 'from sensible women! The *Advertiser*'s cheap to put a notice in, and all of them looking for steady local men.'

Dutifully, I put down my toast and peered at the ads. The advertisers were requesting photos from their respondents.

'Now, I need your help, Jacinta, and I know I can rely on you.'

'My help! I hope you're not putting an ad in about me.'

She stamped hard with her iron, which gave out a ferocious hiss. 'You, my girl, are still of an age when you're best keeping away from the field and . . .'

I was getting a full beam from the boiled blue eyes, but for some reason she thought better of finishing that train of thought. 'The keys are over there, on the mantelpiece. The green one's Mr Byrne's and the red's Mr Wilson's. Hop upstairs and have a root around their rooms. See if you can find me some photographs.'

'But why me, why can't you do it yourself? You've got loads of legit things you could say you had to be doing in their rooms.'

She sighed, an intimidatingly deep sigh. Mrs Duggan had a way of letting people know that whatever awful tragedies were upon their minds, her cross was the heaviest.

'Because, child, I need to be totally sincere for this

56

operation and since it is only too likely that I will come across material that will throw me off-course, it's better for you to do it. Now, run along and do what I say.'

I had no trouble finding a picture of Mr Byrne because he worked for a construction company and one of their old brochures showed him pretending to shave in front of a mirror surrounded by willow-patterned tiles. Mrs Duggan was delighted by this picture because it showed what he looked like before the moustache. I suggested that perhaps Mr Byrne had thought it unflattering, one explanation for the fact that I'd found it underneath a stack of American pornographic magazines. And since Mr Byrne was now inseparable from his antlers, wasn't it unfair to sell him as clean-shaven?

For the selling of Mr Wilson, a junior environmental health officer specialising in refrigeration, I was more motivated. Mrs Duggan was afraid that he was boring but I knew just how fascinating he really was. Every morning he had a little rummage in my toilet bag and he liked to use my towel. But I found nothing in his room: no photographs and no hidden depths, just the apparatus of his public passions, squash and bird-watching. My commander accepted the situation with another sigh. Steady under pressure, she insisted that since Mr Wilson had nothing physical to hide, she had nothing to worry about in recommending him without a photograph. Glancing over the articles for sale, I told her to put her own ads in.

'What about offering Mr Byrne as a walk-in wardrobe?'

Her pipes rattled with a laugh. For Mr Wilson I suggested hydraulic totems, a cistern, or maybe a geyser? But there was no point, I no longer had Mrs Duggan's full attention. Her washing storm had abated; the machine had stopped vibrating and the air was clearing. It was time for elevenses and any other business. First, there was my mother's progress with Mr Broderick, Tom, who now kept his own toothbrush in our tooth mug. He had been invited to put a deposit

on a holiday in Lanzarote, but before this Ma was hoping I
would look into a matter of such indelicacy that I thought it
best to consult Mrs Duggan.

'She wants me to ask Eugene if he'd mind if she told
everyone he was dead.'

'Dead?' Mrs Duggan frowned. 'Wouldn't you think she'd
feel more kindly about him now that she's got herself another
shoe-returner?'

'He has a difficult mother . . .'

'And what's so unusual about that?'

'A difficult, deeply religious mother with money, so, so it
would be very nice if they could get some of it, to open a
little shop, maybe a chemist's. Ma's always fancied a shop.
If my father said it was okay to say he's dead, she and Tom
Broderick could come back from Lanzarote saying they'd
been and gone to Rome to be married.'

'Well,' Mrs Duggan paused so as to summon up her most
oracular voice, 'I'm sure your father would have no objection
to being thought dead by your mother. He's always been very
accommodating. But there's you to consider, isn't there?
Wouldn't life be a little awkward if you were always going off
to visit a ghost?'

'I hadn't thought of that.'

'No, well, it's time you did, and I think Mrs Morphy will
have to find another way of becoming Mrs Broderick, if that's
what she really wants.'

Even though my mother was at last siphoning a very useful
man, Mrs Duggan couldn't be congratulatory. As far as I
could tell, this had something to do with her anxieties about
my father's future. To me she never talked about how he
fitted into her evacuation plans, but she was inclined to think
that she had just borrowed Saint Patrick from us and she
couldn't return him while Thomas Broderick was a compli-
cation.

When it came to Duggan goodwill, of which there was
barely a trickle on this particular mid-morning, Xanthe, my

father's actual girlfriend, wasn't any better off than Ma. Mrs Duggan was miffed because even after five years of intimacy or at least daily contact with him, Xanthe wasn't offering Eugene permanent shelter under her duvet. My father was not at all put out by Xanthe's independence of him, for shamefully obvious reasons, but Mrs Duggan often chose to be insulted on his behalf: 'Oh yes, you're good enough for her shop window, but you're not good enough to share her laundry basket.'

Mrs Duggan made great play of the fact that she and Xanthe had never been formally introduced. This was opportunist of her because she was the first to tell of the mythical pair of Englishmen on the desert island who aren't talking still on account of the fact that they've never been introduced. Xanthe communicated with the house via intermediaries, usually Mr Byrne. She rarely called in person, and if she did she stood in the porch, like a child, waiting for Eugene to come out.

With nothing but sightings and secondhand information to go on, Mrs Duggan had decided that Xanthe wasn't good enough for Saint Patrick. She had her down as a female vagrant. Apart from Xanthe's image, the eagle's nest of silvered black hair, pantomime make-up and acrylic-spattered tracksuits, there was the artistic lifestyle: irregular hours, irregular friends and the compromising patronage of a Mrs Albert Bugler. Whenever Xanthe's name came up, Mrs Duggan growled: 'By their friends ye shall know them.'

At such junctures, experienced Duggan-listeners knew that if they didn't move fast they were in for parables about Mrs Bugler, whose previous incarnations included a stint in *Patrick* as a fifth-century nymphomaniac. To the rest of us, Mrs Bugler was a mature woman, an interior designer who had put a lot of work Xanthe's way. To Mrs Duggan she was still the sloppy knickers who, for the immediate and comfortable gratification of a gross sexual appetite, used to keep a bearskin rug in the back of her Mini.

59

'A bearskin, Mrs Duggan! Surely not a real bearskin?'

'Oh, I don't know, it was a great shaggy thing. It's a mistake to be so literal-minded. That's not the point.' She heaved herself into the massive chair and held out her mug for a reload from the pot. 'Do you know what, Jacinta?'

'What?'

'There was no end to that woman's wiles. When the film was scuppered, probably on account of her low-class carry-on, she started searching for a husband, a rich one. She used to dress herself up in riding gear, jodhpurs and all, even though she'd never been on top of a horse, and wander round Fortnum & Mason's in hope of being mistaken for a country lady by some landed gent.'

It seemed to me that the go-getting Mrs Bugler should have been a woman after Mrs Duggan's own heart but, obviously, I wasn't getting the point. 'I suppose she smelled of horse shit too,' I said, literal-mindedly.

'Of course she didn't. She wouldn't go that far. But I just wonder if that Xanthe's got a horse at all.'

'She's busy with three pictures, it's called a triptych, and it's for Mrs Bugler herself.'

Mrs Duggan sniffed. She didn't mind Eugene working as a nude model for art students. An expert when it came to the form of racing horses, she also respected it in humans and she knew my father to be a well-made man. Jack Fennessy had picked Eugene for reasons she appreciated. In Mrs Duggan's biscuit tin of *Patrick* clippings there was an interview with him in which he spoke about the nature of filmstars: 'There's no mistaking star quality, even in an unknown, when you see it, any more than there's a chance of mistaking the looks of a great horse in the paddock.'

Eugene never made it out of Fennessy's paddock, but he did put some work into the privilege of Mrs Duggan's tolerance. He kept himself clean and decent, and he was blindingly technical about the gymnastic skills required for the poses that interested student artists. He even had her convinced that, for presentation purposes, he needed his beauty sleep. But what his friend Xanthe was currently doing to him, for Bugler gold, was downright sacrilegious. At the crack of her whip, a smiling or half-asleep Eugene climbed in and out of tombs, carried crosses and walked on water. Mrs Duggan had never seen these sketches and paintings but the gregarious Mr Byrne kept her informed about the capers in the studio above the shop.

'It's not right to use the body Our Lord blessed your poor father with like that. It's cheap and downright wasteful, to my way of thinking.'

When I shrugged she gnawed this old bone from another angle.

'It's always been my hope that she'll get bored with that sort of thing.'

'Mrs Duggan! You can't treat a painter's theme as if it's a spring fashion or something. It's not like that.'

'I'm sorry,' she sighed again, lightly this time, 'but I just wish he wouldn't let himself be a party to it.'

'They get money out of it.' It was best to recommend the association on economic grounds, which she usually appreciated.

'If that's a fact, we can only hope that she'll retire with her ill-gotten gains soon, and give him a decent share in them.'

I took advantage of that natural break to leave the kitchen and scuttle treacherously off to the shop. After Duggan seminars I liked wasting time with Eugene and Xanthe.

Their shop was at the corner of the other end of Hebden Street. The opening hours and the name changed according to Xanthe's concentration on the artistic upstairs work. In the year of Hector and Tom Broderick it was called Fin de Siècle.

Fin de Siècle had one thing in common with the shops of the most exclusive designers. To enter it you had to be already possessed of a certain *savoir faire*. Little was visible from the street, both of the windows being obscured by overloaded clothes rails, and the interior was dimly lit. The shop looked as if it were a front for something besides the sale of secondhand clothes, and it was. You could hide there, or find some consolation.

Once they'd squeezed by the rails of faded frocks, saggy trousers and buttonless coats, Fin de Siècle's customers were rewarded by the sight of themselves in a flatteringly inclined full-length mahogany mirror. This free-standing mirror, whose judicious angle was managed by Eugene, was one of the shop's two distinguishing props. The other was the scabby chaise-longue that ran alongside the back rail. Eugene lolled on this couch while the customers groped among experienced clothes and complained. If you had burst pipes, broken veins, racist in-laws, anti-social neighbours, delinquent children and an unemployable husband, you could toddle into Find the Sickle and tell your troubles to the smiler on the couch. If he was really listening, Eugene knew more than any priest or the staff of the Citizens' Advice Bureau. As it was, the poor mothers of Camden weren't worried about the lack of feedback. In fact they often praised Eugene for his discretion. Even though it was one o'clock – shopping time for solvent women with office jobs – Fin de Siècle's closed sign was up. I pushed the door in to see my father, in a baggy white linen suit, standing on a chair. Xanthe, her mouth bristling with pins, was turning up the trousers.

'Ah,' he said, 'just in time, Jassie.' He raised his arms and turned around. 'Just in time to help us decide what we should wear to Bugo's fiftieth birthday party.'

Wearily, I said I thought they'd decided to go as a pair of wild mushrooms. But Xanthe frowned and Eugene told me that decision had been unmade for two reasons: apart from the projected cost, mushroom outfits would not flatter either of them.

'So what do you think, Jassie, of me as Fred Astaire and Xanthe as a wild witch?'

I didn't say what was obvious, that these identities involved minimal outlay, for he would pass as a dancer in the right old suit and Xanthe was a natural witch. Instead I suggested that they could come up with something more original.

'There is no greater sign of immaturity in the artist than the fear of not being original.'

Xanthe removed the pins from her mouth and looked up at him. 'That is good, Eugene, who said that?' As usual, he couldn't remember, but the point was taken. Xanthe agreed to look over the shop's black stock for a witch dress.

Fred Astaire and the witch's hope of the sort of gain that would make a sociological hobby of the shop was within Mrs Bugler's gift. Whatever Mrs Duggan thought about her, Mrs Bugler – 'Bugo' to her Bohemian friends – was a very important person. Her extremely rich husband owned a famous collection of Victorian female nudes and it was believed that her own taste for two-dimensional male bodies had been developed in a spirit of retaliation. Mr Bugler had made his money in catering and his wife dabbled in restaurant décor, ladies' lavatories being her speciality. For Mrs Bugler, Xanthe had done any number of murals and a naked Eugene had been repeatedly expelled from the Garden of Eden.

Although she was a fully paid-up member of ASH, Mrs Bugler allowed Xanthe to smoke in her gorgeous homes. She had even bought her a special ashtray. Xanthe smoked like there was no tomorrow. The cigarettes were probably responsible for her dry-baked voice and her crisp laugh. While my father was making sandwiches, she began to fish for one. She smoked unfiltered cigarettes that came in soft packets, so this took her ages and in the meantime I was riveted by her beautiful hands. They were large, hardworking hands, but with such perfectly long and straight fingers that if you had come upon her rooting through your rubbish, you would never have taken her for a full-time vagrant.

'Mrs Duggan was just asking me when the pictures for Mrs Bugler will be finished?'

63

Xanthe ignored me, which I didn't mind because that was her way of being tactful about an irritating question. Eugene emerged from the back kitchen with the lunch tray to tell her that Mrs Duggan was only worried about his health, there being no heating in the studio above.

'I do not believe this. Mrs Duggan is a philistine. She is not seriously worried about my model's health.'

Eugene shrugged and smiled.

'You will observe,' he had said when I was about to be introduced to Xanthe for the first time, 'how admirably self-defined my friend is. She has the petty but far from ignoble courage to live without reference to anything but her own imagination.'

Like oysters or Guinness, this was a cultivated appreciation. I was only able to decide that I liked Xanthe because, by contrast with some previous girlfriends, she had never tried to clamp Eugene through me. I'd encountered enough would-be stepmothers over the years. Also, Xanthe was refreshingly indifferent to retail prices and calories. She was a remarkably individual individual. As far as I or anyone else knew, she actually hailed from Bolton, and she surely hadn't been christened 'Xanthe', but she spoke with a clipped, guttural accent, like a character in an avant-garde movie.

The next thing she said was: 'Jacinta will help us on Saturday?'

'Yes,' Eugene turned to me, 'you'll stay on, won't you? There's a drag party at the poly and we're expecting an invasion of students, but we'll have to leave early, if we're to catch the four-thirty train.'

'Oh sure, no problem . . .' I tried not to sound too delighted. I didn't want to give away the image of myself and Hector on the *chaise-longue*, which had started flickering at the very first mention of the Bugler party, a serious dusk to dawn affair with live music, fireworks and semi-resident guests.

*   *   *

64

I spent that Saturday morning helping Eugene to sort out the most glamorous old clothes for the drag rail. Then, like little Hannibal in his father's battle tent, I helped Xanthe with her party toilette. She sat on the *chaise-longue* with her black crêpe lap full of ancient cosmetics and I held up the shaving mirror that Eugene kept at Fin de Siècle while she rearranged the boundaries of her features. A Lake Erie of a mouth was painted fuchsia, and thick kohl borders gave the large brown eyes an even fiercer, witch-like stare. As a more certain gesture to the party identity she painted her short and jagged fingernails to match the lips. Unlike my mother's make-up rituals, there was nothing clandestine about Xanthe's performance. She never hid behind car vanity mirrors or lurked in loos. In Mrs Duggan's opinion the brazen, obvious artifice of Xanthe's make-up let down the whole side, that is, the side of all us other females.

Eugene was looking his understated best. With a new severe haircut, which flattered him because of the implication that large quantities of hair had been chopped off, he presented himself as a polite and passable Fred Astaire. But his Morticia was ready before him and while he was still fussing about his necktie she pulled him into a taxi and ordered the driver on to Waterloo Station, from where they were taking a train to the Bugler country house near Dorking. Soon after they left, the students in search of drag costumes began to shamble in.

Mrs Duggan was not expecting me home that night on account of the Joint's shameless exploitation of child labour. I'd told her I was on duty for a special all-nighter at the club.

It wasn't as easy to lure Hector back to Fin de Siècle as I'd been hoping. His response to my first invitation, for a post-Joint coffee, was demoralising. He was frowning at his trainers, refusing to even look at me, until I told him how my folks were only longing to renew their acquaintance with him. Among the art students, 'Xanth and Euge' were five-star wrinklies. Having friends round at two in the morning was just their style and Hector was anxious to please them. After leaving the Joint we called in on an Indian takeaway, and he wanted our order to include Xanthe and Eugene.

'I shouldn't bother about them, Hector. They'll be coming from Mrs Bugler's party, where there'll be lots of food.'

'Oh yeah,' he said, biting his lip in bashful admiration, 'she's havin' a Mardi Gras band.'

But once we were inside Fin de Siècle Hector realised that instead of taking away two curries and two portions of rice, we had four cartons of rice.

'Ah fuck!'

'Don't worry. There's cheese, and bread, and I'll make us some toasted sandwiches. The others must have been held up.'

While I was making up the aphrodisiac sandwiches he turned on the telly. He didn't even say thanks when I produced them, and Humphrey Bogart was getting the brown-black stare. With his glum profile parallel with mine, I drank straight from the bottle of wine, which I'd paid for. While Hector watched Humphrey, Jacinta watched Hector, so near and yet so far.

I started to fear for my health. I was wondering if there'd been any research on this, the debilitating effect of being steamed up for someone day after day, and that someone only interested in food and an old movie he'd probably seen ten times. I'd been going wild thinking about how I was going to eat Hector, to lick him from his ankles to the nape of his neck, to lie his glossy body across mine, like the *Pietà* Jesus, and look into his face. I would have been grateful for the most feeble co-operation with these desires of mine.

But now he was sitting there eating the rest of my sandwich and I had to ask myself, why him? Why was I stuck to the chaise-longue on account of this inanimate hulk? I began to think of Hannibal, and Napoleon. People, my mother, for example, go on about Napoleon's fondness for tall, slender women, not about the fondness that tall, slender women sometimes have for squat and sallow men. Then I remembered Pauline Fourès.

Napoleon was finally convinced of Josephine's infidelity when he was away in Egypt. The worry was that his troops' morale would fall if they thought of their commander as a cuckold, so the junior generals came up with Pauline Fourès, the blonde wife of a young officer. This Pauline was no walkover. She'd disguised herself as a man so as to follow her husband to Egypt, but when Napoleon put his eye on her the husband was sent away on a mission and she was invited to dinner. Halfway through the meal he spilled wine on her dress, and then he rushed her off to his private rooms to clean up the mess. They came back to the dining table, hours later, to the ribald applause of the French High Command.

I snuggled up to Hector and threw my wine all over his tee-shirt.

'Aw shit,' he said, picking at the damp cloth. I didn't say sorry but I helped him to peel it off. Then, instead of allowing me to nestle in his chest, he insisted on dealing with the stain immediately. We were in the kitchen, showering salt and water on it, when the shop bell tinkled.

At first I thought Xanthe was drunk because she was swaying and groaning, with her hands over her eyes, and Eugene said nothing to us as he ushered her through to the back of the shop and off upstairs. He came down within moments to tell me to find a bucket in case she was sick and to search through her usual handbag for some migraine tablets.

Hector set about showing us what a nice boy he could be. First he covered his chest with a sweater from the shop's pound box and then he made coffee for the three of us.

'Poor Xanthe,' Eugene said, 'she hasn't had one like this for months.'

From the other end of the chaise-longue Hector shuddered sympathetically. 'Migraine, that's terrible, that is.'

'What was the party like?' I imagined that booze, superior

cheese and loud music, or a combination of the three, had brought on the attack. Eugene sighed into his coffee. Apparently, Xanthe had eaten a load of mature cheddar. Also, there had been an unfortunate misunderstanding because it wasn't a fancy dress party. Bugo had changed her mind and forgotten to tell them.

'As it was, I passed as a liberal clergyman, but Xanthe was not altogether at ease in the snake-encrusted dress.'

'Aw, that's really shitty.'

'You think so?' Eugene's question was sincere. Strong feelings, strong language, always took him by surprise. He wasn't to understand that Hector's vehemence was only a form of politeness. Now his eyes were roving round the shop, looking for clues to my friend's presumption. With its volume down, the telly was still on and there were crusts on the sandwich plate. Our scene looked as innocent and boring as it had been and, for the moment, Hector was safely stumped. There hadn't, yet, been enough dialogue for him to realise that, as far as Euge and Xanth were concerned, he was an uninvited guest.

'Oh no, Eugene, I don't think it was really shitty. I mean, Xanthe often dresses like that anyway. To anyone who knew her, she was in character, not fancy dress.'

'Yes, quite right, Jassie. It certainly wasn't vindictive, and Bugo can be capricious. We should have checked.' As he said this, Eugene checked his watch, and then Hector stood up.

'Best be goin' now.'

'Righty-ho.' I rushed to open the door for him. He loitered solemnly on the threshold, but it wasn't the build-up to a carnal farewell. Instead, within Eugene's hearing and probably for his benefit, he offered to walk me home.

'Don't be silly, Hector, there's no need. I can run from here to Mrs Duggan's in one breath.' No need to tell him that I was safe as houses. I'd developed some awful immunity. No one, no man anyway, would ever want to touch me.

*　　*　　*

68

On the following Monday I called in on Xanthe. There were buckets of flowers in each corner of the shop, all kinds: gladiolis, roses, tiger lilies, an azalea. A pale and unmade-up Xanthe told me Mrs Bugler had sent them.

'She finds it hard to make up her mind, but she can afford to be confused.'

'Well, she's sorry anyhow.'

'Yes. Bugo is a good friend to her friends.'

'That's nice.' I must have said this with a significant lack of enthusiasm because Xanthe, who wasn't normally very enquiring, about me, anyway, asked me why I was looking so 'sad'.

'I am sad. To tell you the truth, I'm feeling a bit un-requited.'

'That's too bad . . .'

The door tinkled and we were invaded by a severely pregnant woman. 'This street's so bloody long,' she cried out as she hurtled by us and all the flowers. 'I'm caught short after walking the length of it. 'Scuse me.' We heard the loo upstairs flushing, and then she was down again, beached on to the chaise-longue.

'I know it's a bit of a contradiction, Xanth, but get us a drink, will you?' Xanthe went to the kitchen. 'Goodness! Is it little Jacqueline? No one told me you were about. Show us your teeth.'

I bared them at her. It was Sheila, Eyebrows Sheila I called her, on account of dark bushy eyebrows which contrasted with her springy Barbie-blonde hair and which weren't fashionable when she was going out with Eugene. Sheila had been one of the wifely girlfriends. A dental nurse, she'd paid for me to visit an American children's dentist.

Xanthe came back with a glass of apple juice.

'Look at my investment,' Sheila asked her. 'Fifty quid I spent on that girl's teeth, and that was years ago.' Because it was no longer easy for Sheila to manoeuvre herself from the shoulders downwards, I was being addressed by a dis-embodied head. 'So how are you, anyway?'

'She's got the unrequiteds,' Xanthe said.

'A woman's nothing 'til she's been through that, at least once. Mind you,' she patted the shelf of her abdomen, 'I can't believe I was ever interested in romance, if you can believe that, looking at me. I've got my own final solution in here. I'm carrying it very high, so they say.'

'I wouldn't know.' Xanthe's voice was cool but her eyes were smiling.

'That's what I like about you Xanth', you're so unsentimental. Anyhow,' the blonde head swivelled back at me, 'it's only our mothers we can be sure of. Take my advice and forget him, whoever he is, no man's worth it.'

'It's all very well for you to say forget. I wish I could. I can't. It's turning into a religion.'

'But it's all in your head?'

Xanthe agreed with this. 'Each man is your invention. You elected him.'

'She does, better than the rest of us. God, I used to fantasise about driving nails through Mr Morphy's slender wrists, but she actually does it. You don't believe me? Go upstairs and see! She's a tigress, this one, drags her antelope off to the long grass and tears him from limb to limb.'

'Remember Sheila, it's Jacinta's father you're talking about.'

'I know who you're talking about.'

''Course she does. Don't you, Jacqui?'

I asked when the baby was due. It would have been tactless to have asked who the father was. If there was anything worth knowing about him, Eyebrows Sheila would have told us. She'd bought a man's vest, for maternity purposes, and was talking about names for the boy she was expecting when the shop bell tinkled again. It was Eugene.

'Delightful Sheila!' he exclaimed, bending over the *chaise-longue* to take her hand and kiss the back of it. 'And how are you treating life?'

'Oh, I won't go into that.' She flicked the kissed hand

at him and pinkened slightly. 'You wouldn't be interested, anyhow. I know you. I hope you're looking after this daughter of yours.'

'Jacinta? She looks after me!'

Sheila's head swivelled again, in Xanthe's direction. 'I must be wending my weary way, Xanth'. If you don't mind, got to nip upstairs again, don't know any other safe houses this side of the Camden Road.'

'Sure. Any time. But you must tell us when the baby is born.'

'Oh, you'll hear the roaring and screaming,' Sheila said, putting out a hand so that she could be helped up from the *chaise-longue*. Then Xanthe told Eugene to throw the things on the drag rail into a cardboard box. On a pretext of buying bread for our sandwiches, I followed Sheila out of the shop. I had an urge for some tooth-rotting sweets. Quite suddenly, I was missing Ma and the cheap luxuries we shared together. She understood the comfort of sweetshops. The nearest one also functioned as a newsagent and a stationer. I loitered among deliciously cloying smells, eventually lashing out on a quarter pound of wine gums and an eraser shaped like a taxi.

When Hector's Joint tee-shirt dried it was still stained by red wine, which pleased me because I could hang on to it as a second-order relic. It wasn't a bit of him but it had touched him. Even if I'd felt inclined to return my relic to Hector there wasn't a suitable opportunity.

I still saw him every night. Under the Joint's thundering right-hand speaker we mouthed and shouted friendly banalities at each other. I told him Xanthe had recovered and I had several more of his mints. Once, when he was walking away from me, I reached out to touch the small of his back, but still he had no mercy, and he didn't slow down. Then a dream warned me. I dreamt that I was moving towards him with great difficulty, as though I were treading through water. Just as I got close, he floated away. I began to keep a distance.

71

I was in the neglected ladies' with only *Alfred* for company when a knife fight broke out on the dancefloor. Lloyd told me later that it was so beautifully choreographed, this fight, that some of the punters carried on dancing as if it were that night's special effect. By the time I was back in the cloakroom the police had arrived, and the club closed early. Hector was blamed for the fact that the combatants had got in armed, and I guess he lost his job. I shouldn't think that bothered him very much. When I heard he'd gone to France as a roadie with a rhythm and blues band, I handed in my own tee-shirt. Eugene said it was just as well, that Mrs Duggan had him worried about me doing such a dark and dirty job.

SAINT MACARIUS OF EGYPT

od revealed to Saint Macarius of Egypt that two women in the nearest city excelled him in virtue, in spite of his fasting, his tears and his prayer. He took his staff and left the desert to find them, and lo! they were two homely married women, of whom no one talked, but who were extremely careful not to say spiteful things of their neighbours, who had not the smallest idea that they were saints, and who laboured night and day to make home pleasant to their husbands and children.

5

Xanthe met my father at the last jumble sale she ever went to. After seeing him in action there she stopped spending her Saturday afternoons that way. To get clothes for Fin de Siècle she sent Eugene to the jumble sales on his own.

The good women who collected and organised the old clothes were the same women who stood behind tables in school halls on Saturday afternoons. At five to two, just before the doors opened, they smoothed their aprons and looked around them proudly. The unwanted clothes of their children and their husbands and their neighbours had been mounded up on separate long tables. They had sorted the loot without taking anything very much for themselves and the whole effort was most satisfying if deserving people got the best buys.

But the hall doors burst open for the undeserving, urban vultures with raucous voices and rapier elbows. In a phalanx of over-sized shopping bags these horrid types advanced towards the tables where once engaged they howled with outrage about minor stains and missing buttons.

Eugene was never like that. Although he came early, he had no visible bag and as soon as he was inside the hall he kept well away from the barricades. Instead he sauntered over to the home-made produce table where it was his trick to spend some time admiring the cakes. On the day that Xanthe introduced herself she had first noticed him pointing at a richly glazed fruit cake.

'That's a vintage specimen, a mature fruit cake.'

'How right you are,' the cake lady said. 'You've got taste. It's one of Irene's.'

'Irene?'

'Over there, behind the menswear.' Eugene raised himself to his full height and pretended to peer across the hall.

'How much is she asking for it?'

'A pound. Not even the cost of the ingredients really, and it's a good cause. We're hoping to get a computer for class six.'

'Oh, that's far too little. Let me give you one pound fifty. But, there's just one thing, do you know if there's any butter in it? It's my mother, you see, she's allergic . . .'

'I shouldn't think so. Let me find out for you. Irene, Irene? There's a gentleman here . . .'

Across the hall, hemmed in behind her table, the baker's attention was drawn to my slim, non-combatant father. She eyed him up and pictured him in the cotton shirts that no longer fitted her husband. To hear Eugene's compliments and to tell him her cake's ingredients she had to stand aside from the scrum. Within moments she had invited Eugene to come round to her side of the table. Reverently, he put his cake down. Then he held out his arms until he was staggering under the weight of clothes filched for him from under the eyes of the undeserving.

Just beyond the cake table, Xanthe had been nursing her bruised shins over a paper cup of watered-down orange juice. It was obvious to her that this man knew exactly what he was doing. He knew, for example, that the heavy, labour-intensive cakes were made by the most senior organisers and the most solid citizens, the women in charge of the jumble sale. As Xanthe told me, 'From him I learned that it is through the stomach that men reach women's hearts.'

Not that she ever cooked for Eugene, or any other man. Xanthe concentrated on harnessing his capacity for inspiring the generosity of other women. This gift of his was acknowledged right across the board, even by Ma, who remembered how particularly good he'd been at getting refunds for her dud shoes when the shop managers were female. Like Xanthe, I tried to be a beneficiary. If I'd fancied a trip to Timbuktu Eugene would have found some woman who knew someone who could put me up, or even find me work. After finishing my job at the Joint, it was only a matter of time before I was plugged into the munificence of Mrs Bugler, who knew so many frightfully useful people. At her birthday party, just before Xanthe's migraine attack, Eugene had nobbled a man who was about to stock a new 'Living Viking Museum'. When Mrs Bugler invited the two of us to tea in Dorking this connection was just one of the things that he put on the agenda.

The invitation did not impress Mrs Duggan. 'Tea!' she said scornfully. 'I suppose you know what that'll mean down there. A biscuit if you're lucky.' As far as she was concerned Dorking might have been Outer Mongolia and it was no use explaining that we weren't particularly interested in the food aspect. Nevertheless, just before we left, Eugene stood me in front of the murky hall mirror and called her up from the basement. Since she had already ironed my dress and his shirt, she was unlikely to delay us but he knew that a final inspection would please her.

'Mrs Duggan, I'm about to sell my only child into slavery, so could you please come up and tell me whether she'd be better in heels.'

When a breathless Mrs Duggan appeared to turn me round, I was provided with an inoffensive way of raising a question that had been on my mind ever since I'd found out the facts of life.

'How can I be sure that I have the status he says I have?'

'Status!' Mrs Duggan shrieked. 'Status indeed. I can tell you two things, Jacinta dear. You don't need heels with that little dress, and so far as I know you don't have any brothers or sisters.' That warmed me as little else had since Hector's defection. Mrs Duggan's intelligence system was impeccable.

77

If I'd had any siblings, she would have known their birth weights.

The first response to the fruity doorbell at the end of the gravelled driveway leading to Mrs Bugler's Georgian façade was a chorus of yapping. Our hostess clutched a barrel-shaped fox terrier as she opened the door. Its equally tubby relatives were shooed off by a much younger woman in a velour navy tracksuit. Her breast pocket was embroidered with the words 'Bugler Residence'. Mrs Bugler saw me reading this inscription.

'So much more practical, n'est-ce pas?'

Her first words were addressed to me and the creamy voice that spoke them came from deep within her, like the voice you get when you're trying to suppress a burp. She was a tall, cholesterol blonde, with front teeth that were, in consideration of the diction rather than the ruddy skin tone, nicely hoofish. She was wearing an orange silk jumpsuit and to seize the dog she'd had to place a trowel on the hall table. This made me think that we might have come too early, interrupted her gardening. But once she'd ushered us into the back end of a double drawing-room, Mrs Bugler didn't excuse herself so that she could change. Instead she asked if we'd like our tea immediately, only to ignore my father's 'Yes' as she was beating the sofa upon which the roundy bitch had momentarily settled herself.

Eugene eyed the remaining dog hairs. 'I must get you some glue, the spray-on kind which we use to stop the Christmas tree from moulting. You might apply it to these animals to the benefit of your upholstery.'

'Oh, you are wicked, Eugene.' She pretended to wallop him on the bum. 'Now do behave, or I'll tell this jeune fille exactly why you're so beastly to dogs. He is a dreadful tease, isn't he, Jasmine?'

'Jacinta,' I said, squirming.

Then she sat down, but as soon as we had seated ourselves

she was on her feet again. I don't think she was stationary for more than a moment during our visit. Mrs Albert Bugler was a right Martha, never still, even in the company of Jesus Morphy. She stood up and she sat down. She ruffled her hair and fiddled with her zipper. She clasped and unclasped her hands. She threw her bangled arms round Eugene when he was within groping distance and when he wasn't she massaged the favourite dog.

'Now, dites-moi, Eugene, how's our Xanthe? Did she find her pills and did my flowers arrive?'

'Yes,' he said, 'Xanthe has recovered and the shop still looks like a funeral parlour.'

'Jolly good.'

'Really, what Xanthe needs is a good holiday, but finances being what they are . . .' He sighed, and Mrs Bugler dumped the dog. Her stage directions now told her to get up and walk over to the back window, where there were curtains that could be adjusted. Out of embarrassment, guilt, or a combination of the two feelings, I found myself following her. Below the window there was a meadow of a garden. She said she'd been burying a dog turd out there when we'd arrived, that otherwise gardening was not one of her 'passions'.

'And these days that's une vertu. Ignoring weeds, it's called ecological conservation. So much more convenient?'

'Oh yes, yes,' my father called over, 'and we will have tea, thank you.'

'Goodie! Bertie likes to have his nap after four so if we take tea now he'll join us.'

Eugene said that was all to the better, and he stood over Mrs Bugler as she whistled into a cream-coloured radiophone. Within moments a very ancient, very waxen man in an automated wheelchair was steering himself through the doorway, but as soon as he saw us he went into reverse. We got a wave from one lower arm, a prelate's perfunctory blessing or a feeble gesture of dismissal, and that was that. Mrs Bugler sighed at the favourite dog and decided that we still had a quorum for tea. Eugene and myself sat down again.

As a designer's interior the room that received us was a bit of a let-down. Apart from the faded *Haywain* over a hearth bristling with desiccated flowers, there was no colour. It was a beige desert that smelled of dog and aerosol pine, and the only individual touch was depressingly quantifiable. The layer of comfort in our house in Dublin, yet alone Mrs Duggan's, was thinner and cheaper. Here were cushions piled on to fat and furry sofas, rugs on top of a mowable carpet, velvet curtains flanking a double-glazed window. Even the dogs – at least four of them lolling about like the caliph's force-fed wives – had an insulation value. Their presence gave me a new, innocent perspective on the Mini with the bearskin rug.

For the second time Mrs Bugler read my mind. 'The bour-geoisie,' she said, giving that noun the full benefit of her offensively correct French accent, 'like to see reflections of themselves and their possessions in everything. That's why they like velvet. It keeps the imprint of their derrières long after they have risen. Wouldn't you agree, Eugene?'

Eugene produced an appreciative little laugh. He was so good at pretending to enjoy himself. I tried to match his agreeableness by smiling fixedly. Turning to me, he explained that Bugo's personal taste was very different. 'You should see the London flat, Jacinta, before you make up your mind about anything. Mr Bugler is fond of this house.'

'Yes,' our hostess cried, 'I'm like Persephone in Hades when I'm in Dorking, I'm afraid. Give me Paree or Manhattan any day.'

She said 'give me' as if she were behind a counter and I suppose being bourgeoise in Dorking for a couple of months every year was a small price to pay for the other things she'd got for herself. Indeed, that remark sent her foraging among a shelf of photo albums, and she handed me a volume contain-ing selections from the Bugler Collection, the bulk of which, after a winter in Washington, was currently housed in an Amsterdam warehouse. While I was gawking at photographs

80

of Pre-Raphaelite nymphs, Eugene enquired about the Viking promoter. He'd been doing some research and thought he'd do nicely as a thrall, or slave, lots of whom were Celtic prisoners of war. After all, hadn't he already been a plausible white slave, as the youthful Saint Patrick?

Persephone couldn't have agreed more. 'Oh yes, yes, you were such a wonderful, wonderful slave, so touching. And, yes, yes!' she gasped orgasmically. 'You would make such a terrific thrall, but, *malheureusement*, my Viking friend is talking of . . .' the delicatessen French wouldn't stretch to it, 'of recession.'

Tickling the favourite dog behind its ears, she explained that there was, as yet, no call for live Vikings, that as an economical alternative to real actors the Viking promoter was thinking of recording sound effects to go with latex puppets. Then the tea trolley glided in and she slapped the dog down to free herself for doing the honours.

At that stage I became aware of a warm corpulence behind my back. While I had been surveying the garden one of the animals must have buried itself in my stretch of sofa. By shape and texture it seemed to be another terrier, but I didn't dare look behind me. It was certainly warm, but was it still breathing? Had I killed one of Mrs Bugler's dogs and in so doing destroyed Eugene's hope of further introductions to slavery, Xanthe's chances of being an artist worth investing in, a holiday for the two of them, another little job for me? If the animal were already dead, there was a chance that no one would notice until we had left. But what if it were not so much dead as slowly dying?

'Now do forgive me, Eugene, I can never remember if you take sugar.'

He said he didn't, and then they both looked at me. It was my turn to say something.

'Our landlady,' I blurted out, 'she says people should carry cards with their tea specifications on them, like the ones you carry for being a kidney donor.'

'Your landlady?'

'Yes,' said Eugene, rushing in with the salvage truck, 'Mrs Duggan can be rather eccentric.'

'Ah, Dymphna Duggan!' Mrs Bugler beamed congratulatorily over at us. 'Marvellous lady. I really must see her soon.'

We said nothing to encourage this imperative. By now I was uncomfortably full of tea and biscuits, but I was afraid to enquire about the loo because of what lay behind me. Salvation came with the tracksuited maid who came in to remove the tea trolley. As she was rumbling it out there was a little whimper and, like the lapdog who crawled out from underneath Mary Stuart's skirts after she had been beheaded, a very old terrier began to nuzzle me off the sofa.

'So that's where you've been, you naughty boy!' Mrs Bugler collared the old dog. 'Now this is Fennessy, the elder of my tribe, named for dear Jack.'

'Jack Fennessy?'

'Mais oui, when he died I was feeling sentimental. With the passage of time,' her free arm circled the air, 'one forgets what one suffers for the sake of art.'

'Oh, come now, Bugo, you didn't suffer.'

'Oh, I did, Eugene, we all did. Those prickly bikinis, hours on end, over and over again. Mind you . . .' she stopped for a bit of misty-eye, 'everything is relative.' She heaved the canine Fennessy over so that his grizzled head was level with Eugene's knee. 'Go on, give him a little pat, he can sense your hostility. Dogs are very sensitive, you know. Of course, I've always had a special rapport, but you have never dealt with your feelings, have you, Eugene?'

'With the greatest respect, my dear Bugo,' said Eugene, backing away from Fennessy, 'I hardly think that I should.'

'Oh you should! You should! He's not a wolfhound. Poor Fennessy, poor Eugene!' She looked over at me. 'He had to lie there on the deck, smiling, while wolfhounds salivated all over him. Jack thought it was so erotic.'

'What ship?' For a technical question I was hoping there might be a technical answer.

'Why, the ship that took Patrick out of slavery, in return for sexual favours to the crew, and the dogs. You see, Jacinta, Jack was rather academic . . .'

'Nonsense,' Eugene was standing up, 'there was no historical justification whatsoever for the wolfhounds. It was all a misprint.'

'Please,' I coughed and frightened Fennessy, who wriggled free of his mistress and began to waddle round the room. 'Please explain about the wolfhounds that were eating my father, because if you don't, no one else will.'

'Why, of course. I must get you my scrapbook.' As she rose, Mrs Bugler was forestalled by Eugene.

'No need. She's just being polite. It was a silly, silly business, best forgotten.'

'Well, just tell me about the wolfhounds, then?'

Mrs Bugler started to settle herself for the story, sucking in her cheeks and rolling her eyes, but Eugene wasn't having her version of it. In a low, deadly serious voice, he told me how tradition had it that the ship carrying the young Patrick away from Ireland and out of slavery also carried a cargo of wolfhounds, these beasts being prized exports to the Continent in the fifth century.

'Lovely, just lovely.' Mrs Bugler clapped her hands. 'Just the sort of detail Jack liked.'

'Regardless of the truth!' insisted Eugene. 'If the history didn't fit, Fennessy,' in mentioning that name he had disconcerted the old dog, 'Jack, just fired the historian.'

'It was hilarious, you can't imagine, Jacinta, chaps with beards and corduroy trousers and cardboard folders, all over the set.'

Eugene raised his hand, just like a fifth-century bishop, and Mrs Bugler collared the dog so that he could continue.

'One historian in particular caused great offence, to our

director, and that was because he had the temerity to point out that these wolfhounds are only referred to once in Saint Patrick's own account of the voyage, and this single reference, to *canes*, which is the Latin for dogs,' Mrs Bugler was nodding as if she were hearing evidence in court, 'appears as *carnes*, Latin for flesh, in other versions of the manuscript, so . . .'

'Flesh, dogs, it was all the same to Jack.'

'So,' Eugene continued, 'it was far more probable that Saint Patrick was referring to meat, dead animal . . .'

'Seems like a lot of fuss about very little.'

'Oh, you wouldn't have thought that, chérie, if it meant the difference between eating a bacon sandwich or lying down with wolfhounds.'

'Quite.'

At this stage I thought it politic to interrupt the seminar by enquiring about the loo. When I returned from the bathroom, which was, décor-wise, another monochrome disappointment, a walk through the garden had been decided upon. We put on our jackets and Mrs Bugler, with an arm through Eugene's, dragged us through a hayfeverish field. When she congratulated me on having inherited my father's looks, which, considering my more obvious resemblance to my mother, was tactful of her, he told her that I was looking for a casual, temporary job. I was a bit nervous because of all the slavery talk and because he hadn't made eye contact with me since my landlady remark. But, as he'd been hoping, Mrs Bugler did know 'just the thing'.

Mr Eric Lennox, a sensitive American friend of hers, was allergic to house dust and in urgent need of a conscientious *femme de ménage* for his London base. On account of his business as an 'art consultant', Eric spent much of his time in other cities, relying on her good self to fill the cleaning vacancy. Before dropping us off at the station she would give me the keys to his dear little house in Pimlico.

*   *   *

The trip home was bleak. I decided that I was very corruptible because after the Buglers and their puffy house, the ordinary people on the return train, for the most part grey women with herds of carrier bags, looked dispiritedly mean and poor.

'Right you are, then,' said Eugene, 'one mission accomplished. You'd better buy yourself an overall and open a bank account.'

'Huh, it's not exactly a seat on the board, is it? I was hoping for something a bit more mental. You could have told her I can read and write.'

'Just have a go. There's cleaning and cleaning, and she'll keep an eye out for how you're doing.'

'Yeah, and that's just what I'm in need of, isn't it, a few more women to be keeping an eye on me.'

'There's more to the world than Mrs Duggan's kitchen, you know. It's a chance to broaden your horizons.' Then he tried to close the conversation by picking up the newspaper behind his seat. He was far too pleased with himself for having achieved nothing more than a few compliments on his servility and a cleaning job for his daughter.

'I suppose you're right really. I mean I've never met a real dilettante before.'

He snorted and flexed the newspaper. Then, with clenched teeth and a head held as stiffly as a ventriloquist's dummy, he produced Mrs Bugler's indigestion voice. 'They're not your ancien régime, that's not real decadence, if that's what you're thinking.'

'I don't know what else to make of it. As you know, I'm not au courant with a wide social circle.'

'Poor Jassie, you were old before you were born. You should work on your sense of humour, learn how to have some fun.'

'That's really encouraging. Ma says I'm joyless and you think I'm no fun, just because I try to make sense of your ramshackle lives.'

He sighed and put an arm around me. 'Don't be a silly girl. I'm sure it is hard to figure us all out. Do you know something?'

'What?' I was waiting for an important emotional revelation, but that's not what was coming. He told me Bertie Bugler didn't need a wheelchair for anything more than laziness. The chair was a sort of Trojan horse for him, enabling him to get off planes first and to avoid situations that bored him. I was thinking about the insult to my injury, being considered boring by a voyeuristic old plutocrat, when the woman across from us leaned forward.

'Excuse me, but don't I know you from somewhere?'

I thought she might be a friend of Mrs Duggan's, but Eugene knew better. Relaxed and smiling, he allowed her to inspect him at close quarters.

'I know! You're Cortes, aren't you?'

Ma found Eugene in a book shop, Mrs Bugler and Mrs Duggan met him when he was still Saint Patrick, and Xanthe spied him in a crowded school hall. But this woman before us knew him as Hernando Cortes, conqueror of Mexico.

For about eighteen months Eugene Morphy was the star of an endearingly imperialist television commercial for Miller's Chocolate Ingots. From a magnificent white horse he had surveyed the procession advancing towards him down a wide, water-lined causeway.

First came Montezuma's lords, gorgeously attired, but barefoot. Behind them came the imperial litter with its pallium of green feather cloth. Rich cotton wraps were laid upon the ochre ground. The litter stopped and in sandals of gold Montezuma himself stepped out.

Cortes dismounted and his triangular blue eyes met the emperor's almond-shaped black-brown ones. He walked forward and opened his arms, and Montezuma raised his hands. When Cortes gave the emperor a necklace of beads threaded with gold his courtiers kissed the ground. Then, from the glittering city at the end of the avenue, a messenger came running. He handed Montezuma a packet of Miller's Chocolate Ingots, which the emperor, on foot, gave to the conquistador. At this moment a dark chocolatey voice said: 'Miller's Ingots, the chocolates that inspired a conquest.'

I could remember every detail because this commercial was treasured visual evidence of my absent father. Something about the high budget encounter, or Eugene, had also touched our fellow passenger because even though they gave her migraines she continued to eat Miller's Ingots. Eugene said he was sorry to hear that, and he autographed her cheque book. Then, while they lapsed into a general conversation about how nice the weather was for the time of year, and whether it would last, I thought about Ma's sofa and the Murphy/Morphy stake in Fin de Siècle, both of which derived from the chocolates that inspired a conquest and caused migraines.

When we reached Waterloo our companion handed her heaviest bag to Cortes. Like a bad-tempered terrier, I followed them up the platform.

It wasn't easy to speculate about Mr Eric Lennox's personal life because his London home was a monument to sensory deprivation. Mrs Bugler liked to feel her body's impact all around her, but her friend lived like a ghost. He had paid someone else to turn a five-roomed Victorian cottage in Pimlico into an open-plan laboratory: all white and black and grey, with surfaces of glass, marble and chrome. Even the books were hidden behind flat metal blinds, and the only picture I could see was a wall chart showing various yoga postures for sexual continence.

After a first, superficial patrol I was very cheerful. As far as I was concerned, the place was already immaculate. But when I saw the inside of the cleaning cupboard, the arsenal of aerosols and tins and squeezy things, the two models of vacuum cleaner, the dustbusters, the fittings for researching underneath the bed and above the cornices, the special polish

87

for the bathroom tiles and the telephone cleaning kit, I panicked. Even the cloths were intimidatingly exquisite. Mr Lennox had standards of hygiene I couldn't even imagine, let alone honour. He wanted the place kept so that a forensic scientist wouldn't be able to find evidence of human occupation in it. Along with that idea came thoughts of the crimes to which I might find myself an unwitting accomplice. I sat on the white marble floor of the bathroom and calmed down by reminding myself that Mrs Bugler would hardly have recommended me for anything sinister. Then I went to the kitchen and poured myself a drink of grape juice. Emptying the fridge of all the food and drink left since Mr Lennox's last stay in London was a pleasant responsibility.

Apart from the money, which was paid directly into my own little account, I began to enjoy having this antiseptic den to retreat to. The Lennox place was double wrapped for double protection. From within Mrs Duggan's solid enough house you could still hear the whine of milk floats, the crackle of imperfectly tuned door intercoms and the howls of toddlers bullying their mothers. But the only sound I ever heard in Eric Lennox's cottage was the sound of irritable French and Italian women complaining into his answering machine.

My twice-weekly routine was simple. For each visit I'd take on a new, special task, like washing the skirting boards or polishing the brass taps, in addition to the general dusting I always did on account of his allergy and the fact that it was the first and easiest thing for him to check. Then, when I began to feel tired, I'd turn on the vacuum cleaner, or my radio, and stretch out on the double bed. Under an Egyptian cotton sheet I rinsed myself in the most perfect misery.

When I think of the hours I spent weeping for Hector, hours when I could have been improving my French or making myself beautiful clothes, I feel like Mrs Duggan does about waste. They say you spend a third of your life asleep but I reckon another third of mine has gone on crying. I wasn't holding a candle, I was lurching under a caber for a man I could no longer describe, let alone talk about. I was so frantic to hold on to the precious, evaporating essence of my beloved that I couldn't fix his external form. It was as though I'd been the victim of an assault in the middle of a dark night, so traumatised that I couldn't supply my rescuers with any useful clues as to the attacker's identity. At first I'd hoped for a postcard. When nothing came I had fantasies about a sudden reunion. I'd open Mrs Duggan's door one morning and there he'd be, smirking on the doorstep. But mostly I thought, nothing else will happen and I'll never know what happened.

After the thinking and the crying I'd sleep, sometimes for hours and when I woke up I'd soak in the sunken bath. I justified that part of the routine on the basis that it was the best way of cleaning it. But on one fateful day, as anyone could have predicted, I overslept. I was in my knickers, lying on that bed when, like Goldilocks, I woke up to realise that I'd been found out. The upper, bedroom floor was open-plan and in the far corner I could see Eric Lennox on his exercise bike. Though he was as busy as a hamster on its wheel he must have heard my eyelids lifting because he stopped and looked over at me. I shivered when I realised that I'd been using his gym towels, thick little grey ones, for the dusting, because that's what he was using to mop his brow.

'So I finally get to interview my new cleaning lady? Funny how they're often called Jacinta.'

'It's not that funny.' Poignant was the word I was searching for. He was the first person in months to get my name right, and that was only because of its international association with scrubbers.

'No? I'd say it was a kind of coincidence.'

'I'm afraid it's only an index of the menial status of females born into the One True Holy Catholic and Apostolic Church.'

'I don't get you.' That was to be his catchphrase. I started to put my clothes back on – he didn't seem to notice my

89

nudity – and explained that as far as I knew I'd been named Jacinta to keep my pious and potentially generous granny happy, that the original had been one of the Fatima girls who had seen visions of the Blessed Virgin in the year of the Bolshevik Revolution.

'Now that was a real coincidence. This celestial vision appears to tell the world, through these little children, that they must all pray for the conversion of Communists. I mean there were so many things she could have chosen to make an appearance about . . .'

'Huh, but it's some kind of a plant, right?'

Then, instead of giving me the sack, Eric invited me to dine with him. He had already loaded up the fridge. While I decanted various salads, the sort of things that made Mrs Duggan worry about the future of humanity, he was changing. He came downstairs in a brand new suit – everything he had was new – and we sat down to a classy, multi-cultural feast. Sat down is the word. Although we were both equipped with individual knives and forks and plates, I was the one who cleared the table. While I was eating he raked his beansprouts and put a little bit of cream cheese at the edge of a blade-thin cracker. By the time he'd worked his way through the whole cracker he'd managed to use up more calories than he'd consumed. Then, while he was polishing a pair of bronze-rimmed spectacles, I started to flatter him with curiosity about his important work.

'The answering machine's been busy. Sounds like several women are after you.'

'Uhuh. I'll check it later.'

'Are most of your clients female?'

He put on his glasses and the lenses glinted at me. 'I can be more specific, Jacinta. Most of my clients are widows.'

'Gosh! Is that a cause or an effect?'

'Well, I guess . . . I guess you could say it's a cause. Most of them are the surviving wives of dead, very successful painters.'

I nodded knowingly, as if every shelf in the land had a handbook on it about how to be an art widow.

'So you're a sort of an agent?'

'Uhuh.'

'I suppose Mrs Bugler will need help with Mr Bugler's collection when he dies?'

'She might.'

'She likes art, doesn't she, and artists, of course?'

'Yep. Mrs Bugler likes artists all right.'

'So what do you actually do?' Genuine curiosity had taken over.

'Oh, I handle copyright, reproduction rights, stuff like that.'

'It must be very demanding.' I was thinking about the emotional demands, those aggrieved voices in the answering machine.

'Not really,' he said, shrugging modestly, 'it's just like shuffling cards. Anyone could do it if they knew how.'

That led naturally to my own humble business. Eric was satisfied with my work – he no longer sneezed as soon as he was over his own threshold – but there was one additional thing he thought I might be able to help with. His shirts needed ironing and he didn't have an iron, or a valet. Well, that was no problem. I stuffed them all into a Harrods bag and told him they'd be with the best ironer in north London within a couple of hours.

SAINT PETRONILLA

aint Petronilla is said to have been a daughter of Saint Peter the Apostle. He took her with him to Rome, where she became paralysed, but Simon Magus having asked why, if he could perform miracles, he allowed his daughter to remain infirm, Saint Peter answered that 'It was expedient for her.' Then he added, 'Nevertheless, to show the power of God, she shall rise from her bed and walk.' Then he called her, and she rose, and was restored to her full health.

A certain officer or 'Count' Flaccus having greatly admired her beauty, sent soldiers to her, to ask her to be his wife. She replied sharply, 'If he wants to marry me, let him not send rough soldiers to woo me, but respectable matrons, and give me time to make up my mind.' Whereupon the soldiers withdrew abashed. But before Flaccus had obtained matrons to convey his offer, Petronilla was dead.

6

Mrs Duggan did not like to be taken unawares. When she stepped out over Hebden Street's pavement of half-masticated chips and puréed dog shit she always carried a sugar-pink, beaded handbag. This dainty little thing was like a standard, or a flag of truce: it warned people of her approach. It also worked as a signal of entitlement to archaic courtesies at bus queues and pedestrian crossings.

When Amelia spied that transvestite's bag and its mighty bearer lumbering back from the High Street she hurried up. Amelia was an estate agent's scout and she had identified Mrs Duggan as the last elderly owner-occupier of an entire house in Hebden Street. Most of the other houses had been subdivided into flats.

When Mrs Duggan saw Amelia and her briefcase she hurried up too. Usually, she liked hearing how much her big old house would fetch. After sessions with estate-agency people she could tell us all how good she was to be keeping a full house instead of retiring to Mayo on the proceeds of an emptied one. But she was busy that morning, and she knew already how much the house was worth, so when Amelia stood by her gate Mrs Duggan's horns were lowered.

'Oh, hallo, em, I'm from Bishop & Cullen's Kentish Town office. I'm sure you've heard of us.'

'I have. I've heard more than enough for the time being, thank you.'

'It's an old family firm, established in this area for three generations, and I wonder if you'd like to see our terms for sellers.'

Something about Amelia's body and Amelia's hair saved her from a casual goring because Mrs Duggan stopped and said, 'Well, as it happens, I am thinking about selling, but it's an awful prospect, I can tell you.'

This was music to Amelia's young ears. Recession and depression meant that she wasn't getting very much practice at her job, and, as we found out later, she was only in the property business for the practice. Now she dug into her briefcase, hunting for the literature about how Bishop & Cullen could help with profitable evacuations.

'We can help you,' she assured Mrs Duggan. 'We have a special scheme for looking after all the final bills and forwarding the post. We can cancel the milk and even supervise the transport of your pets.'

'Ah now. Unless you're planning on greasing my stairs . . .'

'I beg your pardon.'

'It wouldn't be easy to shift my pets. You'd need a fully equipped dormobile.'

At this stage in the parley other scouts would have dumped their brochures and run back to their office sanctuaries, but Amelia had mettle. 'Look,' she said in an unhurried, threateningly businesslike fashion, 'I am quite certain we can assist you. I shall leave our literature and we can meet to draw up a moving plan when you have had a look at the options.'

'Oh, that's very kind, very kind indeed, but won't you come in for a cup of tea?' Mrs Duggan took hold of one of Amelia's skinny arms and led her inside to admire the house's original features. This was the beginning of a sordid friendship. Before long it was discovered that whereas Mrs Duggan was burdened by a surplus of men, Amelia was exercised by a scarcity of them.

*   *   *

Mrs Duggan lured Amelia inside because she *looked* as if she could well be of help in dislodging Mr Wilson. Looks were very important. Amelia's growth went into her hair. Even when they were held aloft in a high ponytail, her metabolic, mouse-blonde curls tickled her sharp shoulder blades. This hair made it easy for Mrs Duggan to picture Amelia with the arseless Mr Wilson, whose head was surmounted by equally pubic curls.

Ever since she'd seen a televised debate about the identity of Van Eyck's *Man in a Red Turban,* Mrs Duggan thought it important to be able to have such a picture in her mind's eye. For forty-five minutes an American scholar with interesting spectacles had argued that this painting is a portrait of none other than Van Eyck himself because (a) painters of his day habitually depicted themselves in red turbans and (b) the face is so like that of Mrs Van Eyck. Throughout that programme, Mrs Duggan had sat bolt upright in her big chair. Long an observer of the resemblance between dogs and their owners, she could now blame the slab-like degeneration of her own nose on her husband and call his early death a mercy for her looks.

It was as plain as the freckled tent of a nose on Amelia's face that she needed a narcissistic challenge. A readymade man would be wasted on this girl. She needed a half-fledged one to mould in her own image, and Mr Wilson, didn't I have to agree, was just the job for her. But, I felt obliged to ask, just because it's probable that Van Eyck looked like his wife, did that mean they were happy? Had the physical solidarity anything to do with emotional sympathy? Wasn't it possible that the Van Eycks looked alike to us because they looked like all the fashionable and successful fifteenth-century people?

'I mean to say, whenever Ma's told she's the spit of Natalie Wood she just says that everyone of her age with brown hair gets taken for Natalie Wood at some time or other. It's just whatever you call it, the spirit of the age.'

'Never mind about that. I'm not worrying about Mr

97

Wilson's happiness, or Amelia's for that matter. I just want to get this show on the road, and get on with my retirement plans.'

I didn't dare ask her what, if any, real plans she had for this mystical retirement. Instead I found myself agreeing, in a practical rather than a scientific capacity, to pose as Amelia's friend when she came round to vet Mr Wilson at his dinner. Mrs Duggan thought he had nothing to lose by displaying his marvellously virile appetite.

It was like the start of a school play. There we were, me and Amelia and Mrs Duggan, all seated round the kitchen table, waiting for Mr Wilson. Twiddling a side strand of the hair, Amelia sucked up to Mrs Duggan.

'It must be nice for all these chaps to have such a creative landlady. Jolly unusual these days to be able to come home to a cooked supper.'

Mrs Duggan subsided into her chin. 'Oh, now, I enjoy it really, and they're mostly very appreciative. Jacinta's father, Eugene, is the only one who doesn't always take his dinner here, and that's really on account of the irregular hours he keeps.'

I'd never heard a body titter until I heard Amelia's laugh. 'Oh yes! I know who you mean. Eugene. I've met him at the junk shop. So you don't keep tabs on all your lodgers!' We were then treated to a little speech about the callous manikins in Amelia's loveless office. For reasons I had no difficulty in appreciating, they resented her commitment.

'I'm not really that committed,' she insisted, 'I don't have to be. It's just something I seem to be able to do for the moment.'

'And that's fair enough for a girl of your age. Now, if Jacinta here would only concentrate on something, we'd all be a lot easier in our minds.'

Whatever else she was, Amelia wasn't stupid. She wouldn't be drawn in on this odious comparison. She looked away from me and continued. 'Actually, Mrs D., I've decided that I want to live in the Mediterranean during winter, and come back here for summer. I'm learning about the property business so that I can set up on my own, and keep myself that way. I'm having Spanish tuition.'

'Oh, isn't that nice. And you could practise the Spanish with our Eugene because, you know, with his rôles, he had to do a bit of that.'

'Rôles?' Amelia may have thought Mrs Duggan was talking about some kind of sandwich.

'Oh, yes, indeed,' she continued, 'his dramatic rôles.' Momentarily forgetting about Mr Wilson, she couldn't resist a little boast about her gazelle. 'That's where the benefit of a classical education comes in. He has the Latin, you see, and once you've that,' she flapped her arms, 'sure you can be a High Court judge, if you have a mind to it.'

I had to intervene. 'Well, he makes a little go a long way anyhow. He can just about rise to Adios amigo, and the Latin came in handy when he didn't want to be eaten by dogs.'

'Dogs? Does Latin work like that?'

'Not at all. I don't know what Jacinta's thinking of.'

'Sin and sex, that's what I'm on about. My father, as I'm sure Mrs Duggan will get round to telling you, was once Saint Patrick in a film, which was never released, and for that, he had to do a lot of frolicking in his pelt, with dogs as well as hairy men.'

'Jacinta, how could you? As I understand it, the film was very artistic, tasteful. They all wore costumes, all of the time.'

'As I understand it, the costumes were the equivalent of barbarian fig-leaves. That bearskin you're always on about, the one in the back of the floosie's Mini, it was the one she had to loll on in Tara's great hall, you know?'

Mrs Duggan laughed nervously, very nervously. 'Amelia here will be getting very confused. She'll think we're not full shillings if you carry on.'

99

'Oh no!' chirped Amelia. 'I find it absolutely fascinating.'

But the fascination didn't please Mrs Duggan. 'Well, we could do with a little less of it round here.' Dirty look at me. 'D'you know, I'm thinking there must be lots of opportunities for environmental health officers in Mediterranean Spanish-speaking parts.'

'Em,' Amelia ventured. She was not to know that Mrs Duggan had lurched off the subject of films and pagan orgies to the prospects for Mr Wilson as a live export. Just then, she heard him upstairs.

'Oh, come in, come on in, Mr Wilson,' she called up, 'I have got something for you, just a bit behind-hand today on account of Jacinta's friend here.'

She made a flustered fuss of clearing away the tea things before setting down his mess of stew and dumplings. Mr Wilson put his nose in the stew without even glancing up at Amelia. Because he'd been swimming after work he looked even damper than usual and there was also something fishy about the unappealingly functional orifice into which he was forking his stew. Strange that, I thought of telling Mrs Duggan later, if the sympathetic theory had anything to it, surely this greedy ornithologist should have looked more like a bird than a fish?

To me Mr Wilson was an altogether horrible prospect and while he chewed, Amelia was restless. It was plain that she had seen enough. He was starting on his seconds and she had shut her briefcase when Mrs Duggan landed her with a fresh mug of tea. She wasn't going to let her get away that easily.

'We thought you might settle a little question for us, Mr Wilson, arising from Amelia's recent holiday in Dalmatian parts.' This was Mrs Duggan's signal for Amelia to place her trump, a snapshot, on the table in front of him.

'We were wondering,' I did my bit by saying, 'whether that's a great white heron in the foreground. A man with binoculars told Amelia it was.'

100

'No,' said Mr Wilson after a cursory glance at the picture, 'it's only an egret.' That was it. He wasn't even interested enough to ask Amelia whether she regularly consorted with binocular-clad Dalmatians. She stood up and said she really had to be going. It was then that Mr Wilson tried to scrape the dashed hopes off the rocks.

'I'll take you to the station,' he said, giving out his lip-flap of a smile, 'there's a lot of funny types around at this time.'

Mrs Duggan's agreement was vehement. She said the types were all waiting for the winos' night-time refuge to open, that, like starlings, they tended to gather around Hebden Street at that hour of the evening. Amelia and Mr Wilson were taking their leave when my father came in.

'Good gracious,' he exclaimed. 'My favourite size ten in Mrs Duggan's kitchen.'

Amelia tittered again and looked coyly back at Mrs Duggan. 'She's been telling me the truth about you.'

'Has she indeed. The end of the world must be nigh.'

'Go away out of that, Eugene. Let the girl go home. Mr Wilson's waiting to take her to the station.' At that Amelia really had to go and we were left with the kitchen to ourselves. Eugene put a bottle-shaped brown paper bag on the table. It was Spanish champagne.

'Eugene, how did you know? That's just what we ladies deserve.' Mrs Duggan fetched the good glasses, garage glasses acquired with Mr Byrne's petrol stamps, and told Eugene about Mr Wilson's sudden gallantry. 'Don't you think they could be brother and sister?'

He shook his head in mock disgust at her machinations, and my collusion with them, before slowly uncorking the champagne, which didn't pop.

'This is Xanthe's present to us and we are instructed to celebrate her good luck with it.'

'Xanthe?' I said, hoping, expecting, that some very prestigious gallery was going to give her a one-woman show.

'Xanthe and the Bugler Foundation for Artists.'

'Has she won something?' Mrs Duggan's eyes were gleaming.

'She has indeed. She's won a travel fellowship and she's going to Lanzarote to develop her interest in volcanic landscapes.'

'She's not taking you, then?'

'No, she's not.' He said this vaguely, pretending it was the first consideration of his special eligibility as Xanthe's travelling companion. 'I'm not a great one for the sun, which is not in any case to be recommended for ageing Celtic complexions.'

This news didn't make Mrs Duggan very happy. She knew very well that the criteria for getting a Bugler Fellowship were probably flexible enough to have included Eugene if he'd been bothered. She took a very careful, very audible sip from her bubbly glass. Then she thumped it back on the table and forefingered the left-behind man towards her. 'Don't you dare come home to give an old woman a turn, Eugene Morphy. Are you really telling me that woman is running off without you? Aren't you supposed to be her inspiration?'

She was looking at me when she said this, but I could only look at Eugene, who had on his pained, misunderstood expression.

'Come now,' he said, fixing the glass back into Mrs Duggan's hand, 'Xanthe is planning something of a working break for herself. Her grant includes the cost of a new camera. I do think we can respect her project and wish her the best, don't you?' He raised his glass at me, but Mrs Duggan wouldn't raise hers.

'Wish her the best indeed!' She drained her glass, pushed it down to the far end of the table, and began to sound on about Lanzarote. 'She'll be needing all the good wishes she can get, I can tell you that. Lanzarote indeed! They'll be giving away fellowships in hell next. Oh yes, you can laugh if you like,' it was me sniggering, 'but I can see it. Come along now, folks, mingle and melt with sinners from all walks of life . . .'

My father refused to be engaged. He poured himself another glass of champagne and inspected it with a very actorish appreciation. Angrily, Mrs Duggan watched this performance.

'I don't suppose you've ever listened to a word of sense, Eugene Morphy, but I for one have never understood what that girl's been up to, or what you've been seeing in her.'

For all Mrs Duggan's known scepticism about Xanthe as the right spouse for Saint Patrick, this line was not entirely predictable. Usually she applauded winners. Her own mantelpiece was always littered with competition entry forms and she liked her daily flutter on the horses. But Mrs Duggan, who seldom took more than a small glass of sweet sherry, was now under the maddening influence of a glass and a half of Spanish champagne.

'I'm sure Xanthe doesn't expect you to understand what she's up to, Mrs Duggan, and, with the greatest respect, I don't think you should try to read my mind as easily as you read horoscopes.' My father, jaunty when he'd first stepped down into the kitchen, had now crusted over with coolness.

'You, my not so young fellow, have no reason to be so civilised about it all. I suppose you'll be wanting your room for good now that your artiste,' Mrs Duggan put a great relish on that word, 'won't be around to put mustard on your chops. But if you think I'm going to be here for ever, taking your phone calls and thumping your pillows, you've got another thing coming.'

I gasped as he told her, in his low, slow voice, that she didn't have many faults but one of them was not being able to mind her own business. He was not the only one who would prefer it if she would leave him out of her romantic connivings.

'I hate to say this, Mrs Duggan, but the truth of the matter

103

is that it would be far better, far far better,' he looked up and out over an imaginary audience, 'if you stopped pretending that you've been put upon by your household.'

'Don't you dare talk to me like that, Eugene Morphy. You've been using up my hot water for twenty years . . .'

'You like it that way. You've refused anything I've offered you, and you invited the others into your house. Why don't you take up some kind of charity, do something useful with your time?'

That broke her. She burst into tears and went on about the one foot she already had in her grave. He handed her a tea-towel before picking up his jacket again and walking out the door.

'Wait!' I called out. 'I'll come with you.' He turned and said I should stay with the 'old dear'. Just as soon as the front door slammed she stopped crying.

'I'm sure he didn't mean a bit of it.'

To my surprise she gave me a very sober nod. 'Not to worry, just drawing him out, that's all. It would be healthier really if he showed a little bit of resentment.'

'You're probably right.' That's what I actually said, but I wanted to say 'no comment'.

'You know what I'm thinking,' she persisted, 'I'm thinking that pair don't have any sex . . . sexual intercourse at all.'

'I don't think it's any of our business, really, I don't.'

I was confused by all the geography as much as the politics, and I did want to be proper and dignified on my father's behalf. But after so many seasons spent gossiping with impunity about him I could not immediately take up this new mode. She did, however, notice my new reticence, giving me one of her don't-mind-me-I'm-only-a-foolish-old-woman shrugs. Then she shuffled over to the plastic sandwich box in which Mr Byrne's dirty socks were kept. Like the snake that lies over folkloric treasure troves, these socks guarded her savings account books. Now I discovered that one of them contained two thousand pounds in my name.

'I've been putting this by for your twenty-first, Jacinta, fifty per cent of whatever I've won when he's gone to the bookie's for me. But it's right for you to know it's there now. Maybe you and him could take a little holiday, but somewhere nice, mind.'

She had me in tears now. I couldn't bear to replace the savings book below Mr Byrne's socks, so I put it back on the shelf and thanked her. She said nothing more. As soon as she'd hoisted herself into her chair and found the television's remote control, I washed my face and hared off for the shop.

The clothes rail that normally obscured Fin de Siècle's Hebden Street window was half empty so I could see Eugene sitting up on the chaise-longue. He was watching the same quiz as Mrs Duggan. Xanthe was gone to her yoga and her cat was eating its dinner from the Italian glass ashtray bought by Mrs Bugler. He looked lonely but comfortable, like the little old shoemakers in fairy tales. I was so glad I hadn't asked him if he'd mind being considered dead.

Although Cortes's horse neighed spiritedly, the conquistador himself did not speak during the Miller's Ingots commercial. The voice I had to match my father with was usually backed by the raucous chorus of the Goat's massed regulars. That was the pub Eugene rang me from on Ma's meeting nights, and that's where Mrs Duggan first picked him up. She still had a dowager status at the Goat on account of a stint there in charge of the catering and she still saw the world through pub glass. There was, for example, no better proof of the special sanctity of the Mother of God than the fact that she had first prodded Him into His mission on earth at the wedding of Cana.

'She noticed, and she probably hadn't a drop taken herself, that the wine was running out, not him.'

Since the Xanthe and Fin de Siècle stage of his career, Eugene was no longer a regular at the Goat, where the other Giant Elks met. But his social credit was still good and when

Mr Byrne saw me peeping through the velvet curtains that hung beyond the back bar's door, he called me over to his corner and pulled up a chair. I felt sorry for his valentine lover, lately a victim of one of Mrs Duggan's dirtiest tricks. Under cover of a viciously anonymous brown envelope, this adultress had received a pair of those hellish socks. I'd heard this from my father, and it went some way towards explaining his uncompromising wrath with Mrs Duggan.

Quite apart from my sympathy, and the peculiar value of those socks for the safety of my own person, I had other reasons to be fond of Mr Byrne. Avuncular without being sleazy, he asked me straightaway if I were going to help with the shop while 'she' was away. 'She wouldn't want to waste the fare by coming back too soon.'

'No,' I said, 'no indeed, but she'll surely be back within a couple of weeks.'

'Is that so?' said Mr Byrne amiably. Then he twiddled his antlers and adjusted his mighty shoulders so that he could fling one of his conversational gauntlets at the man in the dirty sheepskin coat who was just sneaking by. 'Have you got rid of that car of yours yet?' Sheepskin responded with a rueful 'no' and Mr Byrne, who thought he'd been asking too much for his 'dog' of a car, rubbed his hands gleefully. But there were no hard feelings, and Sheepskin soon joined us. While Mr Byrne was off selling raffle tickets in aid of a kidney machine for a local teenager – he was the sort to take on charitable appeals as well as, more discreetly and selectively, appeals on behalf of the families of Irish political prisoners – Sheepskin expressed friendship and goodwill by telling me how much he liked Miller's Ingots.

I was on my third spritzer, courtesy of the many friends of Mr Byrne, when Mr Wilson slithered in and took the seat beside me. By way of a greeting, he knocked one of his knees against mine.

'Oh, hallo, Mr Wilson.'

'Why don't you call me Pete, like your friend?'

'Oh, I don't know,' I crossed my legs and brandished my glass in the rest of the company's general direction, 'traditions die hard.' There was no point in telling him he was on Mr Byrne's seat because he knew as well as I did that Mr Byrne tended to circulate. In fact there was a double ring of drinkers around the foul-socked philanthropist's table by the time he got back to us. Reaching in for his pint, Mr Byrne told the ones who didn't know already, who I was and how I had a great destiny in front of me.

'What's that?' I asked, wondering if he could possibly be meaning a life interest in a secondhand clothes shop.

'Ah now,' he winked at me, 'the old lady's told me all about it. Aren't you going to study classics at some ancient university?'

'I don't know about that,' I said, though in a friendly way, 'it sounds to me like something Mrs Duggan should be doing, not me.'

He roared with laughter. 'That's Eugene's little girl for you.' And the men I was for, including the Pete Wilson still beside me, smiled with him. Because Mr Byrne was kind I didn't mind how loudly he talked and I was on his side with regard to the antler-moustache. But this Wilson person was another matter, another matter entirely. If there was anything in his bud – and his reluctance to budge from the seat next to mine, even when it was his round, indicated that there was – it had to be nipped bloody fast.

When God was around He did things for girls in my position. Faced with an unwelcome suitor, Saint Bridget got such a convenient distemper that she, temporarily, lost one of her lovely eyes. But divine intervention didn't always work like a credit transfer. Quick-thinking Oringa had to find some walnut juice to stain her skin with, and the gorgeous Ode cut her nose off with a razor. What could I do? I called over to Mr Byrne: 'Hey! Is there a chance of a few packets of crisps?'

Mr Byrne was a little put out by this bawdy request, but being a true gentleman he immediately asked if I wanted salt and vinegar, plain, or cheese and onion. I plumped for the onion, and three bags full. Neither walnuts nor razors were to hand at the Goat and I could hardly shove my benefactor's socks into Mr Wilson's ghoulish face, but I could munch the most pungent crisps, my mother's favourites, with my mouth open. She and Mrs Duggan would have been proud of me. When, after much serious banter, Mr Wilson was prevailed upon to go to the bar to buy a round, I refused another drink and shot away.

I was gloriously drunk and while I was in that state of muddled grace the Paraclete descended. He came upon me not as a dove but as a scowling cat who shot out from Mrs Duggan's porch when I was fumbling with the key, and instead of the gift of tongues I got an Idea. My mother's shoes weighed her down. They had cost too much, emotionally as much as financially, for her to be able to shake them from her ankles like so many millstones. At the same time, their presence in our house rebuked her, like empty bottles rebuke the alcoholic. Since Mr Broderick's initiation the removal of the shoes had become a vexing priority, and now I knew the perfect outlet. They'd fill Fin de Siècle's front window for three months if we were unlucky, a week if we were lucky. It would be a summer project for my father while the art colleges were shut and a small but uniquely satisfying way of improving the fortunes of the Murphy-Morphies.

SAINT FEBRONIA

f all the histories of virgin martyrdom, there is scarcely one more touching and beautiful than that of Febronia, as there is none described more fully than hers by a friend and witness of the sufferings.

7

Next morning, I went straight to Eugene's room to tell him about my shoe idea. He was already awake and sitting up in his bed, like a chirpy risen Christ. Mrs Duggan had got him out of it to answer a phone call from the advertising agency handling a relaunch of Miller's Ingots. A new wrapper was to say how 'naturally delicious' they were, and Cortes was to be resurrected for the accompanying campaign. I didn't want to put him down, but I couldn't be complacently glad.

'Thing is, you don't . . . at least I don't think you look very like a Cortes any more.'

'I beg your pardon,' he did a feeble cough, 'I'm not that decrepit, not yet, anyhow.'

'No, no, but you couldn't pass for thirty-five.'

He laughed like he didn't often, a loud, eruptive laugh, and quietened down to say that he knew he couldn't be the conquistador in his prime any more than he could get away with paying a child's bus fare for me. He didn't seem surprised to have a little greatness thrust upon him after so many years.

The old Cortes commercial, which would remind consumers of the chocolates' classic status, was going to be repeated, but the new wrapper would be featured in a follow-up commercial starring an elderly, less than dashing Cortes. Apparently the conqueror of Mexico had an unhappy later career. He retired to an estate in Spain with a couple of his sons, but the new emperor and the royal court ignored him. The commercial's director envisaged greying locks and filthy

111

stubble rather than the fierce thatch of black hair and the handbag of a beard that Cortes had sported in the vintage commercial. That sounded all right. It was uncomplicatedly good news.

Eugene could dimly remember Maria's shoes and the catastrophic effect of the first oil crisis on the price of them. I was authorised to winkle them away from my mother. In the meantime Fin de Siècle would have a face-lift. Improvements had been on the agenda for some time. Xanthe wanted to hark back to a romantic epoch of unemployment and heavy clothes, a 1930s look: black skirting boards and a lot of yellow. We agreed to go to a DIY store together and to start the work while she was away in Lanzarote.

It seemed that in less than twenty-four hours my life, my family, had taken on a new wholeness. It had become possible to connect the shoes with the shop, my mother with my father. As eleven o'clock approached I was reluctant to take off for Eric Lennox's laboratory, but Eugene prodded me.

'So glad it's not too arduous. The other apprenticeship had Mrs Duggan worried.'

I kissed his forehead. 'Yeah, it's okay. Money for old rope really.'

'I don't know.' He shifted in the bed and slyly smiled. 'Xanthe used to do for him but the arrangement did not endure.'

'Xanthe! You could have told me that before.' I was annoyed. Just when we were enjoying real complicity, he came up with an item that could have a bearing on how I handled Eric Lennox.

'Oh, do not sigh, do not weep,' he flicked his wrist at me, 'there is nothing for you to worry about. It was the vegetation that vexed her, house plants she was obliged to sing to.'

'Well, that is strange because he hasn't got any now.'

'No?' He looked amazed. 'There you are! We can only assume that her Billie Holliday caused them to expire.' Then

112

he stroked the chin that he was under director's orders not to shave and slid back under his pastel-coloured shroud.

Mrs Duggan was sloshing bleach around the tiles inside her front gate. I stepped gingerly over the wet area and was out on the pavement when I saw our mascot wino, 'Hopalong', flapping his arms encouragingly at a red BMW which was attempting to land near the kerb.

On the same principle whereby she allowed one cat to shit in her yard as a way of deterring all the others, Mrs Duggan sponsored Hopalong as our official drunk. She'd picked him because even when he was pissed, usually by the early after-noon, he only behaved as if he were mildly stoned – chattering and crooning in a mystical rather than an obscene or violent way. When he wasn't somewhere on Hebden Street, Hopalong was in the West End giving his rendition of 'The House of the Rising Sun' to the accompaniment of a two-stringed guitar. This was a very efficient little number for him because his excruciated listeners often paid him to move on, back to Hebden Street, that is.

New cars like this red one were unusual in Hebden Street. As Hopalong guided it in at a slant about fifty yards up the road from Mrs Duggan's, I saw Mrs Bugler behind its wheel. We were in for the threatened surprise visit. I was certainly surprised to see first a pair of slender legs in the sheerest of tights and the sort of shoes that transfixed my mother. Beneath those baggy orange dungarees I had never sus-pected such elegant scaffolding.

I ran back to warn Mrs Duggan. 'It's Mrs Bugler,' I shouted, 'she's coming to see us.'

Mrs Duggan took off her rubber gloves and hid the yard-brush behind the bin. Then, like Cinderella's stepmother watching the advance of the princely shoefitter, she stood trembling in the porch. Mrs Bugler's hand reached for the gate-catch. Behind her, Hopalong was staggering under a huge cornet of gladiolis. He had one last rapturous sniff

113

before handing them over. The gate swung open. Then and only then did Mrs Duggan straighten her back and pluck off the gold shields that were always barnacled to her ears. 'Well, well, well, after all these years. You know, Hilda, I've always meant to give these back to you.'

Since the days of Tara and the Mini with the bearskin rug, Mrs Bugler, *née* Hilda No-knickers, had done a course on how to be a gracious First Lady among enthusiastic but incomprehensible natives. Still smiling, and still clutching the ear-rings, she allowed herself to be led indoors. Once in the kitchen, she put the ear-rings down and took hold of Mrs Duggan's hands.

'Dymphna! You haven't changed a bit. You look marvellous. Have you been away? I've been thinking so much about you.'

'I certainly have not. I've had too much to do. I've been here all the time. But you're looking very well yourself, Hilda.'

I backed out of the kitchen and pounded upstairs. Eugene was in the bathroom. I banged on the door and he came out in my dressing-gown.

'Get decent and downstairs as quick as you can. Mrs Duggan's squatting on Mrs Bugler in the kitchen. Oh hurry, please! You've got to hurry.'

Eugene wouldn't hurry his toilette for anyone, and since he didn't get to hear Mrs Duggan's stories about the floosie in jodhpurs as often as I did, the meeting in the basement wasn't a crisis. Still, he promised me that he'd be downstairs within minutes and I tore off to Pimlico. Hopalong was left to deal with the motorists whose access to Hebden Street had been impeded by the outrageous position of the red car.

Eric Lennox was just as elusive as Hector had been, but his discreet arrivals were less disabling. At the Joint I had been a nervous doe, raising my face every now and then to sniff the wind and scan the high grass for predatory movements.

At the Pimlico housette I was more like one of Amelia's birds, a businesslike heron in a Dalmatian marsh.

There was nothing obviously animal about this fastidious employer of mine. With his rapid, regular movements – you could almost hear facial muscles clicking when he spoke – his lustrous shoes, his clothes without stain and his neatly folded blond hair, Eric Lennox was a machine-doll of a man. Not so much a stuffed shirt as a finely pressed one. I imagined that this shirt-becoming quality had something to do with Protestantism, or Christian deviation from the Reformation onwards. It's exactly the look perfected by Mormons. I'd never met a Mormoness but the males who glued themselves to my mother's doorstep had a similar fluorescence.

Eric did have his own ethnicity, indeed he was a constant reminder of the connection between the Protestant ethic and capitalism. All those generations of do-it-yourself Bible-perusing had not gone to waste. This multi-lingual T. S. Eliot researched anything and everything: cleaning equipment and the washability of all that he owned; food; sound systems; computer accessories. For him, to buy was to pray, and though I had lived all my life among anarchist consumers I was not alienated by such methodical ways. As Mrs Duggan would have put it, he was an education for me. I had muffled the glint in her eyes, which had come on with the first bag of wrinkled shirts, by telling her, with complete conviction, that Mr Lennox was hardly ever about.

But on this red BMW day I was ambushed in Eric Lennox's upper room by a Swiss cheese plant of sparkling syntheticity. Then, in the bathroom bin, folded rather than crumpled, I found the exercises for sexual continence. I was being warned about an imminent extension of duty, but I was more excited than frightened. Would I succeed where Xanthe had failed?

From our first encounter Eric knew I liked napping in his house but I did not dare, ever again, to avail myself of the master bed. Considerately, he had compensated me with a bed-sized shelf which, like his desk, could be pulled down from the wall. Although it had a mattress, this was the perfect guest bed because after one night wedged into it no one would want to stay. On it I felt like a packet of bacon waiting to be picked up in Sainsbury's, but Eric Lennox never picked up bacon. He did nothing spontaneously. I was lying on that shelf, relaxing after a spot of dusting, when he crept upstairs.

'Hi, Jacinta.'

'Oh, hallo, Mr Lennox, Eric, I was just about to do those blinds.'

'Aw, don't bother.' He straddled his wheel-less bike and, with his hands behind his neck, nonchalantly asked me if I knew any good fantasies. Now, I must have spent a budgie's lifetime worrying about the allocation of the vast sums of money which might fall upon me from fantastic sources. How, for example, could I provide Xanthe, and through her my father, with the means for a dignified old age without offending her current dignity. First off I would have to find a way of buying a space on a wall in the Tate. Then there was Ma, a gifted extortionist but a lousy taker. If she'd been awarded a fellowship like Xanthe's she would have immediately suspected British Intelligence.

I knew, of course, that Eric didn't want to hear about these domestic fantasies, so with my feet dangling over the edge of the shelf I said, 'Actually, I'm a dab hand at . . . at stories, but they don't work for everyone. I mean, you must have a fairly good idea of what you enjoy.'

I slid off the shelf for my briefing, a whispered 'how about a crowd scene?' He wasn't too fussed about the quality of the crowd. We spent a perfectly civilised twenty minutes considering rock concert, airport, football stadium, carnival, demonstration, even riot crowds, and we could have proceeded with any one of these options until, with a bit of market research that I congratulated myself for, I came up with a classic.

116

'I know! What about an eighteenth-century outdoor execution scene?'

He was dubious. I had to tell him something about the sort of turn-out you got for public executions and then he became interested enough to remove his glasses. While he went to the bathroom, from which he returned in his gym-robe, I got back on my shelf. I supposed that he wanted his storyteller horizontal so that she couldn't monitor the audience participation, and I didn't resent this wish. I fancied my shelf as a pallet, like the ones used by apprentice bards in ancient Ireland. They learned the repertoire lying down in their cells, where, in total darkness, they recited, over and over again, the genealogies of the ruling families and the stock long poems. While he was setting up a cassette recorder, I made a very dignified business of clearing my throat. This was Jacinta Murphy's first audition.

My raids on Mr Byrne's pornographic library had given me the execution scene formula, but the really dirty details were my own. Eric would have fainted in Xanthe's kitchen so, I reckoned, a full-blown eighteenth-century crowd, even in the open air, would drive him wild. In my best mid-Atlantic Shakespearian accent I regaled him with the street vendors' lurid cries, the whining dogs, the sweat, the ladies urinating over the open gutters, the bloodstreaked aprons of the fishwives, the vermin hopping from one indifferently filthy body to the next.

I was hoping to get away with clouds of atmosphere, the last-day-of-the-world tensions that are conducive to random intimacy. It was difficult for me to site myself, and my assailant, precisely within the crowd around the scaffold. Of course, I couldn't be a dog or a child. I had to be a voluptuous wench and even though she wasn't voluptuous, Mrs Duggan's Amelia came into my mind. I became a sluttish Amelia in a street-sweeping skirt. Directly behind me, in the pressing, sweaty crowd, there was a man, but I never saw his face. Instead of moving off when I became aware of his hard-on, I stayed put. As I was working out what exactly this faceless opportunist could get up to behind me the telephone buzzed.

I stopped and listened to the usual answering message clicking into action. Eric turned off his tape recorder and walked over to the phone. Sitting up on my shelf I watched him standing over it, waiting to hear who was phoning. He tightened the belt of his gym-robe and gave a tiny groan as one of his widows said something imperious in French. Then he turned to me, 'Okay, Jacinta, just carry on.'

I lay back on my shelf and tried to continue where I'd left off. But it was no use, I'd lost my tone, I'd lost Amelia. I was about to turn round and knee the faceless rapist in the groin when Eric spoke into the void.

'What about the fastening of the skirt?'

'I don't know Eric, to be honest I'm really jaded. I've had enough excitement for one day.'

Dead cool, he found his glasses and, without a trace of embarrassment, he began to tell me how I'd gone wrong. He didn't appreciate the authenticity.

'You can leave out the stuff about sheep-stealing and the victim's last words, Jacinta. We're not after a documentary, are we?'

'No?' I resented the 'we'.

'What you're wearing, how you respond physically is more important.'

His disregard for the historical details, for the plight of the condemned man, bugged me. He didn't want to know about the miscarriage of justice, or the vile laws, that had brought this man to the scaffold and 'in future' it would be no good varying the scene by changing the execution victim into a Jacobin or a Narodnik or a highwayman. I'd started off wanting to succeed where, presumably, Xanthe hadn't. Now I had a few glimmers on how she'd fallen down on the job, but I was no longer keen on a 'future' on that sliver of a shelf. However, I didn't want to do myself out of the cleaning job, which was well paid, so I couldn't be too rude.

'Right you are Eric, but the thing is I don't think I'm really cut out for what you're after.'

'Oh no, Jacinta. I think you're good, really I do. You could be really brilliant. We just need to prioritise, okay?'

'Well, I want a cup of tea, then.'

'Sure, sure,' the creep was almost jovial, 'I'll make tea, and then we'll start again.' Although he made rose-hip tea for himself, he had gone to the trouble of getting in sugar and full-fat milk for me. But once I was with my mug, it was back to the shelf. While he clutched at his towelling girdle I racked my poor brain. Then I had it. How right Mrs Duggan was when she recommended the hardback book as a chastity shield. Once again, the saintly lives came into their own.

'I'm thinking you might enjoy a martyrdom, Eric. Lots of people did. The incidents of martyrdom can be varied at pleasure.'

'Uhuh. Well, shoot.'

I cleared my throat. 'We could start with Febronia, a really stunning eighteen-year-old virgin martyr . . .'

'Febronia. That's some name, huh? Sounds kinda phoney, cheap, like a detergent.'

'There you go again, having a dig at the millions of poor girls who've been given martyrs' names. I'm sure it was a perfectly nice name in the time of Diocletian.'

'Try me.'

Febronia got off to a great start. Within moments I had her in the arena before the grim tribunal. She was stripped and her hands and feet were bound to four stakes so that she could be stretched over a fire. In this position she was scourged so that her blood hissed on the charcoal. The crowd began to plead for mercy but Diocletian's henchman, Selenus, would have none of it. He ordered Febronia to be taken off the barbecue and put on the rack, and then her sides were torn with iron combs.

Eric was holding his glasses. He looked more curious than aroused, but he didn't tell me to stop.

119

Selenus ordered the surgeon, always on hand for martyr-
doms, to cut off Febronia's tongue but the onlookers persuaded him to compromise, so he just extracted seventeen
of her teeth.

'She's dead now, right?'

'Oh no! She gets tied to a stake and has a breast cut off,
and her long hair is the only thing covering her bleeding white
body . . .'

'I think we can assume she's dead before she gets to the
stake.'

'I thought you'd find it interesting.'

'It's not what I'd call relaxing.'

'Sorry.'

'Okay, don't worry,' he sighed, 'I won't ask you again.'

This time I made the tea. His cup shook in his hand and
although I was as exhausted as Febronia, I was sorry for
him. He was more like a bored child on a wet afternoon than
a sex monster. I felt I couldn't leave him miserable and so I
mustered myself for one more story, the tale of my mother
and her shoes. One thing you could definitely say for Eric
Lennox, he was a great listener.

Whenever Ma was listing the things she didn't like about
herself, she started with her size seven feet. She was
ashamed of them.

'Of course it's not rational. Big feet can be very handy.
For example, if Henry the Eighth had been bothered to look
at his wives' feet he might have got himself a few more live
heirs.'

'I don't get you, Jacinta.'

'Feet and pelvic capacity, they're connected, you
know.'

'I didn't.' He didn't dare look down at his own feet, or over
at mine, but a manicured hand was measuring the precision-
draughted Lennox nose.

'Yeah, it's one of the first things you get asked when you
get pregnant, the size of your shoes, I mean. I'm not sure if

there's any significance in it for men.' (I'd have to check that with Mrs Duggan.)

'So your mother's got big feet.'

'No. She's average for her height, but she still feels bad about them.'

Eric was asked to picture Ma as she sidled into a shoe shop. She went straight for the size three rack, figuring that if, in a purely formal sense, she liked the smallest version of a particular shoe, she'd be able to handle it in a size nearer her own. I said nearer, not her own. She wasn't capable of asking outright for her size, and she bought the shoes that she could get her feet into, not the ones that fitted her well enough so that she could walk.

My mother's shame was not unusual, so it was reasonable to suppose that a habit of buying small shoes was common to her generation. This is what brought me to the marketing breakthrough. I proposed to sell Ma's surplus shoes by presenting them as being a size smaller than they were. My father would be put to work erasing all evidence of actual size, and we would tell the customers that they were all five and a halfs, not six and a halfs. I had already observed that a large proportion of Fin de Siècle's regular customers were women who had not been able to cope with retail prices since around 1973, the very women who had the most severe anxieties about the size of their feet.

'You can just imagine how delighted they'll be to try on good-as-new shoes that fit them beautifully.'

Eric was well able to imagine that. It was more than probable, he thought, that our customers would feel a sense of solidarity with a shop that only sold shoes that fitted them. After we'd run out of my mother's shoes, it might be worthwhile investing in some more, and doing the same thing with the size indications. The whole prospect seemed to cheer him up. He even found his CIA trenchcoat and invited himself to take a look over our Fin de Siècle.

*　　*　　*

While Eric, with the twitchy hands clamped into the pockets of the big coat, watched the taxi meter, I travelled in stately comfort across an entirely foreign London, a cleaner, grander city of wide streets and hard stone. I watched the flocks of thick and gleaming carrier bags waiting by the pedestrian crossings and thought about the luxurious lifestyles of their bearers. When finally we were wedged into Hebden Street I was feeling very seduced. 'Pull yourself together, Jacinta Murphy,' I had to say to myself, 'this sort of thing can be just as tempting as a pair of mean brown eyes.'

Fin de Siècle was in its most challenging state. The Crimplene dresses on the everything-for-a-pound rail, which was out on the drizzly pavement, were being pawed by two babies in a double buggy. Their mother was bent over the £2 box. Inside the shop, Eugene, minus socks and shoes, was sitting on the hat teachest eating a fried-egg sandwich. Behind him two schoolgirl truants were feeling up a man's mock silk dressing-gown, working up the courage to drive a hard bargain, and in the darkest corner our best jacket customer was groping for a new exterior. This woman came every other week. Fin de Siècle jackets were the siege towers in which she could advance towards a hostile world.

You could smell the fat from the egg pan and Eric, who wouldn't have lasted long in the eighteenth century, immediately sneezed. One of his hands held a fine cotton handkerchief to his nose while the other shook hands with Eugene, who did abandon his squelchy sandwich. I wanted to seize one of our half-spoked umbrellas and drive the riff-raff from our temple, but with him there they wouldn't have budged.

'How kind of you to take my daughter home,' he said, as if our limo had just swooshed up a gravelly avenue.

'That's okay, sir,' said a very American Eric in the same spirit of make-believe. You'd never have guessed that Little Dorrit Murphy had been doing overtime as a personal pornographer. Then Eugene cleared the top of another teachest and told me to put the kettle on. To my alarm, Eric said he'd love to have tea, but he backed off when my father informed him that only the straight stuff, hundred per cent pure tanin, was available. I ran out to the chemist's, the nearest source of herbal teabags.

When I got back, Eugene, in between little banters with the delinquent schoolgirls, was telling him how the shop was 'organised'. Eric said he was charmed, it was all very charming to him: 'But this Aladdin's Cave aura, these collectables,' he gestured at the box of old cutlery underneath the men's suit rail, 'they confuse serious customers. Leave a tenth of this stuff on display, and store the rest till you can use it.'

I told him about our decorating plans. 'We're trying to shift the real rubbish this week, and then we'll put the rest up in Xanthe's studio while we paint.'

'That's her studio?' Eric pointed upwards and with a flap of trenchcoat tails he was off through the back and up the stairs. Leaving Eugene to dangle the teabags, I headed up after Eric. Xanthe's studio was out of bounds to casual visitors. Even I was rarely in it when she was there, never when she wasn't.

I found Eric staring wildly around another allergy factory. The light flooding in through clean front windows showed up cornices draped by cobwebs and ragged walls whose pattern of cabbage roses was barely veiled by a thin wash of white emulsion. Where it was not covered by a dull, autumn-patterned carpet, which smelled as if it had rafted a thousand incontinent cats, the floor was calloused with blobs of acrylic paint. But if these immediate sights and smells were banished, it was possible to credit Xanthe with orderliness. Before going away she had tidied up. Under a trestle table her paints were neatly stacked, alongside pickle jars full of brushes and knives, and a tower of emptied ashtrays. Against the back wall there were three empty canvases. For pointers to her recent preoccupations we could see, pinned to the wall above the table, the Turin Shroud, Michelangelo's *Pietà* and several bathers by Degas. For evidence of their reference value there was, folded against the opposite wall, a door-sized, hinge-linked triple portrait of Eugene Morphy.

Eric began to sneeze again. 'Lot of dust,' he said, jerking an elbow at the triptych, 'that should be covered.'

If you were liberal about it there were social advantages to life around my father. I did, for example, know the etiquette of viewing works of art in front of their makers. If you don't understand a painting, and the art of Xanthe's friends usually required captions, you ask questions. With any luck, the work will then acquire meaning in terms of its creator's experience, and you can proceed from there. Hector was a case in point. He made sculptures that were inspired by medical cabinets or bathroom cupboards. I had seen photographs of these rats' nests of tampons, blisterpacks, glutinous cough mixture bottles, garotted tubes of toothpaste, and so on. When you knew that his mother worked as a medical receptionist, and that the bathroom cabinet simultaneously represented her work and the secretive, sinister things about women from their sons' point of view, you could negotiate Hector's projects.

Although it alienated me for other reasons, I usually had no problem understanding Xanthe's pictures. The recent stuff was figurative, and the figure in question was my own flesh and blood. Besides, Mrs Bugler was used to commissioning paintings like curtains. Like a Medici, she specified the subject and the mood and the size, and she paid by the metre. As far as I knew, Xanthe had made this triptych for her personally, but until now I'd avoided it because I didn't want to make myself liable for an informed critique with Mrs Duggan.

Now I watched Eric Lennox examining the martyrdom, in three stages, of Eugene Morphy. Compared with Febronia, he got off lightly. In the first section, he was standing, naked and with his hands behind his back, before a tribunal of women. Many of the faces belonged to Fin de Siècle regulars. Eyebrows Sheila had a fat baby on her lap and our Jacket

124

Lady was sitting beside her. Behind these two, wearing a self-portraitist's squint, Xanthe herself was standing tall.

The second, middle image had Eugene on the rack. Like a good dental patient, he was being terribly co-operative, glancing down at his ankles as they were being tied, by two punkish girls, to the far end of the grille.

For the third image, the tribunal gallery was emptied of spectators. Three disconsolate wolfhounds were nuzzling the Eugene who was elegantly slumped at the foot of the execution stake. This picture had me searching in my mind for encouraging platitudes because in it Eugene's eyes were as shudderingly shut as the eyes of the face in the Turin Shroud.

I turned to Eric and said, non-committally, 'That'll be Mrs Bugler's latest acquisition.'

'Uhuh.'

'You like it?'

The hands being stuck in their pockets, he could only hunch his shoulders. 'It's busy. You know these people?'

'Some of them. Can't see Mrs Bugler though.'

'What about you? Are you in there?'

'No. She hasn't put me in.'

'Huh. Guess it's not finished.' The hands were out and he was grinning awkwardly. 'Tell me, does your father live here?'

'Not really, not officially. He keeps some stuff here, and he's downstairs just about every day.'

'What makes him sexy?' The grin had evolved into an unAmerican grimace.

'Don't ask me. My mother used to say it was the way his bones were arranged.'

'I got bones.' Eric rolled up one of his trouser legs to expose a hairless shin.

'Yeah but . . .'

'But what?'

He had me stumped. 'Actually, if you want to know what

125

I think,' it had just occurred to me what I thought, 'I think he's pathetic.'

'Pathetic!' Eric squeaked.

'Yeah. Really pathetic, you know, like he makes people, women, feel sort of sorry for him. But you're not like that. You've got money.'

'I thought they were supposed to like money.'

'Well . . . they do actually, but it's the spending that's nice. You've already bought everything you need. You buy takeaway food and pay people to clean up after you.'

'Okay, I get you.' That was a relief. I hadn't got round to mentioning things like a sense of humour.

'Anyway, do you think Mrs Bugler will like this?'

'That's not for me to say.'

I tried not to worry. If Eric cared enough about the triptych to suggest a dust-sheet, it could probably be sold to someone else. He was disappointed, even annoyed, when I didn't let him rifle through Xanthe's bedroom for a suitable covering.

Downstairs my father was still lost among his customers, sartorial chickens who were scurrying, this way and that, all over the shop. I sent him off to borrow a sheet for the triptych from Mrs Duggan, and Eric had to go with him because it was the same direction as the nearest minicab office. In the meantime I cleared the premises.

The double buggy's owner was deliberating about when she could come back about the dress she'd been mauling ever since I'd arrived. She said she could never make up her mind while the babies were awake but I knew she was really paralysed by Eugene's absence. He flattered customers like her into buying clothes, which, if they were not irredeemable self-haters, they sent off to the very next jumble sale. Fin de Siècle stock circulated like small denomination coins. We frequently acquired garments already familiar to us. Sometimes Eugene even managed to sell them again to the same customers, and that was just one of the wonderful things about the secondhand clothes trade.

126

If he didn't feel up to a bit of convincingly nonchalant flattery, Eugene reduced prices. But this lazy strategy often disabled the sort of customers we got. Instead of scenting a bargain they smelled a rat. I told the double mother that if she wanted this dress she'd have to buy it there and then because we were going to shut for a few days and much of the stock would be dispersed. She gave me fifty pence and scarpered. Then the Jacket Lady emerged from behind a rusty rail.

'Was that the VAT man?' she whispered urgently.

'No, he's an international art consultant.'

'Goodness. Is that how they look? I was sure it was pestilence or VAT.'

She wouldn't be bargained off. Eugene always had to tell our Jacket Lady how neat her shoulders were before she could buy her fully lined fixes. I was hanging up what she'd been trying on when Amelia ghosted in. That scary hair was down in curtains around her face and she had a tub of brown rice and two plastic forks by way of legitimating her unbusinesslike visit, obviously not the first. I revved up the rudeness. Seizing one of the forks, I dug into her rice. Between mouthfuls I told her that 'the old man' had eaten recently and that 'we' were too busy to entertain visitors. For a moment she shrank back under the dusty curls, but then she recovered herself to say, with a sickening confidence in the importance of her opinion, that the Cortes revival was great news.

'I think the beard really suits him. He's got such an ascetic face.'

'Yes, yes. But he's talking to my stepmother-in-commonlaw's agent right now, so it's not really a good time to call.'

If she had a conscience it was ticking as she wafted off the set. I didn't tell my father she'd called but I was certainly going to tell Mrs Duggan. She had conjured Amelia up for Mr Wilson and before she got her fuzzy spirals over

Eugene's naked toes I wanted her exorcised good and proper.

A few days later, so that no one could see the bare inside, we rubbed window-cleaning fluid on Fin de Siècle's windows. Then we moved everything worth selling up to the studio. At the bottom of the hat tea-chest I found volume seven of the *Lives of the Saints*. 'Oh Christ! Mrs Duggan's been looking for this. I must have left it here.'

Eugene took it from me and blew the dust from its spine. 'You can hide it somewhere in your room. It's probably best if she doesn't know it's been circulating.'

'Has it?'

Of course it had. Where else had Xanthe got the sequence of his martyrdom? Out of loyalty to her, I hadn't wanted to let Eric Lennox in on the full complexity of my reaction to the triptych. But I was, to say the least, curious about the extent of its subject's co-operation.

'That triptych's a bit of a death mask, isn't it? Did you just fall asleep for her or what?'

He chuckled. 'I suppose I must have. I often do. I think it's rather good actually, my only tragic rôle.'

So it was just another rôle and with Cortes alive and kicking in front of him, he hadn't internalised it. I got back to work.

We washed the woodwork and spread newspapers on the floor, and then the sun came out. Since May we'd been living under an asbestos mat of a sky so this was a big event. We took off our painting clothes and I rummaged through the stock upstairs to find a cotton dress for me and another old tracksuit for him. He put on his straw boater and together we set out for a picnic lunch.

I'd found five pounds' worth of change in the pockets of the men's clothes we'd moved upstairs. Unlike the women's dresses, the men's coats and suits, which were bought by women, rarely needed cleaning. They'd belonged to men who'd died, or disappeared – husbands who'd walked out, lodgers who'd left in a hurry. Men were always disappearing, that's how it seemed to me. But because of my father's special visibility to other women, other women besides my mother and myself, that is, he got treated as a cosmic stand-in for all the sons and lovers who'd absconded. When I say special visibility I mean that he wasn't like the other sober men on the daytime landscape: postmen, window-cleaners, drivers, builders, telephone engineers, men with obvious functions.

The supermarket Eugene patronised, if that was the right word for a blessed freeloading, fairly hummed with the souls of vanished men and the women who worshipped there still shopped for them. I saw them all the time, collapsible widows who still bought one giant pork chop and one dainty one; monumental matrons with horde-sized packs of hamburgers for the sons who had long since left home.

Of all the valentines sent to Mrs Duggan's house the one from the supermarket cashiers had been the least anonymous and the most cheerful. Their indulgence of Eugene didn't bother me but I didn't like it when he cashed in on it. When I saw him making eye contact with the check-out women, I pulled him by the elbow and reminded him that we'd made five pounds already that morning, that there was no need for us to make off with unpaid protein. (I'd caught him before putting smoked salmon under the bread and winking it through the check-out.) Although he pretended to ignore my remonstrations, he did allow me to pay.

The canal water was black and syrupy, the path smeared with pigeon shit. But there were no dogs and enough nettles to hide any evidence of them. Possibly because they didn't like being sprayed by the water, dog-owners avoided the canalside. That was one reason why it was my father's favourite walk, why he'd suggested it.

'And quite apart from the absence of dogs, it's not beautiful, not in any pastoral sense anyhow.'

'Why's that such a boon?'

'There are no distractions. It's good for contemplation.'

What had he got to contemplate, I was wondering, but I
didn't ask because I had a new grievance of my own to nurse.
Just when I was getting Hector under control, what should I
find, under the *chaise-longue*, but a cryptic postcard from
him. It was a picture of Bordeaux city centre but it had been
posted from Barcelona. The message was banal: 'Having a
lovely time. Viva Espana!' It was addressed to 'all at Find
the Sickle' so the 'you' was offensively plural. No matter how
I contemplated it, that postcard was annoying me. A cheated,
hungry Jacinta escorted Eugene Morphy to the canalside
nature garden.

It was deserted. What remained of a pair of swings was a
bright yellow gibbet and the bin was choked with bottles.
Our bench was dedicated to one 'Bill', founder of the community action group which had saved the garden's site from
developers. I wondered aloud about Mrs Duggan's Bill,
usually referred to simply and coldly as 'Mr Duggan'.
Eugene said he'd barely met Mrs Duggan's husband, but
that was of no import because she hadn't liked him anyhow.

'No, but some people get retrospectively sentimental. Not
you, of course. Xanthe's only been gone for a few days and
you're interviewing the understudies.'

'What could you be referring to?'

'I'm referring to the brown rice mission and you know it.'

He dusted bread crumbs off his lap and affected mild irritation. 'I gather you've not been altogether kind to little
Amelia.'

'Little Amelia! Little Amelia's . . .'

'Little Amelia's got a waist,' a critical glance at my middle
showed that he had a sting in him, 'so unusual in girls these
days, and her equally slender uncle is none other than Herbert Miller, titular head of the great chocolate dynasty.'

130

'Ahah! So this Herbert knows that Hernando Cortes is a personal friend of his niece?'

'He does. Until the fair Amelia took it upon herself to remind the people concerned of my continuing sojourn in this valley of tears, they were, by all accounts, envisaging a rather pastel and blandly animated relaunch for Cortes and the imperialist chocolates.'

'What's in it for her, then?'

'What's in it for her? What mercenary language is this? If there's anything in it, it's beyond the cash nexus. Indeed, you might even say that, in my own humble way, I am an instrument of reconciliation, affording Amelia the appearance of being sympathetic to the continuing prosperity of her dynasty in these harsh, health-minded times.'

While I was playing with a rubbery wedge of Emmental he told me how he worried sometimes that I was getting as mercenary as my mother and as corroded as Mrs Duggan. 'What you must understand, Jassie, before she takes complete possession of your youthful senses, is that I've never owned Xanthe, and she's never owned me. We are friends, partners, or whatever you want to call us, and that has precious little to do with the Amelias of this world.'

'But why don't you live over the shop?'

'I have no desire to live in a shop! Besides, the arrangement as it is is a perfectly good one.'

'For you maybe. What about Mrs Duggan?'

'What about her? I can't see her retiring. Can you? Of course she likes to ruminate. Don't we all? But, you know, she hasn't been in Ireland for twenty years. Amelia has a gut feeling that she won't sell up.'

'Oh really. I suppose she has to keep that in the briefcase.'

'What?'

'The gut.'

He snorted, but he'd run out of righteousness. I sat beside him silently supposing that maybe it was selfish of me to be wanting all the grown-ups to settle down on my terms. If I'd

131

felt like being totally honest I'd have told him what a relief this gut feeling of Amelia's was. By now, Hebden Street was my home. When the retirement of the century was first mooted my mother had panicked, there being a remote possibility that Eugene would end up on our doorstep. She'd suggested museum status for the Hebden Street household. Young owner-occupiers would pay to smell the Lifebuoy soap and to watch Mrs Duggan, in her best nylon housecoat, frying kidneys. If Britain was becoming a mega theme park, if redundant ironworkers found apprentices in museums of industrial archaeology, why shouldn't Hebden Street get in on the action? The house already had one ageing actor in it, and he was watching me, waiting for my next move.

'Why did you leave us, me and Ma?'

'Why are you asking that now?'

'I'm just asking. It's a simple question.'

'I'm afraid I cannot offer you a simple answer. People don't live rational lives.'

'But I'm not talking about people. You're supposed to be my father.'

'And you, young lady, are supposed to be my daughter. I would recommend a little deference, some due regard for the dignities of old age.' He tilted his hat towards our bit of sun and leaned back against the bench. I took the rest of the bread and walked over to the edge of the canal. A family of coots saw me coming. The five downy babies had orangey-red heads. I cast the bread on the water and the adults seized it. Touchingly, they didn't gobble it up themselves, like common ducks. They tore at the bread and distributed it among their young.

'Isn't that sweet,' I called back at him. 'They're a real family. Look at them! The mum and dad are sharing the bread with their babies.'

He got up and as he stood beside me his face was wearing a sickly smile of pure condescension, just the job for one of Xanthe's industrial blasphemies. For a moment I thought of pushing him into the smelly water, but he moved before I did. Tugging at my elbow, he drew me back from the edge and said: 'Have I ever told you, Jassie, how becoming that fringe of yours is? Now, a little abstention, from cheese for example, and a little concentration on something in particular, and you might really have a future.'

'Phewie! Hallelujah!' Between the gasps I was mopping my brow, flouncing my hair and beating my breast. 'Thanks be to God and everyone else, he's only worried about my weight.'

But he wasn't reproached, or even amused. He just looked at his watch.

'Okay, Miss Begotten. Let us be about our proper business.'

That afternoon, with the radio on at full blast, we put the first coat of gloss paint on Fin de Siècle's skirting boards.

SAINT WALTHEOF

aint Malachi, an Irish bishop, came to Kirkham on his way through England to Rome. The prior saw he was in want of a horse and gave him his own horse, a sound, rough, grey cob, and said he was sorry he could not give him a better animal, but it was the only one he possessed. Saint Malachi gladly accepted it: 'Dear to me shall be the gift of a kind heart.'

This horse eventually became quite white. It was a question agitated between English and Irish monks whether the horse was bleached through the merits of Saint Malachi who sat upon him, or of Saint Waltheof who gave him.

8

Mrs Bugler told us that she'd pointed her car in Fin de Siècle's general direction because she thought Eugene might be lonely while Xanthe was away. But really she was bored, grounded in Hades on account of the ailing Bertie Bugler's faith in a variety of local therapies.

She pushed her way into our seedy little lives with presents: a new cover for the ironing board, a box of spinach seedlings for the yard and, on the third visit, a fox terrier puppy, one of Fennessy's great-great grand-daughters. This little bitch was better off than I was. She came with a trust fund for veterinary bills, an elegant shit-scooper that doubled up as a walking stick, and a retractable leash that was supposed to be symbolic of the way in which Mrs Duggan kept her lodgers.

The puppy settled herself into Mrs Duggan's lap and the wise men pottered about offering encouragement and congratulations. Mr Wilson found a box for her, Mr Byrne volunteered to take her for walkies and Eugene was benignly indifferent. When pressed about his tolerance, he said he was hoping that the little dog would be of therapeutic value, a worthier as well as a more appropriate object of Mrs Duggan's callous regard than any of the lodgers. There was some problem with the name. A Carthaginian one was in order but Dido was too tragic, Tanit too gruesome and quite apart from their sex, neither Hannibal nor Maharbal nor Hamilcar rolled off the tongue. No one knew the names of Hannibal's sisters and his wife was a cipher, so we called her by the family name of Barca.

Mrs Duggan was powerful enough to resist the Bugler descent, but she chose not to. It had been easy for her to keep up with Hilda's affairs because her subsequent emotional history had been reported in the newspapers with the most useful racing columns. Now Mrs Duggan saw herself as a noble enemy, not quite forgetting but more than willing to forgive. Typically, she invoked great historical precedents for her magnanimity. Hadn't Hannibal entertained his Roman adversary, Scipio Africanus, after their Punic War? And Napoleon's Josephine, didn't she eventually invite the mistresses round to tea at Malmaison?

But what was Hilda being forgiven for? It was Mr Byrne, a reliable informant about most things, who told me what the war had been about and how the gold ear-rings came into it. Apparently, back in those nipple-sucking, bearskin days Hilda had seduced Saint Patrick. The only extraordinary thing about this achievement of hers was the fact that she'd spent a night or several nights in Mrs Duggan's house, which was out of bounds to all women who were not close friends of its owner, blood relations of its occupants, or fully accredited fiancées – Mrs Duggan was always the first to inspect the engagement rings. She had been away on one of her rare trips, visiting a recently bereaved (now dead) sister-in-law on the Isle of Wight, when Eugene and Hilda had consorted under her roof. They'd even used the Duggan marital bed, and Hilda had left her best ear-rings, rose-gold shields, on the bedside table. Mrs Duggan had picked them up and put them on, and she told everyone that she'd found them in her bathroom.

One warmish Tuesday afternoon Dymphna and Hilda removed themselves to the back yard for tea. The yard still smelled and by now it was bristling with half-buried hatchets, but Persephone was more comfortable there than she was in the dark basement kitchen.

Previous Bugler–Duggan summits had opened with the

ear-rings ritual. Mrs Duggan would take off the rose-gold shields with a terrific flourish of repudiation and press them into their original owner's hands until she had spent enough time saying she'd never missed them. After twenty years on a vigilant landlady's lobes the gold had a rosier hue than Mrs Bugler remembered. It had to be agreed that Mrs Duggan's skin had a truly miraculous, alchemical effect on precious jewellery.

On this particular afternoon a weary Mrs Bugler must have decided to clear up the ear-rings business once and for all. I had just come from Fin de Siècle and was in the bathroom above the yard when I heard my own name. If I didn't flush the toilet, they wouldn't suspect I was there.

'I think we should give them to Jacinta,' she was saying.

'But her ears aren't pierced,' said Mrs Duggan.

'We can arrange that. Eugene won't raise any objections.'

'No, he won't object.'

'He won't even notice. I have to say this, Dymphna, entre nous, he's the dearest, beautifulest man, but he never lived up to my expectations.'

Mrs Duggan lost no time in considering this vague slur. 'Oh, don't I know, Hilda. Maybe that's the problem, people, women, hoping or expecting too much of him. Why they can't be happy with him as he is, why they have to rush around making him in their own image . . .'

'It's only natural, Dymphna. You treat him like a child. And that's not a criticism.' (Mrs Duggan was probably looking indignant.) 'You're as right as anyone could be. At least you haven't had expectations, and so you haven't been disappointed.'

'Yes,' said Mrs Duggan, valiantly searching for some common ground. 'And I know that he's not the worst. Bill Duggan, for example, he never lived up to the most miserable expectations.'

I didn't hear Mrs Bugler's sigh of sympathy but I did hear how, unsurprisingly, Bertie Bugler also failed to arouse

139

expectations. That was one of the reasons why Mrs Bugler found such consolation among artists. 'Just to do what they do, they have to have no sense of reality, the wildest expectations.'

'Well, that's very nice for you Hilda. I'm sure you have the most interesting conversations.'

'Oh, yes, I do. Men do a lot more talking than they used to.'

'God help us!' Mrs Duggan exclaimed. 'It's not as if we were suffering in the silence.'

Barca must have made a bit of a kerfuffle then because there was a lot of chair-scraping and yelping and Mrs Duggan reproached her friend for spoiling the dog. 'It's all very well for you, Hilda, just having the icing off the tops of the buns, but it won't do for the animal to be expecting everyone's dough.'

'Oh, I do like a nice dog. You can read a dog like a book. Not like men! No indeed.'

'Now just leave her be, Hilda. She needs her sleep and it's nearly five. Jacinta'll be back soon, so we can tell her about the ear-rings.'

'Good show.'

I flushed the loo and, as loudly as I could, traipsed down into the yard.

'Jacinta! Hilda and I have just been thinking it would be nice if you were to have the ear-rings.'

'But my ears aren't pierced.'

'Well, they should be. A girl of your age should have pierced ears. It's far more economical. If you don't have the holes you just lose the ear-rings and it's not worth having decent ones. I'll sterilise a needle and do it for you myself.'

I leapt away from her. 'They've got UN committees to deal with that sort of thing.'

Mrs Bugler laughed. 'Sit down, Jacinta. I wouldn't let her attack you. You can have it done painlessly in any high street.'

Mrs Duggan harrumphed back into the flimsy garden chair,

140

which had been won by Mr Byrne in a Goat raffle and which Barca was now asleep under. 'She's too soft. What on earth are we going to do with her? I think she should study the classics. She's studious when she wants to be, and she has the qualifications.'

'Please, please don't go into that, Mrs Duggan.'

Mrs Bugler took pity on me. 'What a stuffy, dusty idea, Dymphna. There's more than one way to skin a cat. Look at me!'

We looked.

'I've achieved enough without going near a library.'

'You surely have, Hilda, but, as you've probably noticed, the times have changed. I was wondering, myself, if you had any ideas about how to get Jacinta a start.'

Mrs Bugler spent a moment getting Mrs Duggan's drift. Then she chickened her arms and declared, sorrowfully, that her wings were clipped.

'Stuck together, more likely,' said Mrs Duggan, 'and by something unmentionable.'

Mrs Bugler hooted with laughter and the dog's eyes flickered open. Crumbs rained off her cotton-jersey undulated middle as she stood up to give us her ideas on classical education.

'From the bed to the purple, that's what I say! I like to think I've had just about the most classical education going. And I'm not the only one. Look at Theodora, or the Dragon Empress!' We all had a good look around, to see if there were any whorish ghosts in the immediate vicinity. 'The other girls made mistakes, falling in love, getting pregnant, but not me. Marriage, the joint account, that's the ticket.'

'To what, Hilda, to what!' Mrs Duggan was not impressed. She wasn't even amused. She stood herself up so as to push Hilda back into her chair. 'Now sit down again. I know what you're saying, and there's no doubt, no doubt at all, that you're better off than most of us, but this is serious, very serious, and Jacinta here knows it.' But before she could

141

move on to my other possible vocations, I found a spanner to throw in the works.

'What about your triptych, Mrs Bugler? You know we've been doing a bit of clearing up at the shop.'

Mrs Duggan groped Barca under her chair and glanced angrily over at me.

'The triptych,' said Mrs Bugler, 'it's just wonderful, isn't it?'

'Yeah, but what's happening to it? Mrs Duggan wants her sheet back.'

'Oh, now, Jacinta. I don't really miss that old sheet at all, not at all.' The hypocrite. She was forever going on about the dust-sheet.

'Well, when Xanthe's completely finished, it's a matter of transport. It's a wonderful painting and it's going to have a wonderful home.'

'Where?'

She turned to face Mrs Duggan, 'Do you know what I'm thinking, Dymphna? I'm thinking the triptych might just suit my study in the Highgate flat. I need a screen.'

'Will it fit?' said Mrs Duggan anxiously. I wanted to ask if it was bank statements that she studied.

'Oh, I can make anything fit. So many people come to my pied-à-terre and admire the work I keep there. Time after time people say, "Bugo! Why are you so selfish? Why do you keep the best paintings for yourself?" But, of course, I'm far too selfish to share everything, too selfish by far. I do so love having my very own images to contemplate.'

'That's not selfish at all Hilda, not at all,' said Mrs Duggan, 'I'm sure we're all entitled to our little pleasures. But to get back to Jacinta here. What are we going to do with her?' She then outlined the other possibilities: a computer programming course (Ma) or an improving time abroad in an as yet unspecified country (Eugene). Mrs Bugler went for the second option.

'Oh Paree, Paree,' she shouted, 'you must go to Paree.

I'm like Persephone in Hades in England. Give me Paree any day. It's the place for an aesthetic woman.' It wasn't clear what she meant by that, whether she meant 'aesthetic' in blatantly subjective or deeply objective terms. She suggested that I talk to Eric Lennox about openings in the art world, for which a knowledge of Paree was one primary essential. I liked this idea. My mother, Mrs Duggan, they could guide you through thickets of men but they hadn't as much as a sniff of money, the only real lifter.

'Maybe I'll do that. I mean I'm surrounded by art and that, but it doesn't seem to connect with money, and Mr Lennox knows about how to make the connection.'

Mrs Duggan frowned at me for mentioning money. 'And where did Mr Lennox study?' she asked. When Mrs Bugler said he'd gone to Harvard she told us the Interesting Fact that this august institution has the smallest specimen of Giant Elk, so then we had to explain the current elk situation.

All was quiet on the elk front. There was nothing that we knew of on Mr Wilson's romantic horizon but he'd become even meaner of late, using the washing-up liquid instead of buying shampoo, and we had reason to believe that he was saving up for a life-determining experience in truly foreign parts. At first we'd thought he'd taken to drink, for he'd come home one afternoon looking even sicker than usual and unsteady on his feet. Then Mrs Duggan found an appointment card for a tropical clinic in his tracksuit pocket and on this evidence she was able to discover that he'd had a bad reaction to a cholera jab: 'And he doesn't need them if he's off to Blakeney Point.'

As for the most incorrigible elk, Mr Byrne, he had started wearing the fancy shirt given him at Easter by the unfaithful valentine wife.

'And you probably know, Hilda, as well as I do, what that means.'

Mrs Bugler assured Mrs Duggan that she did. When a man started to wear the clothes his lover had bought him it was

143

a sure sign that the relationship was finished. That got them back to the subject of Eric Lennox, whose shirts Mrs Duggan so admired, and Mrs Bugler said that as soon as he returned from his business in Japan I really had to consult him about my future. Then, perhaps because she felt excluded by the Lennox connection, Mrs Duggan said she was in the mood to read our tea-leaves. Mrs Bugler was very enthusiastic, declaring that teabags had all but extinguished that skill in the land, but she put me on line first.

Mrs Duggan got out her reading glasses and peered into the bottom of my teacup. 'Now let me see,' she said, staring at me more than the tea-leaves, 'you're run down because you're distracting yourself with too many bad influences. You should pay more attention to what age and experience have to say.'

There were no prizes for guessing which particularly aged and wise person I should be paying more attention to. Mrs Bugler coughed tactfully and leaned forward for a verifying look into my cup: 'Marvellous, really marvellous, Dymphna. Don't you think a holiday in Paree would be good for her, for both of them. They could stay in my apartment there.' The 'they' included Eugene. To my relief, Mrs Duggan forgot about me for a few moments.

'*He* needs a break. A change of scene would do *him* the world of good.'

In the silence during which we all considered how good a holiday in Paris would be for Eugene, there must have been some telepathic unison in our thoughts.

'And Xanthe,' Mrs Bugler asked, 'have you heard from her?'

'Not yet,' I said.

'Not at all,' said Mrs Duggan, 'but what would you expect? Haven't we all been thinking the same thing about it?' I disowned this effort at communality with an 'I don't know what you're talking about' stare, but she continued anyhow. 'At least George Sand took Chopin off to Majorca with her, but

144

that Xanthe woman, oh no, she wasn't having any of it, left poor Eugene behind with the cat.'

'I don't think he wanted to go, Mrs Duggan.'

'Yes,' said Mrs Bugler, 'I think Jacinta's right. I am told that he doesn't enjoy the sun.'

Mrs Duggan could change tack in a gale force wind. 'No,' she said by way of a subversive agreement, 'he's probably just as well off, leaving her to roast in splendid isolation.'

'Oh, I don't think that's quite true, Dymphna. As I understand it, some of her young colleagues, that sweet German girl, forget her name, and darling Hector, they planned to join her. They had exciting multi-media plans and it all sounded like jolly hard work to me.'

Darling Hector! How did she dare to mention him? I owned that name. I'd dragged it down to the bottom with me and I hadn't given anyone else permission to use it. I thought about bluffing more hurtful information out of Mrs Bugler by saying, 'Oh, Hector, you mean my friend Hector who's been keeping me awake for the past two months? He did tell me all about these travel fellowships that were up for grabs, even asked me to come along, but really I thought my place was in this stinking tapeworm of a street with Eugene and the fucking dog.' Instead, I bent down to rub Barca behind her ears. I tried to stop myself from imagining a naked Hector on a black beach. No wonder Xanthe had bought a wide angle lens.

When my eyes had stopped smarting I looked up and mentioned skin cancer. This was not an explicit part of Eugene's known dislike of hot places, and he was making no objections to central Spain as the location for the elderly Cortes shoot, but I went on about the ultra-violet rays. This was a mistake. Mrs Duggan was too happy to share my concern. She made a great business of congratulating Eugene on his escape. Only mad dogs, eccentric Englishmen and leathery old bats like Xanthe went out in the midday sun and Lanzarote was nothing more than a giant ashtray. But for a passing obsession with suntans this volcanic island, to which neither she nor I had ever been, would have been left to its resourceful population of peasants, lizards and mosquitoes.

As grist for her anti-Lanzarote mill Mrs Duggan was even unscrupulous enough to take an unhappy experience of Ma's Tom Broderick. When they had been on their holiday a mosquito had bitten him on his left eyelid, so that for several days he was virtually blinded by a monstrous swelling on his face and my mother had had to lead him around like a cantankerous old bear. When I'd told Mrs Duggan about the bite the significant thing had been Tom Broderick's less than stoical way of coping with it. Also, it had been an Interesting Fact that, on the whole, biting insects preferred women's blood, which meant that there was something very amiss about his hormones. But now we got torrents of sympathy for 'Tom', victim of a particularly depraved and vicious ecosystem.

For a moment Mrs Bugler looked worried, but then she got us back to sense and civilisation by telling us that there were no mosquitoes in her flat in Paree. I thanked her very much for the holiday suggestion, but said I'd have to take a rain check on it. Then I asked Mrs Duggan to read Hilda's leaves. They indicated that she was also too busy, gadding about in every direction, and that she'd be better off if she spent more time with her nearest and dearest. Mrs Bugler didn't take offence. She shook her frothy head, clasped her hands against her chest and said that this reading was simply too clairvoyant for words. Mrs Duggan smiled her magisterial smile.

My mother wanted to see me in the flesh again. Friday evenings saw me pilloried to the phone box beside Fin de Siècle while she ranted on about my lack of upwardly mobile fibre. My ex-schoolmates were frantic with form-filling while I was still pulling the fluff from my hairbrush. It was all very well for Eugene, grazing like a tinker's horse on other people's verges, but that wouldn't keep me.

146

Ma went on about my prospects when she was worried about her own. Computer engineers were crawling round her office, threatening the files on the dead with obsolescence, and the holiday with Tom Broderick had dented her optimism. Until Lanzarote Ma had believed that climate as well as religion were the opiums of all the Celtic peoples. It was the sunless weather that made them sceptical of schemes for social justice. If this doesn't seem to make much sense in historical or geopolitical terms it has to be remembered that my mother always argued from a vague particular, even if that particular, Tahiti in this instance, wouldn't stretch very well to anything general. She had imagined that under the blazing rays of the Lanzarote sun, boring old Thomas Broderick would metamorphose into a social democratic Romeo.

Instead he was reborn as a lumbering mass of complaining flesh. Some of the things Ma had selected him for – his method and his reliability – became odious. She watched him aligning their beach mats into an infuriatingly precise matrimonial parallel. She had to submit herself to a sunbathing programme of unsensuous scientificity. As she slapped high-factor lotion on to her lover's upper back she found herself cringing in distaste. At least women distributed their excess flesh all about their persons.

On day five things looked up. Just before noon Tom Broderick, who had been constipated until then, had a shit. He walked to the beach with a new sprightliness and he was enthusiastic about his lunch. But later that same day the mosquito had struck.

All this made me despair of simply requisitioning the old shoes. I had to go myself to sort them out, and hear her out.

When the campaign to get a Tom Broderick began, our house was the only one on the road, a suburban road south of Dublin city, without new aluminium windows. Such windows were well in place when I got home. Also, many of the things that hadn't worked before now did. For the first time in many years the front gate closed, the doorbell rang and the cold kitchen tap no longer wept. But even though Tom Broderick's insides and outsides were back in working order my mother wasn't happy on account of a male frailty as detrimental to her nerves as snoring or any foot and mouth problem.

Nothing short of a general strike or an international sabotage operation could put a stop to his appetite for a certain kind of information. Wherever and whenever he could, Tom Broderick got his news. Ma's morning lift to the hospital was accompanied by news from his car radio, and so was the lift home. Then, from six-thirty onwards, which is when they arrived at our house in the evening, he sat, his big pink face horribly rapt with attention, beside the radio or in front of the television. He couldn't get enough of the details of catastrophes, natural or otherwise. Was he expecting, at any moment, advance warning on the Day of Judgement, his summons to an examination in human misery in all of its ramifications? Ma didn't know, but she had tried to tolerate this habit and to understand it affectionately as a male thing, just like shaving. After all, it was a man's world, a manmade vale of tears we lived in, so wasn't his obsession with the misdoings of his peers only natural? But after the holiday her tolerance was so far stretched that she was afraid it would snap before the final payment on the aluminium windows.

She didn't like the sheer quantity of news. One morning radio bulletin and one evening television bulletin, plus a glance at one newspaper, were more than enough to remind her that she was better off for not being Kurdish. But what most offended her about Tom Broderick's habit was his passivity. Ma snorted and heckled her way through every news bulletin. When the news was bad, she was there in spirit, among the teargassed and batoned crowds; when it was good, she stood in great civic squares to greet released political prisoners. But Tom Broderick was content to be a witness. Whether Ma was full of hope or deep in despair, he just couldn't understand her relationship with history.

148

I solved that problem by giving him headphones that were compatible with the radio. The good thing was that he accepted them and put them on without a murmur. I didn't find him very inspiring. It was hard for me to respond to conversations beginning with 'Well now, Jacinta, do you think the interest rates will go up again or what?' But Ma still claimed to like the sound of his razor and to find his movements and habits reassuringly predictable. Also, I think she was touched by the artless compliments that poured out of him. He applauded her way with packet soup, noticed when she'd washed her hair, exclaimed with admiration when she put on an unfamiliar old sweatshirt. He was a profoundly resistible man but nobody else had worked so hard to be pleasing to her.

The headphones weren't compatible with the telly, but Ma could absent herself from the sitting room when Tom was glazed over. In fact she decided to help me sort shoes while he was on his second helping of a special report about post-hurricane relief efforts in the Bahamas.

At first my mother's offer of help worried me. If she were tangibly reminded of the shoes, she might waver in her willingness to give them to Fin de Siècle. Besides, I was proposing to deal first with the weapon shoes. The best and the worst moments in my mother's life were punctuated by these purchases – slingbacks, dagger heels, wedges and platforms – which had the most charged and negative associations. They were in cardboard boxes under the bed in my room. She followed me up there, insisting that even a couple of hours' respite from the news had given her courage. She also had a bottle of Lanzarote wine for us to share.

Although we had no crisps, and wine instead of cider, it was just like old times. It was while we were sitting on the bedroom floor, drinking our wine and pairing up the weapon shoes, like harbour womenfolk gutting fish, that she told me about her meeting with Xanthe.

*   *   *

149

The setting, Gatwick airport, was just like the settings I had considered for Eric Lennox's stories. My mother and Tom Broderick were waiting for the announcement of the revised departure time of their flight on to Dublin. She was restless and bored, and not inclined to dissipate what she had by way of a holiday karma by reading English tabloids. She rose from her seat and left Tom to damage his brain and dirty his fingers with the alien newspapers.

For a while she wandered about, just watching people. Ma liked watching people. She smiled at a newly-wed woman fingering her unfamiliar ring, and got a dirty look from the husband. She smiled again, more shyly, at the overalled woman who was pushing a wide brush against all the expensive litter, and she got no response. Then she fingered the tee-shirts and the sarongs in the airport shops and she checked her horoscope in several magazines. She was about to rejoin Tom Broderick when she saw the back wheel of a catering trolley running over the left foot of a tall woman in a baggy purple tracksuit.

It was the simultaneous accident to Xanthe's handbag, a gawping tapestry nosebag, which really aroused my mother. 'Gawd, I felt so sorry for her, storked by a trolley and everything in that hippy bag all over the floor.'

For Ma this was like being publicly disembowelled. A handbag was a repository for a woman's secrets: in a police state they would have to be transparent. You wouldn't want strangers, especially male ones, to be guessing at your menstrual cycle and your medical history, to know the price of your make-up and the state of your finances. The contents of this particular bag were fascinating. While Xanthe rubbed her foot, Ma pecked at a stubble of ancient lipsticks in brass holders, vintage, swollen tampons, a stapler and several batteries, a packet of clingwrap, a half-pound of pure henna, a Swiss army knife, plasticine, pencils, dirty notebooks full of dirty doodles, tissues and buttons, an invitation to a private view in Spitalfields and a half-paid electricity bill, the regu-

150

lations for the Tate Gallery's library, a miniature bottle of whisky, bus tickets, a turdish banana, a plug-in mosquito killer, a wooden afro comb, a heart-shaped bottle of purple nail polish and a photograph of Eugene Morphy, fully clothed.

'I know him,' she said as she handed this item up to its owner.

'That is not unusual,' said Xanthe, intimidating behind a pair of rhinestone-studded Fin de Siècle sunglasses.

'I do know him! I'm the unfortunate who married him. But that was before he went off to distribute himself in England.'

Lake Erie twitched as Xanthe managed a conciliatory smile. 'Yes,' she finally said, 'your daughter looks like you.'

'Do you think so? I worry about her, really I do.'

Then Xanthe told her again how I looked like her, as if it was the balance of my looks that caused the anxiety. When all of the bag's contents, or what she wanted of them, had been restored to her, she hauled my mother off her knees and together they went to one of the airport's coffee bars. Without consulting her, Xanthe strode over to the smokers' section. The ashtray on their table was somewhere beneath a pile of sweet wrappers and used plastic spoons.

'Disgusting, isn't it?' Ma said as she slid their tray on to the slimy table, but a silent Xanthe only looked above and all around them. Already, Ma was feeling foolish for having accepted the invitation to a coffee. Not for the first time, she had let curiosity get the better of her. Xanthe started rooting in the nosebag and eventually she produced the heart-shaped bottle of purple nail polish. Then she splayed the fingers of her left hand and painted each of the ragged nails with a lascivious precision.

'I've never seen that before, anyway.'
'What?'
'Nails being done like that, all over. You're not supposed to cover the half-moons.'
'Why?'
'Maybe it's better,' something stopped my mother from

151

telling Xanthe that painted half-moons weren't sophisticated, 'maybe it's healthier . . . for the nails' growth, I suppose.'

Xanthe was frowning as she blew upon her handiwork. It was quite obvious that the health of her nails was the last thing on her mind. She took a sip of her black coffee before starting on the other hand. Sometimes, for my sake, Ma diluted her disappointment in my father with the deficiencies of men in general, and she smothered all the other women in a sneering pity. But Xanthe was not a candidate for the usual barbed compassion. For a start, she was older than Eugene, and the bag's contents said it wasn't money that was being lavished upon him. Feeling very unsophisticated, Ma raised the only thing she and Xanthe had in common.

'Can't take coffee without milk and sugar myself. But I believe Eugene takes his coffee black now – he was a sugary-tea man when I was his sock sorter.'

Xanthe frowned again and wiggled her hands. At that moment passengers bound for Arrecife were summoned to their boarding gate. It was when Xanthe rose in response to this announcement that Ma realised the missed opportunity. She could have talked about Lanzarote.

'But then again, what I'd have told her wouldn't have been very relevant, would it?'

'Maybe not, Ma, but I'm sure Xanthe didn't mean to be unfriendly. She's not a talker.'

'No, you're right there. But I got that awful feeling, you know?' She looked over at me balefully. 'I mean I'm sitting here telling you all about her, and she's probably never given me a second thought.'

I did know that awful feeling, too well, but it would have hurt her more if I'd told her that. Ma liked to think I wasn't as vulnerable as she was. Calmly, I took her glass and refilled it, and then she smiled slyly to herself.

'Still, she didn't seem that bothered about him either.'

'She's an artist.'

'Bully for her. What's that supposed to mean?'

'She finds him useful. She says he's her aesthetic object.'

'I suppose that's one way of coping. She has to be some kind of voyeur type. He's a bit of an effigy at the best of times. Co-operation is the most you'd get out of him.'

'Ma! You're talking about my other progenitor.'

'Oh, I am sorry. You must excuse me. Forgot myself, thought I was talking about the man I married.'

'Well, how's Tom, then? Is he more than co-operative?'

She grabbed her wine. 'Honestly! You never win. He can be such a boring old shoveller.'

'I don't think Xanthe's got that sort of interest in Eugene. She's very tough.'

'Thought she was the type to do well for herself all right. I mean, there can't be that many of these Bugler fellowships going.'

I didn't tell her how it was, in fact, quite easy to get one of these particular fellowships. When we heard the final news-tone downstairs, the wine was finished. We were in the kitchen, nursing the kettle, when we heard a bullish roar coming from the living room.

Ma rushed out into the hall. 'What is it, Tom? What's happened?'

'You missed it, Maria, you missed the ad for Miller's Ingots.'

I sat between them on the sofa until the next commercial break came up. It was the old Cortes ad, the one with Montezuma, and Tom Broderick very sweetly asked me if I'd like him to video it. I was thinking about this when Ma lassoed my eyes.

'Oh no, Tom, we don't want any of that. We've had enough of that sort of carry-on already, haven't we, Jacinta?'

She became pointedly nostalgic about the financial benefits of the first Miller's Ingots campaign. The sofa, for example, look how scruffy it was. That dated from the first campaign and it was time we got another one. Then she turned on me sharply to say that I had to make sure of my own cut from

153

the new commercial. I shrugged and said I had to work in the shop while Eugene was away in Spain and that, quite apart from what I'd be getting for this, I had the shoes and another little earner in Pimlico.

That night, in spite of the wine, I found it hard to sleep. As I rummaged round, looking for a soporific read, I came across Ma's address book. Tom was still under 'B' and Eugene wasn't in it at all, which was probably fair enough: Mrs Duggan's particulars covered his knowable ones, as well as mine. However, under 'J' I found the telephone number of Eric Lennox's house, which is where I tended to be when Ma was able to phone me from her office. For some of the entries she'd started using her hospital RIP stamp because, just above my Lennox number, Jack Fennessy's ranch in Arizona was obscured by three blotchy black letters.

Now this was a very interesting, not to say momentous, way of arranging things. My mother was a pathologically efficient woman. According to her system, if Fennessy was under 'J', that meant she had had carnal knowledge of him. All my life I'd believed that my name had been inspired by my grandmother's piety and the Fatima connection. Until I stared at the page with 'J' for Jack and 'J' for Jacinta, I hadn't any other data on my namesakes. The questions I wanted to ask were worth another bottle of wine, and another session alone with my mother, as soon as possible.

I didn't have to invest in more wine because next morning, while I was still in bed, she barged into the room with two cups of tea.

'Where's Tom?'

'Sunday. He takes his mother to Mass.'

'That's nice.'

It was, for me anyway. To keep the Victorian mother sweet, Tom Broderick's stayovers in our house were scheduled around an unusually demanding postgraduate degree. This course involved numerous fieldtrips to faraway places, including Lanzarote, and collaboration with a fellow student, Maria Murphy, who had in her custody some very obscure software. But until Ma had come into my room, I thought that the studious Tom Broderick would be with us for the whole weekend.

'I don't know if it is or it isn't, nice. But let's be thankful for small mercies – no news until Monday morning.' She noticed the address book, which was beside my pillow. 'God, you must have been really bored last night.'

'Actually, I wasn't,' I said, sitting up properly, 'it's very interesting. I hope you'll leave it to me.' I opened the book and confronted her with the meaningful J-section.

'J is for Jack . . .'

'Yeah, well, you couldn't be more of a Jack than he was, a Jack-rabbit and a Jack of all women.'

'And J is for Jacinta.'

'Yeah. So?'

'So, is that just a phonetic coincidence or what?'

'What's come over you? Is that Duggan person putting more ideas into your head? It's a coincidence, and a very ordinary one, if you ask me, not like the coincidence of me meeting that nail-biter at Gatwick Airport.'

'So, in spite of the fact that he's been filed in here under his first name, Jack Fennessy never fancied you?'

'Of course he fancied me!' Vanity always got the better of her. 'And the fact that I was married didn't make a blind bit of difference, but if you'd met the horse of a wife he had at the time, you wouldn't have been surprised.'

'But you didn't stay in touch, after I was born, and the film was done?'

'No . . .' She realised that she had walked right into it, having said just enough to make herself liable for the question on my face. She stopped and stared at me for a few moments.

'Now listen to me, girl,' for emphasis, she took my mug of tea away, 'Jack Fennessy had eleven children when I was counting and they were the official, paid-for ones, so if you're reading anything into anything, stop! Stick with the father you got stuck with Jacinta Murphy, because, believe me, he's far more exclusive, and,' she gave me back my tea, 'he has one great advantage.'

'What's that?'

'He's not dead.'

That was probably the nicest thing she had ever said about Eugene. It filled me up with a warm and nurtured feeling, which lasted for hours.

SAINT CHRISTINA THE WONDERFUL

nother of her freaks was to climb the poles with wheels set up outside the town, on which robbers and murderers had been broken, and to writhe her arms and legs in and out of the spokes, with more dexterity than delicacy, after the fashion of an executed criminal, and thus hang for hours to the wonderment and applause of the children. Or she would climb the gallows where the dead and rotting criminals hung, and forgetting her olfactory delicacy for the occasion, fasten a rope between the corpses, and dangle herself between them. All which, of course, was done to relieve the souls in purgatory.

9

Armed to the teeth with Ma's slingbacks and stilettos, I got back to a summerish London. There was sun enough to force a sickly carnival. The back yards and the parks shimmered with exposed white flesh, ice cream vendors appeared like mushrooms and Mrs Duggan's big metal bin stank like Lazarus. Although nothing like my mother's sunkist revolution was in the air, Hebden Street had become more of a street, less of a wall with windows.

In the middle of this thaw the new Fin de Siècle sparkled. Out on a baked pavement the least faded cottons fluttered under bright yellow dress rails and the permanently open door exposed an intimidation of light and space. It worried me slightly. Our best spenders were like Western tourists in search of squalorous underdevelopment: they'd enjoyed the musty smells, the erratic hours and the unpredictable prices of the old Fin de Siècle. As for the others, the ones looking for sanctuary, they might be inhibited now that their fumblings among secondhand clothes could be seen from without. Eugene said he'd leave the stock thinned and the door wide open only until the smell of paint had worn off. I was also curious about how his visibility would affect sales, and him. No more egg sandwiches and pedicures for Eugene Morphy. Propped up on the *chaise-longue*, which was scheduled for an upholsterer, he was as exposed as a goldfish.

I disgorged the first bagload of shoes on to the stripped wooden floor in front of the *chaise-longue*.

159

'Ah,' he said, rubbing his hands, 'Maria's sins. There will be more joy in heaven about the resale of these shoes than there's been over any amount of cash refunds.'

Xanthe bounded down from her studio. A week after her return from Lanzarote she was still startling to look upon. The face, arms and legs had the sheen of a Peking duck, and the grey hairs had been henna-blasted to copper. It was an aggressive, healthy animal who inspected our shoes. Xanthe approved of such good clean stock, but she refused to lend us a scalpel for erasing the sole size-marks.

'This is not a good idea.'

With his hands over his head, Eugene crouched down and whinged: 'Please, Miss, it was her idea.'

'I thought they'd move faster if we rubbed out the sizes.' There was no point in explaining the idea properly. The free-range, unbounded Xanthe wouldn't understand my mother's hang ups or appreciate their generality.

'A stupid idea, to mutilate these shoes. They are perfectly good. No one will worry about catching an infection from them. They must keep their history.' She stood squarely in front of Eugene and lit a cigarette. He smelled work.

'If you're imagining, my dear Xanthe, that I'm going to sit here and tell the next customer that this here crippler,' he had a candy-striped slingback dangling from his wrist, 'was bought in compensation for a bad pint at the Flowing Tide and subsequently stigmatised its owner when she wore it on a Dublin May Day march, you have, I'm afraid, another thing coming.'

'This is a good start, excellent.' Xanthe was so pleased, she was showing her teeth. 'In fact, this is what should be done for everything. We will be in the antique clothes business. We will sell the history.'

'But they're not exactly cheerful histories,' I ventured. 'The suits, for a start. They've come off the backs of men who've died, or gone off with other women.'

'The things for men are not as important.'

160

'But the women's clothes are even more depressing. I can't see me saying, "Oh, that jacket looks really terrific on you, but of course it was bought by someone who was a bit low and overweight, and when she lost a few pounds she put it in with her jumble."'

'No! Good, strong stories must be invented to go with everything.'

'Can I hinterest heither of you ladies in these 'ere shorts,' with the scalpel Eugene had speared a pair of men's shorts, 'I 'ave been reliably hinformed that they was worn in a Cambodian prisoner-of-war camp.'

Xanthe snatched the shorts and tucked them under one arm. 'I have just had a very good idea and you will not spoil it. Jacinta will help.'

He aimed the scalpel at the back of the *chaise-longue* and said he was off to place a bet for Mrs Duggan. I pulled the scalpel out and gave it to Xanthe. She sat down and studied the hairs on one shin against its blade. She didn't shave her legs. She didn't have to because of the honorary Frenchness. People, Mrs Duggan, thought she didn't know any better. I was jealous because the tanned Xanthe seemed to match Hector.

'How was it there, anyway?'

'It was very nice.'

'No mosquitoes, then?'

'Mosquitoes?'

'I'm told they're a problem.'

'Perhaps they are for some people. Bugo gave me a machine for them.' This was Xanthe at her friendliest. She ran back upstairs to fetch her photographs. Soothingly, there were no people, no basking Hectors, in them. In fact, to my eyes, the pictures were only marginally superior to my mother's snapshots. I'd already seen these camels, volcanic barbecues, walled vines and black beaches. But then I thought, if this is all she has to show for her working fellowship, what was she really up to?

'I'm glad you had an interesting time. It's been very boring here.'

'Eric is very bored?'

'I don't know, really. I wouldn't know. Is he always like that?'

The lip-lake wobbled into a smile. 'Like what?' she asked as she clicked her cigarette lighter.

'He doesn't exist very much, does he? I mean he hardly eats . . .'

'He would like to be eaten.'

The enigmas were wearing me down. 'Why did you chuck the cleaning job in?'

'Oh, it was boring,' she exhaled, 'the rich are boring.'

'But Bugo's rich, and she's not boring, is she?'

She had another little think about that, and then she agreed with me. 'No, Bugo is not so boring but she is very bored.' That was as much as you could get out of a conversation with Xanthe.

While I was out buying a shoe rack Xanthe stayed downstairs in the shop. I came back to find that the strappiest white shoes had been sold. By four o'clock on the same day all the cream pairs had gone, and for more than we'd first thought of asking. Xanthe thought we should invest in a real cash register. I didn't ask her what history she'd given the sold shoes.

Nobody mentioned the triptych, which, so far as I knew, was still sticky under the floral sheet we'd borrowed from Mrs Duggan. Next morning its subject raided the shop for suitable hot-weather clothes. He was adjusting his straw hat in Fin de Siècle's big mirror when I came in with the last of the weapon shoes.

'What are those people called, the crowd who pay for Bibles in hotels?'

'Gideon.'

'Don't you think the world would be a kinder place all

162

round if there were more flattering mirrors about? I must recommend a universal mirror charity to Bertie Bugler. If people liked themselves more, they'd be happier, wouldn't they?'

'They could certainly learn a lot about that from you.'

'That's no way to talk to a man about to do a Second Coming.'

'I'm sorry. I really hope it goes well for you.'

'Of course it will. It's a cinch. No armour, no horse, no dogs. I simply have to skulk somewhere along the imperial coach route.'

'That's great. You're great at the skulking.'

'Do you think so?' He was great at accepting compliments too.

'Yeah, but speaking of skulking, I haven't seen Amelia about since I got back.'

'No,' a sudden look of vagueness gave him away, 'yes, she's not been about recently. I think she's on holiday.'

'That's nice. Mrs Bugler wants us to have a holiday. She says we could have her place in Paris.'

'How very affable of her, but, I should warn you, Mrs Duggan doesn't travel well.'

'No! Me and you having a holiday together, father and daughter-like, that's what she was thinking of.' To keep things nicely brittle, I opened a packet of crisps. Eugene loathed crisps.

'Now, Jassie, you, more than some, are what you eat, and potatoes make potatoes.'

'What a load of crap!' I was crunching away.

'Must you be so vulgar?'

I licked my lips. Now was a time for playing the alternative-father card, but vanity stopped me. Whatever else he'd been, Jack Fennessy was no sylph. In any of the pictures I'd seen, so far, he had a big spade-shaped face and tree-trunk legs that pinioned the poor horse under him. Besides, Eugene

Morphy was only looking for an excuse to be shot of me and there was no point in encouraging him.

'Yeah, maybe I am vulgar, maybe I'm having the petty but far from ignoble courage to live without reference to anything but my own imagination.'

He shook his head in disgust. 'If you're a size fourteen again before the summer's out, you only have yourself to blame.'

I shovelled in the last crumbs and scrunched up the packet.

'I wonder where Amelia's gone. You get interesting birds in Spain, don't you, vultures and that . . .'

He pretended to be very absorbed by the faulty fly on the Cambodian shorts. I didn't push him on the subject of the slender Amelia's probable whereabouts.

Eric Lennox liked temperate summers and rhubarb tarts. Although he continued to wear his CIA coat outside, he adjusted to the relative heat by wearing his shirts without a tie, and baggy cotton trousers which needed ironing. He said he was very pleased to see me on account of the dust which had accumulated during my absence. He'd even brought me a present from Japan, a pair of enamelled butterfly ear-rings in a butterfly-shaped basket box. I had no trouble getting into a rapture about them. They were worth mutilating myself for.

'I don't have holes in my ears, see,' I pointed at my virgin lobes, 'but I've been meaning to have them done anyhow. Mrs Bugler told me a good place.'

I explained what a simple procedure it was and he got quite excited.

'Let's go!' he said.

'But what about the dust?'

'Some other time.'

We directed a taxi to Camden Town. The sign in the chemist's window said 'EARS PIERCED HYGIENICALLY AND PAINLESSLY – £5, STUDS INCLUDED'. I don't know what if any qualifications an

164

ear-piercer has to have but I was reassured by the fact that it appeared to be the pharmacist himself, in surgical gloves and a scientific white coat, who came out to do me. While Eric watched, he pinched my lobes, marked their centres with a felt-tip pen and sprayed them with a local anaesthetic. Then he got out his ear-punching gun and inserted a gold stud into it, so that after he had done first one ear and then the other I had a blob of gold icing on each lobe.

I didn't even 'ouch' while this was going on but I had no chance to admire the reward for my courage because when I'd handed over the fiver I saw that Eric, with his glasses on his lap, was sitting on the victim's chair. The pharmacist looked over at me. It was obvious that my sugar brother had not on the spur of the moment decided to have his own little ears done.

'Eric, what's the matter?'

He opened his mouth to gasp: 'You told me it was a simple procedure. I didn't figure on the blood.'

You'd swear I'd just had his baby, or worse. The pharmacist wasn't sympathetic. He said he was fed up to his back teeth of blokes fainting in the shop and he blamed me for taking my 'boyfriend' along. I had to put Eric's head between his knees and another customer bullied the shop assistant into bringing a glass of water. I put the spectacles in my pocket and sploshed water around Eric's face. Back on the pavement he was still mute and wobbly, and the driver of the first taxi I flagged down asked if he was pissed. It was getting worrying. Eric out of his hamster cage was a liability. I pulled his CIA collar up around his lower jaw and told a taxi-driver who was stuck at red lights that my companion had just had a wisdom tooth out. Grudgingly, he let us fall into his cab.

We were at Euston when I realised that I only had five pounds on me. Eric, with the ghoulish, vacant-eyed face still on him, was hunched up on the seat. His little bag dangled from a limp wrist. With his permission, or at least without any resistance, I opened it. I'd never seen the inside of a

165

man's personal bag before but I shouldn't think the contents of this one were typical. There was a concertina wallet of credit cards, no good for the present situation, a packet of tissues, a mouth-freshening spray, a bottle of herbal indigestion tablets, a comb and a load of Japanese currency. I gave Eric a reassuring look and zipped it up with apparent satisfaction. I didn't want to start frisking him for his sterling. Our driver was the sort who would have thrown Madame Bovary and whatsisname out of their coach. I yelled at his fat neck: 'Hey mister, stop when we've had five quids' worth, will you.'

The traffic wasn't too bad so we managed to get as far as Waterloo Bridge. Even while the cabbie was snorting and snarling Eric continued to stare dully ahead. I kept my shoulders under him as I steered him towards the South Bank. I was being awfully sensible. I thought the air and the sights, so touching in their majesty, would set him to rights and by the time we got down to the river we did have two tongues between us. He perked up more when I told him I was hungry. We sat at a table near the National Film Theatre and he ordered me a chicken salad with garlic bread. Then, obviously feeling better, he said he was sorry for causing such a commotion.

'I guess I thought it might be interesting.'

'Actually, I was hoping that the end result, as opposed to the process, would be interesting.'

He reached over the table, pulled my hair over my ears and croaked admiringly, 'But it was interesting. That guy was some kind of a sadist.'

Who was he to be talking of sadists? 'Beauty often involves pain,' I said, stiffly.

To tell the truth, I wasn't at all sure that anything interesting or beautiful had resulted from my ordeal. Because of his reaction I hadn't had a chance to examine my lobes and for all I knew they were a bloody mess. Before my food arrived I went to the ladies' for an inspection. There was evidence,

166

at the base of the little gold studs, of only a fingerprick's worth of blood. When I returned to the table my still-life of a lunch was on it, but Eric was absent. I looked around to see him leaning sickishly over the wall beside the river. He put his glasses on and returned with another funny look on his face.

'I got my lunettes from your pocket, Jacinta.'

'Oh yeah, sorry, I should have told you to go ahead.'

'That's all right. What I'd like to know is,' he pointed under the table to the other thing that resided in my cardigan pocket, 'what is that?'

Mr Byrne's socks had worked a treat. Eric had pulled them out with his specs and nearly fainted right away again. I had to explain. Otherwise he might have thought they were my socks. He shivered while I told him how ecological a method of self-defence it was. The fate of the Amazonian rainforest worried Eric like nothing else, and I thought his concern for me was similarly intense, similarly distant. The pollution in my life bothered him. My welfare wasn't crucial in macro terms, but in Eric's opinion I was 'too smart and too young' to be cleaning his house and off-loading secondhand shoes.

Of course I agreed with him. He fingered his smooth chin thoughtfully as I gave a rough summary of the various strategies for getting me into the boorjwazee. He said he would discuss Paris with Mrs Bugler. While he was putting Mr Byrne's socks in a bin, I took the tip he'd left our waiter for my bus fare back to Hebden Street.

Mrs Duggan was oppressed by the heat but she had Barca to take it out on. Whenever she mislaid her sunhat, which the dog was fond of chewing, she enquired peevishly about the normal lifespan of fox terriers. She didn't mention my sore ears until I was having my ironing lesson. We were concentrating on a load of cotton blouses for Fin de Siècle, job interview blouses, when she leaned over and pulled back my hair. 'So you've gone and had that done.'

I told her that when the six weeks of boring studs were up I had two pairs of real ear-rings to graduate to. Immediately she was suspicious.

'Would he be one of these yuppies?' (She pronounced it as 'yoopies'.)

'No, Mrs Duggan, I think they're supposed to be better at enjoying themselves than he is.' Then I showed her the Japanese butterfly ear-rings. She couldn't admire them without making a little dig about Greeks bearing gifts.

'Greeks! I thought it was Romans I had to look out for.'

'Same thing. Watch yourself with that shirt-fancier now, won't you?'

Really, what she meant was 'don't give yourself to the shirt-man until you've got more than a pair of ear-rings out of him.' I could appreciate her concern for my welfare, but the U-turn bugged me.

'Back in June I'm sure you'd have sold me to Eric Lennox for a couple of his shirts, never mind a pair of quite expensive ear-rings.'

'Sshh, that's a terrible thing to say. You know I only have your best interests at heart.'

'It might be easier for me to cope with my best interests if you were a little bit more consistent about what they are.'

'Since when has consistency been a virtue? Could you tell me that? The world would stop dead in its tracks if it wasn't for women changing their minds, doing things differently . . .'

'Right! I'll try to remember. It's important to keep on changing your line on fundamental issues, about floosies with bearskins, for example?'

She flicked a damp blouse at me and smiled her deepest, chinniest smile. These days Mrs Duggan was going in for superpower-style diplomacy and the rehabilitation of Hilda/Bugo was only a start. While the elderly Cortes was skulking in Spanish shades, she was warming up to Xanthe. The ironing marathons for Fin de Siècle were a part of the new *entente.* Of course Xanthe and Mrs Duggan had yet to be properly introduced but, probably because Mrs Bugler appeared to be thick with Xanthe, Mrs Duggan felt obliged to insist on a prior acquaintance. Xanthe had done nothing to resist the convergence on her goodwill and the three of them had even formed themselves into the committee for the organisation of Eugene Morphy's surprise birthday party.

It had been Mrs Bugler's suggestion and she'd volunteered to subsidise the occasion. Still stuck in England for the summer, the party was another way of being involved with us. Mrs Duggan justified her enthusiasm for the party plan with another motive. Eugene's birthday party was to be a hook for unattached women, one of whom might be happy to take Mr Byrne home in her party bag. (Mr Wilson's plan to melt away entirely by leaving for India in October put him out of the match-making picture.) While I was ironing and bleating about my mother, Amelia, Mrs Bugler, Eric Lennox and the future in relation to each of these individuals, Mrs Duggan drafted the party invitation. She was proposing to insert it in the *Advertiser*: THE FRIENDS OF EUGENE MORPHY ARE CORDIALLY INVITED TO CELEBRATE HIS 48TH BIRTHDAY AT FIN DE SIECLE OF HEBDEN STREET ON FRIDAY AUGUST 30TH FROM 8PM.

'You're mad. You can't go ahead with an ad like that.'

'What's the matter, girl? He won't see it, and there's nothing he can do about it in any case.'

'Except refuse to deliver himself up. Just think for a moment, think of all the derelicts who know him, of all the women he's slighted, of all the men he owes money to . . .'

'You've got a point there. It's the others, they have me distracted. I'll scrap this. We'll get enough of a crowd, enough of a mixture anyway, if we just spread the word round the street and the Goat.'

For extra richness to the mixture, Mrs Duggan had her old phone-message books. Some of the females whose messages were recorded there would be invited. Sheila, for example. Mrs Duggan recollected the extraordinarily dense eyebrows and she thought they'd complement Mr Byrne's moustache. Until I told her about Eyebrows Sheila's baby, she'd been straining about the right way of introducing them.

When I'd finished ironing the blouses I put them on hangers to take them back to Fin de Siècle. Halfway down the street I saw Hopalong leaning against the bumper of the Bugler BMW. He stood up, saluted me and waved at the shop. I manoeuvred the blouses inside to find Hector sitting on the *chaise-longue*. My father's records, which were only played at Fin de Siècle, were on the floor in front of his sandalled feet. He was wearing a Joint tee-shirt and his glossy hair had grown almost to his shoulders. Since I was in a clinical state of shock it was easy to sound casual.

'Oh hiya, Hector. Long time no see. What are you up to?'

'Makin' a tape, for the par'y.'

'That's nice. Where are the others?'

'Gone swimmin'. Ladies' Pond in 'ampstead 'eath.' He looked at his watch and then fished some keys from his shorts pocket. 'I'm collectin' them now.'

'I'll come too.'

He helped me to pull the outside clothes rails in from the pavement. Then, while I locked Fin de Siècle, he peeled Hopalong off the car. I sat in the front passenger seat and watched him twiddling the ignition key.

'Stinks of dog in 'ere?'

I nodded as he lowered all the windows. 'I'm sorry I'm no use. It's all Greek to me. I don't drive.'

'S'all right. You can wave at the populace.'

I was stunned. What a sentence! What a long word! The pure physicality of my obsession often worried me. My fantasies about Hector had no captions. Now I was reassured that he did have a personality. I could savour his coppery arms with a clearer conscience.

As Mrs Bugler's sensuous car slid down Hebden Street I felt a faint rush of wind in my hair. Hector turned another knob and we got a blast from *The Magic Flute*. Although this

170

wasn't the right music, an almost American atmosphere of speed, sun and youth lasted until we were stuck in traffic on the Highgate Road.

'I wish we'd keep on moving. I wish we could stay in this car and never stop.'

'Wot?' He cut off the warbling Queen of the Night.

'I said I wish we could just keep on driving for ever.'

He seemed to understand what I was saying, or feeling, because he grunted amiably and smiled into the mirror. I tried to think of another clincher, something for him to make a definite response to, but I was blocked. I'd written him a thousand letters in my head, so I imagined a risk of repeating myself, or boring him. When we got to the top of the Highgate Road, just beyond Parliament Hill, we hovered. Then a parked car behind us pulled away and Hector swung back into its space.

'What kind of tape are you making?'

'Thought I'd start with early Dylan.'

'He'd like that.'

'Then bi' of Motown, bi' of the Doors, bi' of Van Morrison, or Neil Young?'

'I can see them.'

He started the engine. Two sturdy women in loose summery frocks staggered towards us. A tulip-splashed Mrs Bugler was waving a battery-operated hairdryer at a purple-spotted Xanthe's damp and unkempt head. 'Yuhu!' she cried when she'd seen the car, 'it's les enfants.' She wrenched open the back door and told Xanthe to clamber in first. Then they both put on their sunglasses.

'Marvellous, marvellous. Seventy degrees today. Xanthe nearly swallowed a duckling.'

Xanthe laughed. 'Is smoking permitted in this car?'

Mrs Bugler said, 'Ask our charming young chauffeur,' but he shook his head.

Xanthe clicked her teeth. 'Still, I like to be driven to and from the exercise. I don't like running. Swimming is better.'

171

'I couldn't agree more. Does Eugene swim?'

I turned round to tell four enormous black lenses that he couldn't and didn't.

'Can't swim! Can't drive! Honestly! What are we going to do with this useless ornament to society?'

Xanthe's laugh crackled again.

Hopalong had been asked to keep the parking space. We pulled into Hebden Street to see him asleep on the road. Mrs Bugler was delighted. It was so 'deliciously Third World'. She fished in her boot for a coolbag containing ice and a flask of made-up Pimms while Hector coaxed Hopalong awake. The car was properly parked and Hopalong was upright on the pavement, counting out his money, when Mrs Duggan came into view. She had Barca's lead in one hand and her little pink evening bag in the other.

'Yuhu! Dymphna!'

Barca yelped with excitement and strained at her leash so that Mrs Duggan was bent double. We could see her cursing to herself. As she got within earshot she let Barca off the lead. 'I wish you wouldn't make a show of me like that, Hilda. You don't have to live in this street.'

'Oh, stuff and nonsense, Dymphna. Come and have a Pimms with us.' Mrs Duggan had no choice. Barca had frisked up the street and followed Xanthe into the shop. Hector ran after them. He was pulling the records that were still on the floor out from under Barca's paws when we got there. She yelped and rolled over to present him with her pink belly. Dutifully, he tickled it.

'Oh, she likes you, she does,' Mrs Duggan said, but even when Mrs Bugler had set up her Pimms apparatus and was handing round plastic tumblers, she refused to sit down.

'Have a Pimms Dymphna.'

'No thank you Hilda.'

'Have a cup of tea, then.'

Mrs Duggan hesitated. She didn't think much of Xanthe's tea. 'Ah no, I must be on my way.' She moved aside for a customer. 'This place is over-garrisoned as it is. People will be thinking it's a front for something very unsavoury. Don't you have a husband to be looking after?'

'Bertie's being very well looked after. It's his aroma-therapy day. Lovely girl, single parent. She comes to the house. For goodness sake, sit down. Jacinta will make you some tea.'

She looked over at me but I was riveted by Hector. With Barca still panting at his feet, he was gathering the records into his canvas bag. When he stood up straight and raised his tee-shirt to tickle the warm brown skin of his midriff, I was wishing I were a dog. I would have liked to have rolled over on my back, and for him to have tickled me. I was right back where I'd started.

With a great sigh, Mrs Duggan hoisted herself into the chaise-longue. 'I haven't been introduced to this young man.'

'Sorry. Mrs Duggan, this is Hector. Hector, this is Mrs Duggan. He's making a tape for the birthday party.'

'Well, that's very nice and I'm sure he knows,' after nodding sternly at him, she turned to the others, 'what he's doing, I'm only glad the racket's not going to tear my house apart.'

'He does know what he's doing,' Xanthe said. She had just sold two of the pristine office blouses. I decided to exercise my status as the birthday man's next of kin by formally thanking Hector. 'Yes. It's very kind of you. I'm sure my father will appreciate it.'

'Ah, it's nuffin. Mean, it's like family, innit?' Xanthe ruffled his long black hair and he looked at her to say: 'You and Euge, you're like parents really. Lot of people feel that.'

Xanthe grimaced fondly, but I didn't appreciate the idea of Eugene and Xanthe as some kind of community service, of myself and Hector as honorary siblings. They might as well have nominated Barca as kin. The social dilution of my reunion with Hector was irritating. I got a bit of distance by volunteering to put on a kettle for Mrs Duggan's tea. While

I was in the back kitchen I twiddled the studs in my ears. A cut-price acupuncturist had given Mr Byrne a pin which he prodded into his left ear whenever he felt vulnerable to a cigarette. I was seeing if my sore ears could work as a distraction from the tingling that Hector aroused.

Cradling her Pimms and nestling into the good end of the *chaise-longue*, Mrs Bugler announced that though she had heard 'all about Lanzarote', she had heard very little about Hector's tour with the blues band, which had terminated at Madrid. Now she pounced upon some incoherent morsels about Continental motorways and when he told her that he was soon to be away again, she offered him the apartment in Paree. Between grunts of attention, an uneasy Mrs Duggan watched Barca scrambling under the blouse rail. Just as the kettle began to scream, a familiar floral pattern caught her eye.

'There's my sheet.'

Mrs Bugler bounced off the *chaise-longue* to move the blouse rail. She pulled off the sheet and with Hector's help raised the triptych from its side. Then she opened it out.

'Voilà!'

The first two scenes were unchanged but the last picture, the death scene, had been livened up. Now, like the three Marys by the Cross, Mrs Duggan, my mother and myself were having paroxysms over the Eugene who was still slumped among the slobbery wolfhounds. Mrs Duggan was wringing a gingham apron into a twist and Ma's arms were raised but I was motionless, a sullen heifer with hair in her eyes. Above us, in a deep blue sky, a pair of force-fed cherubs were hovering flatulently.

It wasn't flattering but since no one in the triptych – and Mrs Bugler still didn't feature – had got off lightly, least of all Xanthe herself, it would have been uncool, in Hector's presence, to protest. I could only hope that this was the last we'd be seeing of it.

'So it's going home,' was all I said.

174

'Oh, not quite yet,' said Mrs Bugler, 'you see, I've had a little idea. I think it might make a nice centrepiece for our party? But what do you think, Dymphna?'

Mrs Duggan had seen enough, I could see that, but she stalled by making a very obstetric business of fishing her reading glasses out of the beaded bag. Slowly she put them on and then, as Xanthe made for the safety of the kitchen, she had another stare at the triptych.

'I'm no judge,' she finally said, removing her glasses and furiously polishing them, 'and I don't know what we're supposed to be doing in it, but let's be thankful for small mercies. At least we're fully clothed.' At my nod she turned up the volume, hoping to be heard by Xanthe. 'You're taller than your mother now, aren't you, but maybe,' her voice trailed off, 'maybe that isn't relevant.'

'But isn't it a hoot?' Mrs Bugler insisted. 'The little cherubs were my idea. I think they give it a baroque je ne sais quoi.'

Mrs Duggan was saved from further comments by the cup of tea that Xanthe emerged with. 'Thank you very much,' she said, looking dubiously into it, 'I don't know what to say about that. What do you think, Jacinta, about Hilda's little idea?'

'I don't like it and I'm not having it. The sooner that fucking dog's dinner finds its way to your boudoir the better as far as I'm concerned.'

Mrs Duggan recovered herself. 'Now now, Jacinta, watch the language. There's no need to be so rude to Hilda. Sure it's only a little joke.'

'At whose expense? Not hers.' Xanthe had found her cigarettes and disappeared into the street, but Hector's still eyes were fixed on me. They gave me confidence. 'I'm not going to the party, and I'll make sure he doesn't if that's exhibited at it.'

'Of course we'd respect your decision, Jacinta, but I think, I really do, that you're over-reacting. Eugene would enjoy it as much as we do.'

175

I couldn't pin her down on this 'we' because of a customer, a woman who had already bought many of the weapon shoes and who was now after a pair of satin pumps. But Barca had dislodged the shoes from their rack.

'I'm sorry. They're all jumbled up. You can poke around if you like. I'm sure they're still there.'

'Fine, fine.' She waved me aside and got down on her hunkers beside the scattered shoes.

'Well, I should be going,' said Mrs Duggan, glancing at the customer and picking up Barca's lead, 'there's great drying in this weather and I'm only getting in the way of business here.'

'Sit down Dymphna. You haven't had your tea and you're not getting in the way of anything.' It was true. Entertaining Mrs Bugler was worth more than a pair of secondhand shoes. Still, she didn't want to upset us.

'Don't worry, Jacinta. Forget my silly idea. I'm not offended. If you feel strongly, that's that.'

I shrugged and Xanthe came back inside. To pass her the Pimms flask Hector had to step over the dust-sheet. Mrs Bugler bent down to pick it up. As she was standing in the middle of the shop a mad gleam seeped into her eyes. Then she made a rush at Hector, flung the sheet over him and boomed: 'Hail Hector! Knew you not Pompey!'

Swathed in pastel polyester, Hector was transfixed. We all were. Maybe, like me, he thought he was in for an impromptu haircut. The sheet was covering him like a hairdresser's cape. But that's not what Mrs Bugler was thinking.

'Just look, Xanthe! Isn't he perfect?'

'Perfect for what, might we ask?' said Mrs Duggan.

'For our latest job. Xanthe and I are going to decorate a pizza parlour. Murals on an ancient Roman theme.'

'I take it that he'll be decent, then,' Mrs Duggan sniffed, 'and he won't be getting a chill while he's providing you with your inspiration.'

Hector was staring at the floor and Xanthe was still silent

when our lone customer spoke, rather she made a sound, one of disgust. Holding up a pink satin pump, she studied each of us in turn before passing it to me. Inside the shoe there was a freshly laid puppy turd.

'I'm terribly sorry.' I really was, but Xanthe was businesslike.

'We can give a discount,' she said, taking a swipe at Barca, 'fifty pence each for the shitty shoes.'

The disgraced Barca leaped into Hector's arms and his flowery toga fell to the floor. While Mrs Duggan and Mrs Bugler were examining the defiled shoe I invited the customer to sit down for a drink. She had more than recovered when Mrs Bugler started footering in her handbag. She was insisting that she should pay for the shoes since Barca's toilet training was really her responsibility.

'Oh no Hilda, what comes out of that animal is my responsibility. Put that bag away!'

They got stuck into a tug-of-war over Mrs Bugler's purse, pulling it this way and that, but I knew that Mrs Duggan would win in the end, and that there'd be no compensation. I took Barca off Hector, and dragged her out into the street. Hector followed me.

'I'm goin' now. Got a present for you.'

It was a small jar of green olives in oil. 'There's nothing significant about this, is there?' I was studying the 'extra virgin' bit of the label.

He was puzzled, so there wasn't. 'Eh, sorry it's so small. Couldn't carry much and I gave Bugo the big jar.'

'Oh no, it's very nice. I'm very pleased, really I am.' We were loitering pleasantly when Mrs Duggan joined us.

'Oh, there you are. Come home with me, Jacinta, and bring that wretched animal. You can help me get the washing out.'

While we were pegging out Mr Byrne's shirts I asked Mrs Duggan what she thought of the triptych.

'If that's art I'm a blinking ballerina and whatever else she

177

does that Xanthe can't make tea. I'm spitting feathers for a decent cuppa.'

I was also wondering what she'd made of Hector. In spite of the awful things she was likely to say, I couldn't control my urge to talk to someone, anyone, about him.

'Hector was great with Barca, wasn't he?'

'For a tickle on the tum that animal's anybody's.'

'I think he looks more like Hannibal than a Roman. Couldn't you just picture him leading elephants over the Alps?'

'I've never thought much about what Hannibal looked like.'

'Hector's artistic as well as musical.'

'Is he now? Well, that doesn't come from the mother, any more than those mountain-pool eyes.'

Now we were getting somewhere. 'I never knew his mother was a friend of yours.'

'Friend of mine!' She snorted Barca into the rhubarb bed. 'I don't think anyone got on very well with her, apart from *him*, of course.'

When Hector's mother had been the receptionist at the surgery near Hebden Street she had taken her duties as the person intervening between the doctors and the people who wanted to see them too seriously for local popularity. But she saw rather a lot of a locum who had lodged for a few months with Mrs Duggan, and Hector was one result.

'Where did he go?' I knew that Hector's mother was single.

'God knows. I think he got a job in Scotland, somewhere in Glasgow. Never heard from him, anyway, not even a Christmas card. He was young, you see. I think the family gave her something.'

Then she sounded off about the class of lodger she used to have, filmstars like Eugene Morphy and Zoroastrian doctors from Bombay. She got very academic when I asked her what Hector's mother looked like. She did not want to even guess at the current image of Hector's mother but when she'd been in her natural prime, 'if you could call it that', she'd been a blonde, 'a bit like Amelia, but more yellowish in hair colour.' Then she dumped a fistful of pegs into the bucket and said: 'We haven't seen her about lately, have we?'

'No Mrs Duggan. A little bird tells me that Amelia's having a holiday for herself in Spain.'

On a materialist whim I invited Eric Lennox to the party.

'I know you like crowds and it's sure to be crowded.'

'Thank you very much, Jacinta. I'm very honoured.' I knew he'd feel honoured enough to enquire about what he should buy Eugene as a gift and I told him a full-length towelling dressing-gown would be in order. Eric was really really busy, polishing the biggest leaves on his plant, and I was scouring his shining chalice of a kitchen bin when Ma rang.

'Did you get the forms?'

'What forms?'

'About the computer course.' Ma was still keen for me to join the opposition by becoming a computer programmer.

'No. Not yet.'

'Liar! I'll get another lot and give them to you when we're over.'

'Over here?'

'Over there! I'm coming for the weekend. I'm redundant, as of today, and I'm ringing everyone while I can for free.'

'Oh Ma! Are you all right? Is it okay?'

''Course it's okay, it's bloody brilliant. Ten grand, tax free. There's cables under my poor old feet but I've got plans in my head. Tom has a connection, a crowd who make anti-sun stuff for fair-skinned people. It's called Celtic Mist and he thinks we could invest in it, get the Irish franchise.'

'That's exciting. Maybe Saint Patrick could advertise it.'

I was only joking but she took the suggestion very seriously. There was no question of involving Eugene because Tom Broderick was upset by him. He'd taped the old Cortes commercial and now Ma couldn't go into the living room without seeing Eugene Morphy on a charger.

'It's no use telling him that he never, never had a flourish

179

of hair like that. He keeps buying bloody Miller's Ingots – a hundred and fifty calories a shot, I'm getting fat – and he can't believe I'm putting up with him after having married a vision like Cortes Morphy. Can you imagine?'

I could. 'Did you tell him he's a bit older now?'

She had. She told him anything and everything she could think of that was unedifying about Eugene Morphy but he was still insecure. However, she did have an idea.

'He still doesn't like the sun much, does he?'

'No.'

'So he won't be looking great after Spain, will he?'

I wasn't sure. He wouldn't be tanned, but there was the rejuvenating Amelia factor. I didn't want to go into that with my mother so I let her rattle on about the proper arrangements. While they were in London for the Celtic Mist negotiations, Tom would be introduced to a wasted and sexless Eugene. Ma had already booked them into a hotel in King's Cross, but it was up to me to think of a grotty, badly lit venue for the family get-together.

'You'll have to get him up early, early for him anyway, so he'll look like the cat's got at him. Maybe you should get that old Xanthe witch to come along too,' she said, encouragingly.

SAINT FIACRE

ccess to the chapel of Saint Fiacre remained for long forbidden to women. Following a peculiarity of that sex, several at various periods persisted in attempting an entrance, and a string of miracles is recorded of the manner in which this curiosity was punished. One woman put her foot in at the door, and it swelled to elephantine proportions, and the eyes of another who peeped in dropped out.

10

No one encouraged me to be at Heathrow for the return of Cortes Morphy. I was looking for trouble when I stood in the arrivals hall beside the taxi-driver with a sign reading 'Miller's Chocolate Ingots'.

Amelia in a pink denim mini-skirt saw the sign first. Then she saw me. She nudged him and waved excitedly, but I didn't wave back.

'Greetings Jacinta,' Eugene sighed, 'you've already had the pleasure of meeting Amelia?'

'Oh yes, Eugene, don't you remember, Jacinta and I met at Mrs Duggan's. Look what I've bought her.' She tugged at the fringe of the grannyish shawl hanging from her bag but I took one of Eugene's cases and followed our driver. When we were in the car I asked him how it had gone.

'Eh . . .'

'Fantastic! He was fantastic. It's going to be so moving. Honestly! I really think . . .'

'I wasn't asking you.'

She grabbed his hand. 'Can't you see he's tired. We've hardly had any sleep.'

'Yes,' said Eugene, 'I'm a knacker ready for the knacker's yard and a cup of Mrs Duggan's poisonous tea.' He spoke as slowly and stiffly as he'd walked to the car. Without the Cortes beard, which we'd all got used to, he had a survivor's face. Amelia let go of his hand so that she could scratch one of her hairless, flakily tanned shins. Then I saw what was under her feet. Amelia was wearing the wedges bought by

183

Ma in mortification for Pol Pot and sold by Xanthe to a person previously unknown.

'Oh look! Amelia's wearing the stegosaurs.'

'Actually, they're not as comfortable as they look,' she said, pleased that we'd started a nice conversation.

'Neither's he.'

'Stegosaurian shoes?' Eugene muttered and Amelia grabbed his hand again. 'Oh, you're so exhausted, you can hardly speak.'

'I'm sure you've got your money's worth out of him anyhow.'

He sighed and dropped Amelia's hand so that he could cover his eyes.

'Frankly, Jacinta,' said Amelia, 'you have problems. This is just childish.'

'Frankly, I'd like to see how childish you'd be if I was bonking your old man.'

She looked at Eugene appealingly, but he wasn't coming out from behind the palms to face either of us. It must have been a bit of a let-down for Amelia, but she wasn't the sensitive type.

'Face it Jacinta. Haven't you ever been in love? You, and the past, you don't own your father.'

'So what are you doing in my mother's shoes?' Then, though it's hard to ignore someone you're sharing the back seat of a car with, I did my best. I turned to Eugene and spoke into the gaps between his fingers, which were still covering his face. 'Maria's over. She's . . .'

'Maria?'

'My mother, his wife.'

'Oh! What does she want?'

'She doesn't want anything. She has a new career and a new man and she would like to introduce him, that's all.'

'Oh well. Perhaps we should invite them to lunch?'

Shaking himself free of an imaginary chain, Eugene sat up

straight and joined the conversation. 'For when is this summit conference scheduled?'

'I don't know, yet. She's going to ring today. Mrs Duggan's made a steak and kidney specially.'

'Oh dear!' Amelia smirked. She was a great smirker. 'I'm afraid we can't eat that. We don't eat red meat.'

'Well, we do, so it's no concern of yours, then, is it?'

'Now Jassie, please,' Eugene picked my hand up, only to drop it immediately, as if it were too heavy for him, 'this is just too grotesque. Please please calm down and, as Amelia suggests, try to be a little more mature.'

That was enough to keep her happy. Throwing herself across him, she buried her head in his crotch and murmured: 'You don't have to go back there, you know. We can drop Jacinta off.' Then, with a lash of the wizened hair, she came up for air, and slid across the taxi-driver's window. 'Can you stop first in Hebden Street, Camden Town, and then carry on to Primrose Hill?'

The streets were constipated with lunchtime traffic. I stared out of the window, gnashing my teeth and perfecting terrorist fantasies. Without the weapons designed to serve me in just this circumstance, I could do nothing else. An importunate was nibbling my father's genitals and there were no hellish socks or hardback saints to hand. I could only hate Amelia like I'd hated none of the other women in Eugene's life. To think that they were planning a birthday party for him while this bird-bum was making a gooseberry out of me.

On Amelia's clipped instructions, the taxi stopped in Hebden Street. I got out and with one of his bags Eugene followed me, but the cab door was still open.

'Mañana,' he winked wearily, 'mañana, I'll be in touch. Tell the Grand Duchess that I'll be taking her little cur out for a walk.'

'But, but,' I bleated, 'what about the steak and kidney? She'll be upset.'

'Oh, it'll keep.' He pointed at the bag on the pavement.

185

'I've saved her my washing.' Then Amelia pulled him back into the cab and the door was slammed.

At first Mrs Duggan wouldn't believe it. Was Amelia very ill? That Spanish sun would scorch an angel, never mind an overbred filly like her.

'No Mrs Duggan. She's looking as well as people like her can. He's the one who's looking terrible.'

'Ah well,' she put on the tea-and-sympathy kettle, 'that's it, then. That's only natural. He's come home in disgrace, Cortes the Hasbeen not Cortes the Conqueror, and he doesn't want to show himself 'til he's back to normal. It'll take him a few days to step out of character. That Robert de Niro's never got his figure back.'

'It's not his figure that's worrying me, it's his soul. She says she's in love with him, but . . .' at last, I was in tears, 'could he really be in love with her?'

'Ah Jacinta darling, have a good little cry, while you can. It's a gift.'

While I was snivelling she was loading up the washing machine with the contents of Eugene's bag. But she didn't turn it on. The kitchen was strangely silent. In the gloom, nothing was ticking or dripping, and Barca was sound asleep under the big chair. Mrs Duggan poked one of her arms into the drum of the machine and oared around with it, as if she were fishing for a winning ticket. She could read a man's laundry like she could read tea-leaves.

'It's my opinion,' she said, straightening herself up and turning round, 'that our Eugene's not in love with that glass of water.'

'How do you know?'

'Because he's only ever been in love with himself, and that's the long and the short of it.' She sat down and poured out the tea. 'The poor man, he's doing whatever he can to get himself another ride on a big horse.'

I laughed, with relief. Mrs Duggan's opinion was as

186

ludicrous as it was plausible. Amelia was the key to anything like a spin-off from Cortes II. If Eugene wanted to open a few supermarkets, he had to stay in with the chocolate heiress. I was blowing my nose, startling the dog out of her sleep, when there was a ring on the doorbell. A barking Barca scampered off upstairs, with the two of us in hot pursuit. For a moment, but only a moment, I thought Eugene might have come home. But it wasn't him. Instead, my mother, in stockinged feet, fell in through the door. There was no need for an introduction.

'Howarya both.' She passed me a pair of megalithic platforms. 'Dig them a nice grave.' Then she noticed my red eyes. 'I've come to join the party. Traffic's terrible. Just spent a fortune on a taxi here from King's Cross.'

'Will you have a cup of tea, Mrs Murphy?' Mrs Duggan asked as she led the procession back into the kitchen.

'Maria, call me Maria. Yes, I will, thanks, two sugars.'

'Thanks Mrs Duggan,' I said. 'I did tell you Ma was coming over, didn't I?'

'Yes, you did,' Mrs Duggan looked sternly over at Ma, 'but I thought she'd be escorted, as well as shod.'

'Well Dymphna, I can call you Dymphna, can't I?' Mrs Duggan said nothing. 'Oh, that's a lovely cup of tea. Just what the doctor ordered.' Mrs Duggan looked pleased. About tea she was very sensitive and sectarian.

'I told you Ma. Mrs Duggan doesn't like her first name.'

'Neither do I. But you don't get asked, do you?'

'It's all right,' Mrs Duggan finally spoke. 'You can call me Dymphna.'

Ma knew what a concession this was. 'Well Dymphna,' she said happily, 'I'm not wearing my shoes because they were killing me and I was hoping to borrow a pair of trainers off my daughter here, and I'm not with a man because I've just dumped the one I had in training.'

'Tom?'

'The very same.'

'Isn't he,' Mrs Duggan coughed importantly, 'wasn't he the fellow who could take back the shoes?'

'He didn't, that's just the thing. Never even tried. Those yellow boots . . . I was too ashamed to tell you, Jacinta.'

'It's okay. I know. I saw them in his car.'

'Why didn't you tell me?'

'Are you hungry, Mrs Murphy? Would you like a little something to eat?'

I grabbed Mrs Duggan's line. 'Yeah, something slimming?'

Ma drained her cup of tea. 'No and I'm sorry to be rude, but the truth is that I'm desperate for a kip. Sailor's sleep last night, for all the worry, so if you could show us a bed?'

I had to hesitate over this. The allocation of beds was Mrs Duggan's prerogative.

'That's no problem Maria. If you take yourself off upstairs, right to the top, you'll find your husband's bed, ready and waiting for you.'

'Oh?' Ma was rethinking her request.

'Don't worry,' I said, 'he's not in it.'

'He's still in character, and Jacinta and myself aren't expecting him home 'til he's come out of it.'

'Oh I see,' said Ma. She didn't, but she knew she'd find out later. 'I'll take myself off, then. Hang on!' She began to rummage in her bag. 'I'll leave this with you.' She put a pink jotter on the table. 'It's all in there. Have a read and then, if you're still interested, I'll fill you in on the gory details.'

Mrs Duggan picked up Barca and hoisted herself into the episcopal chair. Closing her eyes, she commanded me to read aloud from Ma's jotter.

There was no point in reading the contents of the first list, which was nothing more than a log of phone calls made by Tom Broderick to his mother within the previous twenty-four hours. As educational prose, the following pages were more interesting. Ma's anti-Broderick lists had been organised under three main headings: Romance, Practicality and

Morality. Although some of the items under Romance had been censored, scribbled over, it was still clear that Tom Broderick left chalky bits of toothpaste by the side of his mouth, that he sometimes wore polo-neck sweaters under his shirts and that he had a quilted anorak which, in windy weather, made him swell up like a balloon.

As the Practicalities we got the omniscient Broderick mother again, and the continual news. Also, there was Tom Broderick's appetite, unqualified by taste or a fear of calories, which was beginning to affect Ma's size. The car was in this section too. As a passenger, she was getting too much news and not enough exercise.

At this point Mrs Duggan proved that she was still awake by interrupting me.

'How much more?'

'Another page, Morality next.'

'That should be under there, the car should. It's not ecological, is it, in this day and age?'

'You can tell her when she's up.'

'Right you are. On again, then.'

Under Morality there was the shoe deception. Ma had found those shoes, the yellow wet-look gladiator boots which she thought he'd returned, in the boot of his car and when she confronted him about them he'd shrugged, then said it had been simpler to give her twenty quid and say he'd got a full cash refund. So apart from being a coward, afraid of a shoe-shop manager, he was a liar. But Ma's vehemence about the shoes was obviously informed by the second big entry in this section, the only news to Mrs Duggan and myself. Apparently, Celtic Mist PLC was a South Africa-based organisation, 'Afrikaner Fog' she'd named it. Although Apartheid was history, Ma didn't like the idea of selling cosmetics designed to protect fair-skinned people from over-exposure to a sun which they shouldn't have been hogging in the first place.

I put down the jotter and Mrs Duggan told me that she for

one was very impressed. My mother was obviously a reformed person, no longer a flibbertigibbet but a sober woman of science and strategy.

'She can stay for a bit, if she wants. She could have your room while you're away.'

'Oh yeah, and where am I going?'

'To Paris, it's all in the white envelope on the mantelpiece. Hilda popped in this morning. She says she's sorry about that tripleditch picture and I told her to think no more about it.'

For a sweetener the envelope contained a return ticket to Paris, a wad of French cash and the address of Mrs Bugler's apartment in Saint Germain.

'I've been thinking that there's no use in you sitting around here, Jacinta, flattening your bottom. You need to see a bit more of the world, and this'll be a nice start. The others have popped over, and we, Hilda and myself, we didn't want you feeling left out.' She closed her eyes again. 'Away with you now. I've had enough excitement for one day.'

Left out! I was feeling too left in. I rushed out of the house and took a bus to Hampstead Heath. Dogs like Barca and men like Eugene were grazing all over Parliament Hill. Instead of thinking graciously about what I should be packing for Paris, I got back to them, Eugene and Amelia. Somehow, I'd been jilted. I'd lost my disposable father. Even if he wasn't, technically speaking, even if Ma had only given him the part because Jack Fennessy was a bicycle, he was the best father I'd ever had.

Hoping to see some coots, I mooned off towards the ponds. It was therapeutic to think about ways of hurting Amelia. A prompt bad angel came up with anonymous information to her employer, the estate agent, about what she'd been doing in empty properties with Eugene Morphy when she was supposed to be taking potential house-buyers round them. The centre-left angel was keener on activating one of Amelia's allergies. Being such a refined girl, she had a lot of these. Next time she ghosted into Mrs Duggan's kitchen, I could sprinkle assorted grains and dusts round and about. I wasn't listening to the good angel.

Ducks with dry throats were quacking with excitement about the bread roll I'd bought for them, when I heard a small boy asking his mother why my cardigan was inside out. She smiled until she was close enough to see my twisted face. I was feeling through the back pocket of my jeans, looking for a tissue, when I found a piece of paper with Eric Lennox's telephone number on it. His place was a proven venue for misery. I could rant and rave there without upsetting little children. If his answering machine was on, it was a safe bet that the Pimlico house was empty. I ran out of the park and into the nearest phone booth.

Eric's answering machine wasn't on and I was so startled by his live voice that I didn't disguise my own.

'Hi, Jacinta. Are you coming round soon?'

'Eh no Eric, actually that's why I'm calling. I'm going to Paris for a week, so I won't be able to do for you 'til the week after.'

Strangled silence.

'What's the matter Eric?' Just when I was hoping that we'd been cut off, he told me his plant, the big one, was a worry to him. It had gone all yellow on him. He'd moved it into his kitchen, as I'd apparently suggested, but there was no obvious improvement. It was just hopeless. No matter what he did, plants just died on him.

'I'm really sorry Eric.'

Another strangled silence.

'Tell you what . . .' No use. We'd been cut off and I'd run out of coins.

Walking home, pondering Eric and his withered plant, I passed an old-fashioned barber's shop. I asked the man inside for a crew cut. I would return to my people as a nearly bald penitent.

*   *   *

191

You could smell the steak and kidney from halfway up Hebden Street. Ma was in the kitchen, peeling the carrots that Mrs Duggan was waiting to chop.

'Oh my God, Jacinta, what came over you? Your lovely hair.'

'I fancied a change, and the ear-rings show better, don't they?'

'But what about Paris?' Ma wailed. 'They'll think you're a refugee from some terrible epidemic.'

I smiled. 'Yeah, well, that's exactly the look I was aiming for.'

'You should have asked your mother before doing that. I'm surprised at you, Jacinta, really.' Mrs Duggan turned to Ma. 'You can't watch them all the time, Maria. But it'll be grown again by the autumn, and she can always wear a hat.' She passed me a sheaf of knives. 'You can set the table for us.'

'For how many?'

'Four. One delinquent, one old woman, one . . .'

'Refugee,' said Ma, 'meaning me, not her. She's got nothing to run from.'

'And one elk,' said I.

'That's it,' said Mrs Duggan, 'one fully grown male elk. I can hear him now, advancing down the hall.'

'Great stuff!' Mr Byrne had stepped into the kitchen. 'I can smell the fatted calf,' he put a hand over his eyes like a big-game hunter, 'but no sign of the prodigal?'

'He's still out prodigalling,' said Mrs Duggan, 'but in compensation his wife, Maria, is joining us for dinner. Maria, this is Damian Byrne.'

Mr Byrne did an exaggerated step backwards, as if, confronted by Ma, he was seeing some gorgeous apparition. 'Well, well, well, this is an honour. Doesn't the Conqueror have great taste in women?'

'I wouldn't be so general about his taste if I were you, Mr Byrne.'

'Of course, of course, Mrs Duggan. Jacinta never got chosen, did she?'

192

'No,' Ma said sharply, 'and I don't think Eugene's done much choosing, ever.'

'Ah. Still, three lovely ladies for me to have dinner with. This calls for a bottle of wine. What do you say, Mrs Duggan, to a spot of Bull's Blood?'

While Mrs Duggan was demurring, Mr Byrne left for the off-licence. Then she told Ma about her opposition to the moustache and Ma looked as if it was the first time she'd heard all about the elks. When Mr Byrne came back with a bottle the table had been laid. His compliments flowed with the wine.

'Magnificent, Mrs Duggan, magnificent! I'm only the prodigal's boring old big brother, but I can tell a good steak and kidney when I'm lucky enough to enjoy one.'

Mrs Duggan looked very pleased and set about producing the rhubarb fool she'd made to follow. But that was nothing on Ma's metamorphosis. All the while, she'd been scrunching up her hair and moulding her lips. It was sickening. There I was, unable to land a dogfish like Hector, and there she was, still trawling men. But in sulking, I was only drawing attention to myself.

'So what's new with our little girl?' Mr Byrne asked. 'You're looking very like that pop star, very what's it, gamin.'

'Gamine,' said Ma. 'And she's off to Paris tomorrow, so we're treating the baldness as a rite of passage.'

'Fair enough, fair enough,' he said, 'when you're a lily you don't need the gilt.'

I flicked some of my wine, and he laughed uproariously, like he always did.

'She's not always so rude, I hope,' said Ma, 'I haven't brought her up that way.'

'No indeed, Mrs Morphy, Maria,' he reassured her, 'and I think we should raise a toast to her future.'

The three of them raised their glasses.

'To whatever the future brings to Miss Morphy, but wait

a bit,' he turned to Ma, 'isn't it obvious what she should be doing?'

He twiddled his antlers and Ma looked admiringly at them, and then he said I should get a proper training for the stage, as befitted the only daughter of Saint Patrick. The others were sociably enthusiastic about this. Without my hair, Mrs Duggan thought I looked like a Joan of Arc she'd seen in a film, and then she said she'd have a word with Hilda Bugler on the subject of dramatic entrances. Ma just smiled an endorsement which had more to do with Mr Damian Byrne than it had with any future of mine.

Mañana came, quietly. By eleven o'clock my Paris bag was packed and ready in the hall and there was still no sign of Eugene. Ma was in his room, sleeping off the previous night's session at the Goat. In case he did show, Mrs Duggan told me to rouse her.

She was wide awake, sitting up in Eugene's little bed with the pink jotter propped against her knees.

'Now this is what motherhood's all for, the day when your daughter brings you a cup of tea.'

'Mrs Duggan sends you her congratulations.'

'For what?'

'For being the first woman to spend the night in Eugene's bed.'

'Nothing to it,' she threw the jotter at me, 'now tell us, where would I buy a German potato peeler round here?'

This item was at the top of a new list. 'I shouldn't bother, Ma, Mrs Duggan likes spending far too long peeling far too many potatoes.'

'Ah, she's a decent old stick really. First thing I'll do, when my money comes through, is buy her a tumble dryer. Stuff comes out with no wrinkles and she shouldn't be doing all that ironing.'

I had to explain about the ironing, how it was Mrs Duggan's form of prayer. Ma was disappointed. I watched her eyes swivelling round Eugene's spartan room. Apart from the picture postcards on the noticeboard, there wasn't much stimulation. A comprehensive list of its contents would have taken ten minutes: clothes (secondhand), books (paperback and stolen), a kettle, coffee paraphernalia, a box-file of clippings, personal documents and photographs, a stack of gift-sized boxes of Miller's Ingots and a noticeboard tiled with postcards.

'God, it's bloody bare in here, apart from that, that scalp-pole,' she was squinting at the valentine noticeboard, 'very discreet really.'

'He's not into interiors.'

'You can say that again.' She laughed. 'What about Damian, what's his room like?'

Since, officially, I wasn't supposed to know what Mr Byrne's room was like, I said I didn't know.

'What's his terrible secret?' she persisted.

'What do you mean?'

'You know! When you meet a nice-looking man of his age, unattached but to all intents and purposes interested in women, there's got to be some reason why he's not in harness.'

'His feet,' I volunteered. 'He has a terrible foot problem.'

'Like myself?' She wiggled her toes.

'No, eh, it's their odour. We, me and Mrs Duggan, we don't mind, but he gets very embarrassed about his socks.'

'That's only a technical problem, easy-peasy.' She was scribbling in the jotter again. 'But come on now, spill the beans. Where did she find him? Was he married?'

'Not to my knowledge, but Mrs Duggan . . .'

'Oh, I get you. Don't tell me. She's frightened them off.'

'That's not really fair.'

'No.' Ma rocked back and forth in the bed. 'I must, I must, I must try to be fair. I know! He's really married to her, isn't he?'

'Not exactly, not literally.'

195

'I'm not being literal! God, for someone who's spent half the year with a secondhand-poetry spouter, you're being awfully unimaginative.' Then, like the wolf who impersonated grannies, she sprang out of the bed. 'Take them away!' With one kick the stack of boxes of Miller's Ingots had collapsed. 'They'll do as your presents for the natives, and gimme your runners. I've got work to do.'

SAINT EDMUND

hilst at Paris Edmund's virtue was put to a rude test. The daughter of his host fell in love with him, and made advances with sufficient want of delicacy to show that she was a girl with no modesty of mind. She even went so far as to steal into his room one evening in exceedingly light costume. Edmund grasped his birch-rod with one hand, her shoulders with the other, and thrashed her bare back unmercifully. The girl danced and wriggled under the lashes, afraid to scream out, lest her father and mother should find her there. Edmund did not let her go until her back was covered with purple wheals.

11

Mrs Bugler's Paree was a sixteenth-century garret in Saint Germain. Minutes passed before I found the building's *trompe l'oeil* of a front door and stepped into a hall filled up by a wide stone staircase. From her cabinet under the mighty stairs the concierge called out: 'Mademoiselle Murphy?'

I had to try the French again. So far, it hadn't done me any good because you can't carry off mouldy French like you can carry off mouldy clothes, but this experience was less demoralising. Apart from the heartening fact that she was expecting me, the concierge was Spanish, a fellow Jacinta even. By using some of the other nouns we had in common, I learned that 'Monsieur Hector' would be returning shortly. With more French nouns and a knee-tapping gesture, which didn't disturb the sleepy Labrador serving as her foot-rest, this real Jacinta told me that she didn't like climbing all the way up to Madame Bugler's place on account of a disability. I was doing my best to promise that we would carry all our rubbish down, when Hector arrived. He had a greasy bag of pizza for us and a bone for the creamy dog.

'Jesus Christ!' I exclaimed, when we got to the top. 'Bugo must be planning the merrie widowhood. She'd need a palanquin and any number of bearers to get her old man up here.'

'Wait'll you see inside,' Hector sniggered agreeably. 'It's just like a li'il burrow.'

To appreciate Hector's opinion no leap of the imagination

199

was required. The low-sized internal doorways of Hilda's burrow had been fitted with velvet curtains, the walls were muffled by kelims and the thickly carpeted floors were covered by more rugs and fat tapestry cushions. Although this very interior interior was more colourful than Dorking's, the effect, without benefit of dogs or bearskins, was similarly emollient. It had been designed for hibernation, some long, delirious sleep.

After just a few days, Hector's trail within a central room lit by one narrow window was marked by a litter of empty juice cartons and battered carrier bags, Xanthe's by takeaway tinfoil containers full of lipsticked fag-ends. The dog's basket in one corner had belonged to the concierge's Labrador when she had been in Mrs Bugler's personal custody. The below-stairs-Jacinta had told Xanthe how Madame Bugler had made her a present of that dog when she realised that Labradors were not easy to look after in Paris.

Hector was ignoring the usual Paris because he'd found a bit of paid work helping with sound and security in a new club, a sort of French Joint, near Place des Vosges. According to him, Xanthe was being just as casually international. She was 'doin' biz' with some 'distribu'ors' in Place d'Italie, but, what she had to distribute Hector couldn't, or wouldn't, tell me.

Hector's routine had him coming back to the apartment early in the morning and crashing out for most of the afternoon. But because of my arrival he'd bought food for two and deferred his siesta. He seemed to like playing housie. He showed me how to activate the noisy bathroom arrangements and how to light the gas under the percolator. There were two bedrooms and since Xanthe's territory was sacrosanct he hoped I wouldn't mind if we had the same room for different shifts. I would sleep there at night and he would occupy it during the day. I thought they were ever so tactful, to be keeping up a celibate front for my sake.

*   *   *

Over the next three days I hardly saw Hector or Xanthe. I woke up to the muffled sound of tinny cars negotiating narrow streets and returned, late in the afternoon, to hear even snoring coming from the padded cell I was sharing with Hector. In between times I did a lot of talking and walking by myself.

Paris, or Mrs Bugler's part of it, was not as distracting as I'd been hoping. There were hardly any Parisians around. The nearest clothes shops were shut and their haughty window models, frozen into summery postures, were looking out and over me, waiting on the return of the people with bone structure and money. What locals you did see were like daylit foxes in London parks, embarrassed about being caught among the August tourists.

I kept myself awake with culture. I ate stale biscuits with a poor Dutch couple on a *bateau mouche* and I fell in with some deeply cultivated Canadians at the Louvre. Then, on my mother's behalf, I went to Les Invalides. Napoleon was her Hannibal. Because he'd eventually had his come-uppance, at Waterloo, she didn't feel she had to worry about what he'd done to Toussaint L'Ouverture.

I'd been walking round and round the little man's massive tomb, a mahogany meteorite fallen from the sky, talking to myself about war and black-haired men, when I heard an English-speaking guide explaining the Egyptian niche. I followed his flock, a group of serious Australians, back upstairs. This guide had charisma, or something besides his English, because before long it was impossible to see his beard waggling on account of a crush of freeloading eavesdroppers. I abandoned myself to the sea of flesh, but when the Australian élite, our guide's paymasters, decided to break for lunch, the crowd fell away. I was peckish too, but my purse, a present from Lanzarote, was missing. I only had what cash there'd been in it and I'd had nothing to eat since breakfast. Highly informed but very hungry, I returned to a cuddly Hector.

*   *   *

201

His hands were clapped, baby-style, under his head. Without their clothes the bodies I'd known were as dull as pebbles out of water, but the naked Hector was still lustrous against a white sheet. I was thinking about slipping off my dress and curling up alongside him, like a snake coiling round a warm rock, but he must have heard my thoughts because suddenly he stirred and sat up. Rubbing his brown stomach suggestively, he announced that he was hungry.

'So am I.'

'Wot 'ave we got?'

'Nothing.' While Hector was groping around the futon for his tee-shirt I opened a box of Miller's Ingots. By the time I'd made some coffee he'd eaten more than half the contents. Studying the muddy portrait of Cortes Morphy on its lid, he said: 'Euge was sor' of dark then, sor' of like me?'

I knew that chocolate box better than he did. 'None of the really dark and hairy actors at the audition could ride a horse.'

'I never knew Euge could ride.'

'Didn't you? He's not usually so inefficient, my father. Anyone and everyone's usually very well informed about what he can and can't do.'

'Yeah,' he said in uncomplicated admiration, 'my mum knew Euge in them days. Says they'd 'ave got along nicely if it 'adn't been for Mrs D. I mean . . . they 'ad been gettin' along.'

It was such a preposterous drift I was a bit slow in getting it. 'You mean?' He did. The chin was out on a meaningful jut and the eyes were on freeze-frame. 'Listen, Hector, you can believe what you like. It doesn't bother me. It would have, but it doesn't.'

'Thought you'd find it in'erestin'-like, me and you, we're sor' of related.'

How was I to tell him, nicely, that I'd started fancying him, and hadn't really stopped, because he was the man least like my official father that I'd ever encountered. I watched him putting on his grisly tee-shirt. Eugene was famous for the bespoke effect of his streelish body on secondhand suits, but in tee-shirts he was all elbows. Eugene was made for tailored, northern things and cold weather. Eugene was tall and articulate and light-footed. Hector the pizzeria Roman was as much of a contrast with Saint Patrick as it was possible to be.

'Yes, that's very interesting Hector, but it's not remotely probable. And even if it was, even if there was anything more to it than what your mother's been telling you, it's all academic, you know?' It was so easy, satisfying even, to watch him shrivelling, like Mrs Duggan's slugs, under the lines I'd been fed. 'It's only our mothers we can be sure of. That's what the history of men and women's been all about, them feeling insecure about the paternity of their children.'

The history bit was way over the head that was in hiding under the tee-shirt. 'But,' he insisted as soon as he was recapitated. 'You got 'is name anyway.'

'But I haven't, have I?' He was confused again. 'I'm a Murphy. Eugene became a Morphy.'

'S'only one letter.' He could spell, anyway. 'You could change it, easy. You got the choice. Wot choice do I 'ave?'

He shuffled off to the little bathroom. While he was examining his face in the mirror, as if he were looking for bruises, I went soft. I told him he was probably the son of a Zoroastrian doctor from Bombay who, when last heard of, was a general practitioner somewhere in Glasgow.

'Shit! I never though' of askin' Mrs D.' Excitedly, he scratched his mane of hair.

'Why don't you? She knows everything, almost. But I wouldn't hope for much because she told me this doctor didn't stay in touch.'

'Don't want to get in touch with 'im.'

'No?'

'No. Just want to save Mum the trouble of tellin' me the actual truth.'

Apparently, the first Cortes commercial was running when

Hector had started making enquiries of his mother and she'd nominated Eugene. It was an 'as well him as another' case. Wretched woman. She wasn't to know how, paternity-wise, the Camden Conquistador was a non-starter.

When he was dressed I sent him out for bread and cheese, which we ate sitting on the floor together. Then I washed his tee-shirt and he punched another hole in my watchstrap. When pressed, he said he liked my new 'hairstyle' and for about an hour we had a sweet, vaguely primeval atmosphere going for us. He was the man and I was the woman and there we were, in a Bedouin burrow, silently servicing each other.

The ethnological fantasy finished when Hector left for his work. For the lonely evening ahead I'd planned a nice dinner out, to be followed by an American film. But since I'd forgotten to ask Hector for some money, I had to set myself up for a razzle without funds. I swigged from a bottle of mouth freshener and painted my toenails with some of Xanthe's purple polish. Then, for armour against the night, I put on her pre-war leopardskin jacket, which I'd returned to Fin de Siècle after I'd been denounced by an animal liberationist on Camden High Street. Xanthe got away with wearing this leopardskin because she looked as if she'd just crawled out of the grass with its original owner and it'd said, ''Ere you are Xanth'. It's chilly in Paris of an evenin', take a loan of my coat while you're over.' I never had that kind of licence but I still had a sort of sitting tenancy in this jacket and the night was cold.

With no money there was no point in taking a bag, but for something to carry I had Hector's camera, which was Xanthe's old one, when I headed off towards St Michel. On a bench near Notre-Dame I ate a banana and watched a ghost of a hippy singing a crucifying song about 'L'Amour' to the accompaniment of his companion's maracas. She was tall, round and Black, barely exercised by the twisting of her feeble instruments. However, the money mat was at her feet, and no one among the audience could keep their eyes off her. Her wide, impassive face wore a Mona Lisa semi-smile, but she wasn't looking directly at anyone. I wondered how they split the takings, if it was fifty-fifty or eighty-twenty, in her favour.

Then I made the mistake of giving up my seat on the bench and while I was standing, men kept coming up to me, or bumping into me, and asking me the time, or if I was Sinéad O'Connor's sister. When I told them I was an only child they still knew I was foreign, which only made them eager for more information, and so I decided, on the same principle by which Mrs Duggan sponsored Hopalong as her official drunk, to be nice to the most harmless pest.

I slowed down for Farouk because of the big lapels on his Madras cotton shirt and his overpoweringly sweet smell. His introduction had taken the form of a skip alongside me and the offer of a guided tour around the Île de la Cité. When I complimented him on his excellent English he proudly told me that he had learnt it in prison. I was touched by this so I agreed to go with him to a café on a street where many of his friends hung out and to sit with him at a window table. I spent about an hour drinking wine and holding his hand while acquaintances of his gesticulated at us from the pavement outside. When he told me how much his family would enjoy meeting me I had to think about shaking him off, but without a pair of Mr Byrne's socks, how was I to do that? Being such a polite fellow, he was sure to offer to walk me home. I told him my brother worked at the Cat's Eye Club, that I'd promised to join him there, and then I shot off.

By now it was much darker and much quieter. The hippy troubadour's female accomplice had left him with an empty money mat. I thought about negotiating for a turn at the maracas in exchange for a percentage, but my French wasn't up to it, so I hurried on. Clutching Hector's camera, I was getting my breath back in one of the niches on the Pont Neuf when Farouk with a less verbal and much bigger friend caught up with me. Ever so politely, he informed me that my lens cap was still on.

That would have been easily fixed if I'd been able to get the cap off, but I couldn't because it was one of these jobs that require a light pull rather than a strangle. Before I did any more violence to the camera the friend, a grinning bruiser in corrugated denim and dark glasses, had reached out for it.

'I'm afraid I don't really know how it works. I've just borrowed it.' Hector's camera was helpless in his hands as he twisted and pulled at it, then aiming it menacingly across the river.

'But you have no film in here?'

I went as blank as the camera and refused to explain myself. While Farouk debated the rest of my night with his friend I set off again. I thought I was well away until, as I was scuttling up the rue St Denis, I saw them sauntering along on the opposite pavement. Farouk crossed over holding the lens cap.

'Hey-ah, there is no great fire.' Like a relay racer, I snatched it off him but I knew there was no point in breaking into a serious run. I'd have to let them take me to the Cat's Eye Club.

I hallelujahed at the glow of a neon 'Cat's Eye' sign and when I found Hector in the dark doorway beneath it I almost fell to my knees. It was hard to tell if he was pleased to see me but to my friends, who were conferring across the street, he was less inscrutable. He glanced over at them with all of the thrillingly nonchalant menace that I remembered from my nights at the Joint and they disappeared without being introduced.

Hector said he was on door duty for another four hours. If I liked I could stick around, but not at the actual door with him. It gave the wrong impression. This was realistic of him. He was more plausible as a pimp than a brother. I had no choice but to descend into the depths of the Cat's Eye Club.

I found myself at the bottom of a mirrored well. Whatever

the clientele were drinking, it must have been powerfully depressant because, apart from a morose couple lurching to 'Hey Jude', they were a shiftless, subdued lot, mainly male and mainly seated in peripheral gloom. But someone down there knew my song. The next track was Martha and the Vandellas' one about having nowhere to hide. I was honour-bound to stand up. I draped my leopard over the back of a chair and swam out into the middle of the luminous dance-floor. The couple were only too glad to fall away for the frenzied tart who'd dropped out of the night sky. Round and round I swooped and stomped, anaesthetising myself with music, the only sensual pleasure I seemed to be able to get. But after Martha there was another dose of Euro-pop. My leopard was still resting and my head was on my folded arms when Eric Lennox loomed into focus. I'd had no fantasies about being in Paris with him but he was so good at taking orders. When I asked him for a spritzer he returned with two.

'I've never had the courage to ask for one of these in Paris,' he shouted.

'Oh really,' I shouted back, 'I've never had any trouble. How are you?'

He dug his hands into the pockets of the trenchcoat and wobbled forward to peer into my face. 'How are you?'

'Fucking great.' I drained one of the glasses, seized my leopard and headed for Hector's doorway, where I came to my senses. There was no point in eluding Eric who, to his literal credit, was solvent in several languages. I waited for him and I didn't interrupt when he told Hector that he was going to make sure I got home safely.

Hector hadn't been unduly concerned about my safety, but Eric wasn't losing any sleep on my account either. When in Paris he was often stuck for sleep and so he was used to walking the night away. However, he'd worn out a record depth of shoe leather finding the Cat's Eye Club. Of course he had a little bit of business to be doing in Paris. His work

was so abstract, he was earning when he was brushing his
perfect teeth, and I was a tax-deductible adventure licensed
by Mrs Duggan.

'She talks a lot of sense, your grandmother.'

'She's not my grandmother.'

'Whoever. She talks sense. She's got a lot of concern about
you.'

'Yeah, well, there's no need.'

He showed his palms apologetically. 'I know Paris. It's
where all the good Americans go when they die. Maybe you'd
like some dinner?'

He was on to something there. The sights and smells and
sounds of Hector were doing wonders for my metabolic rate.
In spite of the pizza and the bananas, my jeans were looser
by the hour. I could afford the meal on offer.

We got into the first taxi to pick up his scent and it took
us to a late night restaurant where they knew him. After
putting away the bread rolls on our table I thought I should
be more of a gourmet, less of a gourmande. Back home, Ma
and Mrs Duggan were waiting to hear all about Paris, and
tales of muggers and buskers wouldn't interest them. I should
have a go at some snails, which were, after all, only slugs
with shells on. Uneasily, Eric watched me eating, but he said
nothing until my greasy fingers had slid down the menu to
Lobster Thermidor. People with graduate grannies, people
like Eric, are born knowing that this is just a way of stretching
lobster meat with egg yolk and milk and mustard and cream
and cheese and breadcrumbs, but I didn't. I was thinking
about the assassination of Robespierre and the other events
of Thermidor, which, in connection with the young Napoleon,
Ma recalled as vividly as Mrs Duggan recalled the last days
of Hannibal Barca.

'I think I'll try the lobster next.'

'Okay, okay, if that's what you'd like, Jacinta, you have the
lobster.'

'You don't want me to have lobster?'

'I want you to have what you want, so long as you know what happens to them.'

I did, as it happened, know a bit about man's inhumanity to lobsters. Mrs Duggan had seen a programme on the telly. I impressed myself and dazzled Eric – his face had a moonish, sweaty gleam – by telling him about the historic experiments of the Royal Society for the Prevention of Cruelty to Animals. Their specially appointed official came to the conclusion that a lobster put into cold water which is slowly brought to the boil collapses and dies painlessly when the heat reaches seventy degrees Fahrenheit. I couldn't remember how the painlessness had been monitored but Eric gave in anyway. Our waiter was sent off to find out exactly how my lobster would be cooked. He came back from the kitchen with a Celsius temperature and had to hover with his little notebook until Eric had calculated its consistency with British standards of animal torture.

In spite of everything he was twitchy as I ate the recently deceased lobster, barely picking at his own walnut salad. I didn't have the strength of character to order a dessert but I did finish the bottle of wine he'd ordered on my behalf.

In silence, we walked back by the river. I was only sober enough to know that I was very drunk.

'You're thinking?' said Eric.

'Yeah. I do that sometimes.'

'What are you figuring on doing?' For a second, my anguish puzzled him. 'Not now, right? I'm taking you home right now. For your future?'

'I'm thinking about drama school. Eugene knows some people still and Xanthe used to paint scenery . . .'

'I've met that leopard before. How's the tamer?'

'Xanthe's okay. She's very self-sufficient.'

'She's got everything she needs. She's an artist. She don't look back.'

'That's bad grammar.'

'That's a quote, Jacinta.'

Then he plucked at my mangy shoulder and pushed me down the rue de Seine. Of course Eric knew the apartment. Mrs Bugler had bought it from a Surrealist widow, an ex-client of his, and when he himself had lived nearby, the Picasso-eyed Jacinta had cleaned for him. He pressed the light switch at the bottom of the stairs but it went out after three flights.

Ahead of him, I was swaying. To stop myself from falling back, into Eric's efficient arms, I sealed myself into a regular Hector fantasy. 'Improved Post-coital Developments' was its working title and in it, instead of mumbles, mints and that miserable session at Fin de Siècle, Hector the Spectre wrote me touchingly illiterate love letters. He was an obvious, even embarrassing lover, desperate to meet me in a proper bed.

But, this time, it refused to happen. No amount of furious rewinding would let me out of the Joint's cloakroom. I was too drunk. Hector was too real. Eric was too close. At a prod from his boney forefinger, I straightened up. If he were the type to take advantage of a besotted female, a suspicion of headlice, or athlete's foot, would send him back to the gym. Onwards and upwards I climbed, without any further assistance.

All of the apartment's lights were on. They stung my eyes. Bonneted by headphones, Xanthe was sitting on the floor with her strong brown legs splayed out in front of her. Her frock was crotch high but she didn't roll it down. A line of ash-coned cigarettes formed a guard of honour for one of her thighs. She took off the headphones and Eric dimmed the lights.

'Good evening.'

'Good night,' he said firmly, 'I've brought Jacinta home.' He shut the door and slid the leopardskin jacket off my shoulders. Xanthe stood up to imprint jammy lipstick on both of his cheeks. I lunged for a carton of orange juice and glugged straight from it. Xanthe took a cassette out of Hector's personal stereo and gestured at me to pass her the case. It

210

showed a smiling, bare-breasted woman in harem pants and it read: 'Soothe Yourself to the Tales of Scheherazade.' With a cigarette wedged between her lips she handed the tape to Eric.

'A little present for you.'

'Why, thank you very much.' As he studied his present, Eric's left shoulder sent a furrow through the kelimed wall. He kept one hand in a trenchcoat pocket.

'Produced at the Playa Blanca Recording Studios, Lanzarote. Distributed by Eros of Place d'Italie. Very neat, but, you know,' he grinned at Xanthe, 'I was kinda hoping I might get a credit, something like, "from an idea by Eric Lennox".'

'The piper can keep the tune.'

'You should try Jacinta on this. She's done something very strange to her head, but she's good, if she gets the right material.'

'Yes?' Xanthe looked over at what had become of me. I was slumping down among the floor cushions. I tried to sit up. Then my eyes rolled and I keeled over again. My body was dragged into the bedroom and thrown on to the futon. As Xanthe removed my sandals I heard her asking: 'Has she been safe with you?'

'Chrissake Zan, the kid's full of snails.'

She gave a low growl of a laugh and wrenched across the bedroom arch's curtains.

I woke up with a sick head and a sore soul. There was a jug of water and two croissants on the floor beside me. I drank the water and went back to sleep. Next time I woke the headache was in retreat. I got up and found more water. There was no sign of Xanthe or her bag, and Hector was asleep on her futon. I was wondering how I could wash unobtrusively in the tumultuous bathroom when I heard a plaintive, snuffling sound. Behind the apartment door I found the concierge's Labrador with a bunch of tiger-lilies at her feet.

211

I stuffed the lilies into the coffee jug and did my best to contemplate them. They were not meant for me. I thought about going home immediately. I'd pack my bag and leave them all, Xanthe, Hector and Eric Lennox, to feel bad-mannered and neglectful. To psyche myself further down, I started to list each of Hector's spontaneous gestures of affection. Since the session in the Joint's lost property room there had been:

1. the postcard from Barcelona, which did include me even if it had been addressed to Fin de Siècle in general;
2. the jar of olives from Lanzarote, which must have been quite heavy;
3. the food he'd bought for my first day in Paris.

A self-respecting girl would have begun packing at the third item but I wasn't one of those. The tee-shirt I'd washed for Hector was drying against the back of a chair. It was soft and white and sweet-smelling, and it came from Lanzarote. There, with Hector's help, Xanthe had recorded her pornographic tape. Since I'd washed that tee-shirt I'd acquired a technical if not entirely innocuous explanation for Xanthe and Hector's collaboration. And if I hadn't disposed of the latest obstacle, the incest taboo, there could be a face-saving advantage to it. Wasn't I entitled to a brotherly embrace?

I put the croissants on the floor by Hector's mattress and laid myself down beside him. One of Mrs Duggan's theories concerned pikes and men, and Hector counted as one hell of a pike. If you had a pike on your line and you pulled too violently you only ended up gutting the fish. I had to be careful as I nudged this one out of the water. I was rubbing the back of his calves with my soles when he woke up. I got a kindling, lazy smile. Then there was a sigh and a gentle swear. I turned round and buried my head against the side of his torso. My arms were around his middle and my mouth

212

was somewhere under his armpits when I felt the top of my tender head being kissed. I was sticking to his warm body with all the fixity of a bee on pollen, thinking about my next move, when there was a bang on the door.

'Mmm Jacinta,' he murmured.

'Gretel,' I said, sitting up and waiting for the door to break for the fist still banging on it. 'Just call me Gretel.'

I threw his shorts at him and opened the door for Xanthe. She marched over to the living room's slit of a window and pushed it open. 'Get ready. We are all going to lunch.'

Hector didn't look ready, for anything. While Xanthe pulled the tee-shirt over his dazed head, I shredded one of the croissants for him. He licked his fingers and wiped them on Lanzarote, and then he saw the tiger lilies.

'Mmm, nice, my fav'rites.'

'I think they're for Xanthe,' I said, looking her in the eye. She glanced at them and him, and then she broke off one bloom for the lapel of her shirt. 'It smells in here,' she said as she decanted the ashtrays into a carrier bag. 'Leave the window open or Bugo will be upset.'

What a bizarre family we were: Hector in Cambodian shorts and his Lanzarote tee-shirt, me in rigidly filthy denim, Xanthe in rhinestone-studded sunglasses, the trenchcoated Eric, who was waiting for us at the bottom of the stairs, as flat and rectangular as his credit cards. Like a compressing line of railway trucks, we almost fell into him as he stopped outside a brasserie on the rue de Buci. A surly waiter in an ankle-length apron led us to the indoor corner table where Mrs Bugler was already installed.

'Ah, les enfants!' she whooped, patting the seats on either side of her. 'I'm really here. Isn't it wonderful?'

Apparently Bertie Bugler was conscious enough to have licensed his Persephone's trip. When my skull and all of our cheeks had been pecked with a vigorous je ne sais quoi she clicked her fingers at Eric Lennox, who began to harass and

213

hurry our misfortunate waiter. His accent was uncompromisingly American, but his French was fluent. He sent back Xanthe's salad because in his opinion there was too much dressing on it and I had to fight to keep a handsome omelette, which no one had ordered but which I had become anxious to defend. As soon as we had something on our plates, he cleared his throat to address the other male present.

'So what are your ideas for the future . . . ?' We all heard the silent 'young man'.

'Hector is just bursting with talent,' Mrs Bugler insisted, 'aren't you, chéri? He's so good with his eyes and his ears and of course,' she lifted up a pliant paw, 'his hands.' But, as I watched Hector, still stuffing his face with his free hand, I wasn't so sure it was talent he was bursting with.

'Yeah,' he eventually obliged us with, 'I'm doin' pills.'

'Pardon me. I didn't quite catch that.'

None of us had. Hector wiped his mouth with the back of his hand and repeated: 'Pills, you know, tranks, Valiums. My mum has them. I'm going to make giant pills.'

So he did have a soul. Even Eric was impressed. He said pill sculptures were a neat idea and that he didn't personally know anyone who had done that before.

'It's brilliant,' I said with complete sincerity, 'I mean there's a whole movement about that, sedatives for stroppy women.'

'Yes indeed.' Mrs Bugler was beaming. 'In fact I've arranged his first public exhibition.'

'Really?' Eric was looking sceptical.

'Oh yes. I've been working on a little plan, a sort of show, at one of the larger branches of Denton's Pharmacies. Maybe in the main window of their Bond Street branch. Bertie has some shares, you know.'

'But that's not really right, is it? If Hector's making a political point, wouldn't that be a bit of a compromise, I mean a contradiction . . .'

'Oh, my dear child. When it comes to the contradictions de la vie, one just wouldn't know where to begin . . .' She glanced over at Xanthe who was nibbling a purple-bladed forefinger with some intensity. Already, the strain of doing without a cigarette was telling, or maybe Eric Lennox liked the nails nice and jagged. Anyhow, Xanthe wasn't going to pronounce on the integrity of having Hector's pill sculptures on display at a major retail outlet for tranquillisers and, quite suddenly, I wasn't really bothered.

As soon as the waiter had removed our plates, Xanthe wedged a cigarette between her lips. We watched her lighting up. Eugene claimed that for smoking, Xanthe had a Papal Dispensation, but Eric Lennox wasn't having any of that. He leaned across the table and wrenched the cigarette out of Xanthe's mouth. Then, with his big coat flapping round him, he did a little stubbing-out dance on the tiled floor. Ignoring this performance, Xanthe smiled to herself, but she didn't immediately search for a replacement.

'Now Eric,' said Mrs Bugler nervously, 'I want you to take us to see Lydia Delgado's Giacometti, you too, Jacinta? I'm sure you would be very welcome. Are you having a lovely time?'

'Lovely, very educational.' I gave her a dopey smile. 'But I'm afraid I have to do some shopping this afternoon.'

Mrs Bugler nodded solemnly. That was the sort of obligation she could respect, and even encourage. She rummaged round in her bag and slipped me another wad of cash. Once again, Jacinta Murphy was a gooseberry, but a bribed and sophisticated species of gooseberry. Eugene was right. There was so much more to life than Mrs Duggan's kitchen. I felt a rush of gratitude for him. The fact that I was lunching with aliens in Paris instead of doing a computer course, it was all down to Eugene.

As soon as Eric had done his acrobatics over the bill, the others sloped off. Then I flashed a smile at our waiter, who was conciliated enough to bring me a large creamy coffee. I was slim and free and apathetic. After months of scraping and gouging to no avail, Hector the verruca had vanished.

*   *   *

215

I went home on my own. At Heathrow I was detained for an hour on account of being rucksack Irish and in possession of an unusual present. I had a Toulouse-Lautrec poster for Fin de Siècle, a set of goats' cheeses for Eugene and a replica of a French Revolutionary sampler for Ma. But for Mrs Duggan and her onions I'd lashed out on a serial killer's sickle knife.

It was time for elevenses when I reached Hebden Street. As I dumped my bag in the hall I could hear my mother's voice from the bathroom.

> A blacksmith courted me
> Nine months and better
> He fairly won my heart
> Wrote me a letter
> With his hammer in . . .

'It's me. I'm back.'

She yelled that she'd be out of the bathroom in a minute.

Down in the basement, mesmerised by the scented clatter of a brand new tumble dryer, I found Mrs Duggan. Under her big chair, on the shawl Amelia had brought from Spain, Barca was asleep.

'Come on in, Jacinta. Welcome back. Give us a kiss. Did you hear the racket up there? She's been bawling her Magnificat ever since the elk took her off shopping in Brent Cross. I don't like to think about what her spirit's rejoicing in. Did you have a nice time, anyway?'

'Oh yes, very nice, very educational, and no mosquitoes. The apartment's sweet, if a bit on the small side, and the cistern makes a terrible noise.'

'A cistern's music compared with the bumps and thumps going on here at night . . .' The hard eyes rested on mine for a moment. 'Still, I'm glad you had a break. It's good to have a . . .'

'What's good?' asked Ma. Because of the wet pearl varnish

on her nails she had to kiss me with her arms extended like a sleepwalker's.

'Paris.'

'Great stuff. Did you get to Les Invalides?'

'I did. No candles to light though.'

Mrs Duggan got her frying pan down and began to hunt round the kitchen for the makings of a valkyrie's breakfast.

'Oh, Dymphna, use the Canadian rashers, in the Marks & Spencers packet.'

'Blinking Marks & Spencers! Do you know what, Jacinta? I've had to buy a new bin on account of the rubbish she's been buying the food in.'

'Ha! That's not the only new thing here, Jacinta. You should see the tiles Damian's got. Between us we're going to turn over the slop room.' Then because her nails were dry, Ma started to prod me. My skull had fuzzed over. They were both glad about that. But I was thinner, that caused concern in Mrs Duggan, jealousy in Ma.

'Here am I, fatter and fatter, and my only daughter's defying gravity.'

'Oh, Ma! Shut up! You're neurotic.'

'And what's wrong with that? I'm a perfectly natural neurotic.'

'Amen,' said Mrs Duggan. 'On the whole it looks as if the little holiday was a tonic for Jacinta.'

'Yes, and now you should have one.' Ma was pointing at the travel brochures on the table. 'Tell her Jacinta. She won't listen to me.'

Mrs Duggan did let Ma take over the frying, but she wouldn't be dowagered that easily. 'I'm not going anywhere 'til Jacinta's properly started. Tell me, did you meet that Mr Lennox while you were over there?'

'Oh yes. He was very kind. Took us all out to lunch.'

'Ah, that was nice of him.'

'Yes, it was.'

'I, and your mother of course, we were hoping he'd take you around a bit.'

'Well, he was rather busy, in fact, and I suppose he and Xanthe had a lot of things to be doing together.'

'Oh my God!' That was Ma's reaction to the egg meandering round an unfamiliar pan. It gave Mrs Duggan a chance to collect herself.

'Xanthe and Mr Lennox, did you say?'

'I said Xanthe and Mr Lennox.'

'So she's tired of pizza?'

'Pizza?' Ma was puzzled. She hadn't heard about Hector and she didn't, yet, know everything there was to know, or at least speculate upon, with regard to him and his female sponsors. 'Anyway,' she said, 'the witch and the yank, shows it's opposites that attract, not the other way round. Look at me and Damian!'

We, Mrs Duggan and I, were both puzzled by this, for though we had never yet considered my mother and Mr Byrne in terms of the physical similarity theory, they were in fact more similar than they were different. It was best not to pursue the subject, which was way beyond our control anyway.

'Mrs Bugler popped over as well,' I said, by way of diversionary information.

'Ah well now, we can be certain she'll be keeping an interest in Jacinta.'

'And Hector. She's looking after him too.'

'What about that husband of hers?' Mrs Duggan asked sharply. 'Doesn't she have to make his appointments with the acupuncturists and the chiropractors and the aromatherapists, as well as those money-gobblers in Harley Street?'

'It was only for a couple of days. But Mr Bugler is on his last legs, or wheels. That's what Eric Lennox thinks, and he usually knows what he's talking about.'

'So she won't have to grease the stairs, will she?' Ma was laughing as she slid fried eggs off the pan. Mrs Duggan swallowed a smile so as to produce a reprimand.

'That's unkind. Hilda does her best to look after him and before you try and get me out of this house, you've got your own affairs to be putting in order.'

'Now that is unkind, Dymphna, really. I'd like for you to have a holiday, and between us we could manage, the dog and everything. Really. Jacinta and I would . . .'

Abruptly, as if its mistress had said something to it, the tumble dryer stopped its clatter. Mrs Duggan waved dismissively at Ma and stood over me at the table. For a few dreadful moments I thought she was going to examine the breakfast my mother had cooked. Ma was probably thinking the same thing. She rushed over with a cup of tea, which was graciously accepted. Then Mrs Duggan smiled malevolently at both of us. 'That young man, that Hector. You know, I think he might have a terrible tendency to put on weight. His father, the doctor, I seem to recall that he was very well upholstered.'

'I can't see what that's got to do with anything,' said Ma, disappointedly. It was time for the presents. She used up fifty calories enthusing over the Revolutionary sampler, and Mrs Duggan said she was sure the sickle knife would come in very handy, but they were too preoccupied with my other present, the little cheeses I'd bought Eugene, for me to be convinced of a genuine satisfaction.

'I don't know, Jacinta,' Ma was elbowing Mrs Duggan, 'don't know if he'll be allowed to eat them.'

'Ah, stop it, Maria. There's no cholesterol in goat stuff, is there?'

'What are the pair of you on about?'

'Amelia, she's got him on some kind of diet. Poor Eugene's not allowed to eat any dairy produce. She has him half-dead with health.'

'What about the party? Have you told her about it?'

'No, not yet. I have to talk to Hilda.'

'Are you sure it's still a good idea?'

'It never was,' Ma insisted. 'I'm glad I'm not going. A, he

doesn't like to be reminded of his age. B, he doesn't like surprises either. C, he won't . . .' Mrs Duggan's downcast face took the steam out of the list, 'but that's a great idea Dymphna, getting Hilda to invite the bad fairy, because when it's a disaster, no one will blame you.'

Mrs Duggan did us one of her super-sighs. These days she didn't know whether she was coming or going. But even if goat's cheese was on Amelia's Index, Eugene could surely eat it in secret. It was of the utmost importance that I gave it to him when she wasn't around.

I found him alive and well, and wearing a new blue tracksuit, at Fin de Siècle. He wasn't alone. The shop was buzzing with customers past, but not present. The ones who'd been on holiday had no money left, and the ones who hadn't been on holiday were skint anyway. Only the Jacket Lady, preening her blazered self in the magic mirror, was there for business. I didn't mind this sort of background. For my best duets with Eugene there was nearly always a female chorus.

'Greetings, Jacinta, dear me . . .' he didn't like my tonsure.

'Don't worry, it's not contagious, and it's a great way of losing weight.'

'Ahah,' he wasn't convinced, 'so, how's the French?'

'Tout va bien, Papa, and I've got a pressie for you, which Mrs Duggan says you'll have to eat in a cupboard.'

He looked down at the little cheeses, individually wrapped in oak leaves and arrayed in a handsome wooden box.

'What nonsense.' He picked one up and gobbled it on the spot. But then he started waltzing round the shop, offering them to the customers. With a grab at the box, I protested. 'This hiways and byways stuff is all right with Miller's Ingots, but I've lugged these all the way from Paris. They're for you, from me.'

'Share and share alike?'

'No, Eugene. Not everything's for sharing. These cheeses are, were, from me to you.'

Shrugging, he handed over the cheese box and sat down on the chaise-longue, where there was a newspaper within his reach. I confiscated that too.

'I need to talk to you.'

'Talk away.'

'I've decided I'd like to go to drama school.'

'To what end?'

'What do you think? I want to follow in your glorious footsteps. I'd like to learn about acting.'

'I've never had any training, of that kind.'

'But if you'd had the opportunity, you might have had less of the resting between jobs, more speaking parts.'

'Oh, I think we should talk about this some other time. Your mother, Mrs Duggan, I'm sure they'll have ideas on the subject.'

'They do, which is why it would be helpful if you were to back me up. I . . .'

'Euge, Euge,' it was a customer, 'got a new zip for that anorak, so if I could just measure it again . . .'

'Certainly, I have it right here.' He started giving his all to this transaction, finding the child's anorak about which there had been at least previous deliberation, holding it up for its potential owner, and discussing the growth rate of all the other members of her family. Standing on the chaise-longue, I began to unfurl the Toulouse-Lautrec poster against the back wall. When I turned round, to get the audience participation, Amelia was in it. She had a talon in Eugene's shoulder and her tracksuit was the same as his.

'Hallo, Jassie.'

'Jacinta's my name.'

'Sorree. Let's try again. Hallo, Jacinta.' Then, in Eugene's direction: 'She's changed her hair?'

'Change? Oh I'd say it was more of an absence than a change.'

Amelia's excess hair was tucked under a sweatband. She headbutted Eugene so that the less shackled bits tickled his

221

chin. 'You're such a sentimental silly-billy Mr Morphy. I don't know what he'd do, Jacinta, if I let anyone have a go at mine.'

Maybe, like him, I'd been born without a conscience. Instead of warming to the sight of Mr and Mrs Herbal Shampoo, I was begging Delilah for a loan of her shears.

'So how was Paris anyway?'

'Eh.'

'I love Paris, though not in August, mind.'

'Oh, I couldn't agree more,' this was our tactful Jacket Lady, handing Amelia the price of her blazer, 'Paris must be seen in the spring.'

Amelia put the money in the till. 'Time for our run Eugene. Maybe Jacinta can stay here while we're out.'

'Em, yes. I'm sure she won't mind. You won't, will you, Jacinta? Stay on a bit, 'til the lunch hour's over.'

'Yes I do, actually. I'm only back since this morning and I thought we might have some time together.'

'I suppose . . .' she looked at Eugene, 'I suppose you could come with us, we usually run by the canal. You could wait in that little garden.'

'I've got a better idea, Amelia.' I let the poster drop and climbed off the chaise-longue. 'Why don't you wait outside, on the street, while Eugene and I discuss this, father to daughter.'

'Fine, fine,' with a toss of the head and a long-suffering look at Eugene, she bobbed herself out of the shop. Eugene wanted to follow his Medusa. He was running on the spot, which made it very hard for me to level with him.

'Are you sure this jigging about is good for you?'

'Certain. Amelia has done the research. We're following a gradual programme. On the later session, Mrs Duggan's hound benefits. We take him with us.'

'Gee, that's nice. Dogs and daughters, they can be dragged along when they get troublesome.'

He stopped the jogging. 'What can ail thee, Jacinta?'

222

If he'd been up to it, a serious interest in my future, or, failing that, a serious defence of Amelia, I'd have had a go at telling him. But I knew there was no point. For years and years I'd watched my mother spitting fire into a dead telephone.

'Nothing Eugene, just a phase I'm going through, delayed adolescence. Don't let me keep you from the agony. Go on, piss off!'

'Right. Good girl. Talk later.' He jogged off and out of the shop. I was having what was left of the goats' cheeses when Eyebrows Sheila slipped inside. To stop me from exclaiming over the sleeping infant clamped to her chest, she put a finger to my lips.

'Only passing,' she whispered, 'just want to check something with you?'

'What is it?'

'Ratatouille or cheesecake? What should I do, for the party?'

'Oh, cheesecake,' I said, authoritatively, 'Eugene adores a really rich cheesecake, you know, butter, cream cheese, the works.'

'Ah, thanks Jacqueline. You're an angel. Couldn't make up my mind. I'll be seeing you, then?'

SAINT LAURENCE

e was ordered to death by cruel torture. He was to be broiled on a grid-iron over a slow fire.

The fire was made ready, he was stripped, and laid on the iron bars. And all who looked on him saw his face, as if it were the face of an angel. Not a murmur escaped his lips, but his eyes were fixed on the deep blue sky, and a light blush suffused his cheeks. The sun shone on his countenance, and glorified it. He seemed insensible to the torture.

'Turn me,' said he, with a playful smile to his tormentors, 'I am roasted on one side.'

And thus he died, without a cry of pain, or a moan, or an expression of anguish on his serene brow.

12

The Devil visited Mrs Duggan in many forms, sometimes as a No. 29 bus. Just to show Him, she caught 29s whenever she saw them, whether she wanted to reach any place on that congested bus route or not. It was a matter of principle she shared with the other carless women who lived around Hebden Street and several of them were on the 29 that was stuck in traffic on the Camden Road bridge early on the afternoon of 30th August. From its top deck they had a good view of the canal below and as they glanced fretfully down they observed a man, a woman and a little dog running along the right-hand towpath.

The passengers saw the man halt. While he was clutching at his stomach, the thwarted dog ran out its lead. The woman stopped to watch the man reining in the animal and transferring its lead from one of his hands to the other. Just as soon as he was free and upright, she set off again. But as the dog shot forward the man tripped over the lead and fell, right into the canal.

There was something balletic about his fall, a slow-motion tilt towards the face of the water, and its immediate aftermath. After first disappearing under the black water, the faller rose for a moment and he was seen to give a thumbs-up sign. His companion's laughter turned to alarm as he lapsed again, and didn't come up. She screamed and ran to the water's edge, while from under the bridge another jogger appeared. He dived into the water to bring up what was already a body without a soul. While Barca circled Amelia's attempt at the kiss of life, the sodden jogger raced towards the steps leading up to the bridge.

That 29 was at the bottom of Gower Street by the time the ambulance team and the police arrived to confirm that Eugene Morphy was dead. When the bus reached Victoria, Barca's howls were commingling with Mrs Duggan's wails. A royal lamentation had begun. The sedatives prescribed by Mrs Duggan's doctor had the same effect as the barbs stuck into a bull before the matador gets into the ring. She was full of blame, against Amelia and Barca, but since Amelia didn't show her face, the dog got the worst of it.

She wanted me in the opera, but my distress had already scabbed. It was to an inhumanly efficient me that Mrs Bugler, who came to take Barca away, relayed all her instructions. She knew about post-mortems and funerals and memorial meetings because her Bertie was forever going to them and because she thought it likely that she'd be arranging his within the next few years. She even had a wardrobe of widow's clothes for all seasons. When Barca was safely in the BMW, she did her best to break Mrs Duggan's monopoly on grief.

'Please get a grip on yourself, Dymphna, for all our sakes, and especially Jacinta's. We're all deeply, deeply shocked. It's a tragic accident.'

'Accident! You think it was an accident, do you!'

I cursed the witness who'd told us about the thumbs-up gesture and, for the umpteenth time, I reminded her that Eugene couldn't swim.

'Jacinta's right, Dymphna. We have to face the facts.'

Mrs Duggan looked at me pleadingly. 'It wasn't an accident?'

'If it wasn't an accident, or an assassination, it was suicide, a spontaneous, typically male suicide?'

I could have put the boot in by harping on about how natural, how artistic this suicide of Eugene's was, quite predictable even. Although they enter the world in much the same way, men and women choose different ways of killing themselves. The sin of despair in men tends to find external, physical expression: they hang themselves, throw themselves off high bridges, drown, that sort of thing, whereas suicidal women go for poison and drugs. But Mrs Duggan didn't want to be reminded of this, always the most Interesting and now the most relevant of the Facts. She wrung out the glasscloth she'd been wiping her eyes with and allowed Mrs Bugler to set out a variety of sombre garments. Eventually, she was persuaded to try on a black linen coat. As it was being buttoned across her, she declared that there was one thing we could all be certain of.

'What's that Dymphna?'

'He's up there now with President Kennedy.'

The assassination theory, and Jackie's style at that other funeral, had led to this happy thought. It was for Jackie's sake that Mrs Duggan had lapsed in her religious observances. It wasn't a matter of conscience. Mrs Onassis had never asked the Church, let alone Mrs Duggan, for its blessing, but that faraway second wedding had precipitated a dispute with the parish priest, she being congratulatory, he being censorious.

Mrs Duggan wore the black linen coat when she came with myself and Xanthe to the hospital. On my instructions Eugene had been laid out in his most conventional dark suit. The mortician had given his face a taut composure that was very lifelike. They stood behind me while I gazed at those lushly fringed eyelids for the last time, and touched his hand. Then I walked away and stood in the car park until Xanthe joined me. I brushed away the cigarette she offered.

'Wish I could feel properly sad, you know?' It was obvious that Xanthe didn't. 'Like Mrs Duggan does.'

'You are not sad?'

''Course I'm sad, what I mean is, I'm sorry.'

'I am too.'

'Yes. But I'm sorry-guilty.'

'You didn't push him in.'

'No. I never pushed him into the canal, but I felt like it. I wasn't very nice about the keep fit, and Amelia, and all that. It's like he was turning into some kind of ghost, before he fell.'

Xanthe's foreign, mascara-caked eyes rested themselves on me. They didn't understand guilt, but the ghost was no problem. 'If this ghost came back to haunt you, what else could you say to him?'

She had me there. I racked and racked my poor bloody brains, but I couldn't, now, think of anything positive, or new, or different. Xanthe snorted in satisfaction and her cigarette was stubbed out under a gold sandal. Her feet were still tanned. After another fifteen minutes we had to go back to peel Mrs Duggan off the body.

Ma was caught on the hop. She hadn't wished for such a sudden recall, on Eugene's terms: 'He would make a drama of it, wouldn't he? Doing an Excalibur in a dirty canal. He wouldn't have the decency to die of a natural cause.' She wasn't sad, or sorry, or guilty, and the next-of-kinship was an embarrassment until she slipped into character. She found herself a new expression, one of gay gallantry masking tragic experience, and she wore it so well, everything she did and said was given the benefit of doubt. Together, we made the funeral arrangements.

For the morning of the funeral God obliged us with a murderous sky which gobbed rain at all the right moments. In the crematorium Ma stood with the Hebden Street party, beside a Damian Byrne whose huddled bulk obscured the sight, though not the sound, of an all-black sobbing Amelia. Both the advertising agency and Miller's Chocolate PLC sent wreaths. There were at least thirty of them, but the Bugler one, a huge Celtic harp, was by far the biggest. Mrs Duggan asked Xanthe to take a photograph of it. She was a picture of mournful dignity in the borrowed black coat but Mrs

Bugler, with her sombrero-shaded eyes and velvet couture weeds, was offensively magnificent. She would have bumped somebody off for the sake of wearing black by day: the strappy suede shoes were what gave her away. Old Mr Bugler was left in the car with the dogs.

Slouch-hatted sleuths always head for the funeral. No honest crime was responsible for Eugene Morphy's death, but the mourners who had taken a day off to attend his funeral could be read for clues to his fate. They were overwhelmingly white, female and blonde. The small chapel glistened with golden heads. With the possibly significant exception of Xanthe and my mother, the deceased man had been indulged by unnaturally fair-haired women.

Mrs Bugler conducted what ceremony there was. In a fruity, headmistressy voice, she thanked everyone for coming and invited them all back to lunch in Hebden Street. Then she introduced me. The reading was her suggestion. She had been hoping for some Shelley, but Mrs Duggan had more gruesome ideas.

According to her, we had a martyrdom to celebrate. The Blessed Eugene had been jogged witless by an anorexic harlot. For proper texts we were spoiled for choice. She sifted through the lives of the saints, skipping over the formula hangings, crucifixions and decapitations in favour of less routine tortures. What about the soldier Hippolytus, tied to the tails of horses and dashed over stones and through thickets of brambles; the teacher Cassian, set upon by vicious pupils wielding slates and iron pens; the sewer-worker Irenaeus, drowned in shit; the actor Genes, assaulted by an unappreciative audience?

'Great stuff Dymphna,' Ma egged her on. 'I'm all for it. Entertainment's the thing. He'd like for us all to have a laugh.' She knew what her enthusiasm was doing. Mrs Duggan wavered.

'Are you sure Maria? What do you think Jacinta?'

'I'm not thinking. I can't think. I just have to read it.'

231

'Oh, it's a great opportunity for her,' Ma insisted. 'A real career break. You never know who'll be there.'

That fixed it. Mrs Duggan shuffled out of the kitchen. We were still sighing, with relief, when she came back with the *Confession* of Saint Patrick.

And there one night I heard in my sleep a voice saying to me: 'It is well that thou fastest, soon wilt thou go to thy own country,' and again after a short time I heard a voice saying to me: 'Lo, thy ship is ready' – and it was not near, but at a distance of perhaps two hundred miles, and I had never been there, nor did I know there a living soul – and then I started on my flight and left the man with whom I had been for six years, and I went in the strength of God, who directed my way to my good, and I feared nothing until I came to that ship.

And on the day that I arrived there the ship was set afloat, and I said that I was able to pay for my journey with them, but the captain was not pleased, and with indignation answered harshly: 'By no means shalt thou go with us,' and when I heard this I parted with them in order to return to the hut where I was staying, and as I went I began to pray, and before I had ended my prayer I heard one of them shouting behind me: 'Come at once, these people call thee,' and without delay I returned to them, and they said to me: 'Come, we sincerely receive thee; make friends with us in whatever way thou likest.'

That's where Mrs Duggan wanted me to stop. I did pause, but only for an unfocused and rather theatrical gaze out and over the sea of faces. Then I carried on.

And on that day I refrained from sucking their breasts for fear of God, but rather hoped they would come to the faith of Jesus Christ, because they were pagans – and thus I had my way with them, and we at once set sail . . .

Unfortunately, Mr Byrne was still my greatest fan. He

forgot himself enough to clap, but Ma was smiling proudly as she restrained him. Now was the time for Hector and his tape. At a signal from Mrs Bugler, he came forward wearing a smart Nehru-style tailored jacket. First, for Mrs Duggan, whose head was bowed, we had Jim Reeves' 'Distant Drums'; second, for me, Bruce Springsteen's 'The River'. After that we got Vivaldi's 'Winter'. This was the Bugler choice and we had reason to believe that it also accommodated Amelia. Xanthe and Ma hadn't wanted anything special. Then the cardboard, wood-look coffin shot into the hole in the wall, the curtains went swoosh, and we all made eye contact.

Mrs Duggan, my mother and myself were the first to dent the spongy crematorium lawn. To accept condolences we stood together while, across from us, Amelia made her pitch. Xanthe moved out of the chapel with the art students, who formed a guard of honour around her. It was like a polling station, only for this election there was no contest. While Amelia and her sidekicks, two or three besuited men, pretended to be busy sorting out the corporate wreaths, we received those mourners who were keen to earn the free lunch.

As soon as it was obvious that our party was going to get the majority of votes, Mrs Duggan defrosted herself. She knew the 29's passengers and the Goat regulars, and she knew the Fin de Sièclers by sight, so she made most of the introductions. But first we met a stranger to all of us, a woman who arranged life drawing classes at Holloway College. She had no idea what a large family Eugene had, of his work for charity, or his career as a filmstar. Ma did nothing to soil the posthumous reputation of Eugene Morphy RIP. After the educationalist, we got another woman, another damp and chastened blonde. Now that Eugene was dead, she just didn't know what to do with herself of an evening. She'd spent her adult winters knitting Fair Isle slipovers for Eugene Morphy, size 38. Apparently, the patterns don't work so well on bigger chests. But having unburdened herself before us,

233

this treacherous knitter hobbled off in Amelia's direction.

'Jesus Christ! Take a look at the opposition.'

Mrs Duggan nodded grimly. 'Hold your horses, Maria.' I held on to her. To the applicant mourners in our vicinity, Ma probably looked as if she'd been overcome by a shot of grief. Mrs Duggan made eye contact with Mrs Bugler, and she flurried over to Amelia, who was now accepting more flowers from a man we didn't know.

'What a sickener,' Ma hissed, 'it's not as if he was cut off in his prime.'

'Easy now Maria. That's only the swimmer, the fellow that jumped in, and he's heading our way now.'

We regrouped to receive the gallant jogger. He took Mrs Duggan's hand and said he was sorry for not having dived in sooner. Ma turned away on him, and called Mr Byrne over. She told him to bring up his car, so that it could lead the return cortège, but Amelia stole the march on us. Her limo was gliding out of the cemetery when Mr Byrne reappeared with Eric Lennox and a man-sized black umbrella.

'Gad, I'm real sorry Jacinta, such a sweet man.' He whined and twisted his head to one side, and lo! I saw that one of his dainty ears had been pierced with gold. He'd missed the actual ceremony but, as he was sure we'd understand, it was Zan-they's fault. Her instructions as to the funeral's timing and location had been cryptic.

'Oh, that's quite all right Mr Lennox,' Mrs Duggan leaned forward and almost tweaked his shirt collar, 'it's very very nice of you to come, isn't it, Jacinta?' Then she pulled off her black gloves and grabbed his hand. Cranking it up and down, she told him she'd heard 'only marvellous' things about him from me.

He pinkened and I could see him wondering how to respond so I told him she was his ironer. That gave him a chance to return the compliments: 'So you're Mrs Duggan. This is an honour. Jacinta tells me you were asked to iron the Turin Shroud.'

But this reminded her of the triptych. 'What about that tripleditch Mr Lennox? Hilda tells me you've found a home for it.'

Eric was on tippy-toe, looking out for Xanthe. 'She's round the back,' I told him, 'with some of the art students.' This information irradiated him. 'Em, it's the triptych Mrs Duggan's asking about. Just, out of curiosity-like, where'd you dump it?'

'I sold it.'

'Yes, but who bought it?'

'My British dentist, for her waiting-room. She does a lot of showbiz people and she figures,' he shrugged at us, 'they'll find it amusing.'

We did anyway. Mrs Duggan had been vexed by the possibility that Amelia had bought the triptych, for private worship. Now, somewhere at the back of her aquarium eyes, the old fire was flickering: 'Now isn't that something, Jacinta?'

I smirked at Eric and Mrs Duggan took his poor hand again, wringing it so vigorously that he almost fell over. He deserved his freedom. I called Xanthe and before lolloping over to her, he dug deeply into his trenchcoat to produce a cheque, for me. I shouldn't do for him in Pimlico until further notice. Then, from over the grass, Mr Byrne and the big black umbrella advanced.

Ma was already installed in the car's front passenger seat.

'Well, girls,' she said as soon as Mrs Duggan and myself were settled in the back, 'that's the first shift done with.'

In anticipation of mournful strangers with wet soles, Mrs Duggan had bought a new doormat for her hall. She stepped out of the car and straight into the double sitting-room on the ground floor. This was where applicant lodgers had been interviewed, and where engaged couples had been allowed to meet, in the good old days.

The most senior respect-payers, neighbours and Goat regulars, followed Mrs Duggan into this room. The others,

mostly Fin de Sièclers and art students, swarmed over the house like the workers storming the Winter Palace. For some of them the funeral party at Mrs Duggan's would be a con-summation of sorts. Eugene Morphy had left them at her porch. Time and time again they'd watched his chiselled body disappearing behind the brown front door. Now they could see the hook in the hall where he'd hung up his coat, the bathroom where he had shaved, the table he'd eaten off.

The hyperactive Mrs Bugler was still chief marshal. Having removed the sombrero, she got down to business. Hector got her car keys because he had to drive Mr Bugler back to Dorking. Mr Byrne was put in charge of the alcoholic drinks table, which had been set up in his room. Mr Wilson was sent off to buy plastic buckets for all the flowers, and when he came back she made him responsible for answering the telephone and ordering taxis. Mr Wilson now spent his evenings packing and unpacking a new yellow rucksack, but he was unable to refer, even in the most practical terms, to what had happened to Eugene. Slithering about on the grande dame's orders, he was in the only sort of social element that he could handle.

I flinched as I heard, twanging up from the kitchen, how a particular establishment in New Orleens had been the ruin of another puir boy. I shot down there and shoved Hopalong out into the damp yard, where he was soon joined by a downbeat herd of art students. Waiting for Xanthe to appear, they smoked and admired Mrs Duggan's anti-slug eggshell sculptures. It wasn't long before Eric Lennox and a woman he introduced as Hector's mother had joined the basement contingent.

Her name was Michele. Too many variables of age and class were intervening for me to see any resemblance between this skimpy, wrung-out woman and Amelia. In fact it was hard to see how Hector had come out of her, or any other baby, for her frame was so narrow and shallow it was an

236

improbable shell for the usual internal organs. Mrs Duggan's exact whereabouts worried her.

'She's upstairs. It's more comfortable up there.'

'My son, 'e told me to come . . .'

'Yes, of course, you're very welcome.'

'Don't fancy seein' 'er though, if she's the same as ever.' I laughed. 'I'm afraid she is.'

'Don't suppose nothing would change 'er, not even a tragical thing like this. If she's above, I'll stay below, if you don't mind.'

Some of the food we were about to receive had been intended for Eugene's birthday party. As Mrs Bugler supervised its delivery, Ma was handling distribution.

'Now let me see,' Mrs Bugler was counting on all fingers, 'back in a moment Maria, when I've found the quiches.'

'Right you are Hilda. Jesus, Jacinta, that one's found her vocation.'

'Wouldn't 'ear a word against 'er,' said Michele, Mother of Hector.

'Eh no,' said Ma. 'She's doing sterling service, up there.' She raised her eyes. Above us, in Mrs Duggan's state room, there was standing room only and, according to the latest summary of developments in celestial parts, Eugene Morphy and President Kennedy were rubbing shoulders with Martin Luther King, Buddy Holly and Jim Reeves.

'That woman's totally disgustin'.'

'Yeah,' Ma said fondly, 'but I wouldn't hear a word against her.' She hoisted the clingwrap off a tray of chicken legs and landed Michele with it.

'She loves kids, as well as animals, Bugo, I mean,' Michele continued, 'bought my son a suit, Asiatic-style – an' 'e's ever so picky – just for today.'

'Did you hear that, Jacinta? What you can do when you have the vowels and the hormones and the money . . .'

''ormones.' Michele was looking dubiously at her tray of chicken. 'Thought they'd be free range?'

237

'Free range! Must write that down. Where's my list?' We watched Ma hopping round the kitchen for her jotter.

'What 'ave I done?' Michele asked, but she got no answer. With a wave of the jotter, Ma banished her and the chicken out into the yard full of ravenous students.

'The shop,' she was scribbling in the jotter, 'we're going to change the name, soon as poss. New regime, new name.'

'That's a possibility.'

'What?'

'New Regime.' She clapped me on the back. 'Good girl. Now stay good and Mrs Bugo might do something nice. If she can fit the boy with mantelpiece shoulders she can buy you a soul.'

'Ma please!'

'Please what?'

'Please don't be so venal, just give it a rest.'

'For your information, I've had one shandy, one watery shandy and . . .'

''Scuse me, but they're all veggies out there.' Michele was back with the repudiated chicken. Ma had no mercy on her, or me. She pushed us both out into the yard with a load of samosas. The students fell upon this food, but Xanthe didn't budge. In battle make-up, with the lake-mouth gnarled into a lurid grin, she stood among them like a scorched tree.

When, largely on account of Eric Lennox and Michele's efficiency, I became so redundant in the basement as to be available for tedious little conversations I sneaked upstairs. No one accosted me as I crept by Mrs Duggan's territory, and Mr Byrne's room was full of uncurious men.

I fell asleep in Eugene's bed. When I woke up, the house had stopped reverberating with the sounds of strangers, but it was still light. With no particular focus, I began to cry. It was, as someone had promised it would be, a relieving experience. But even while I resorted with a delicious privacy to Eugene's sheet as my nose and eye rag, I couldn't help

238

myself from wondering if any research had been done on the normal volume of a bereaved person's tears, if I'd done an acceptable amount of weeping.

From Mr Byrne's room there came a stench of stale beer. I found him wading through a battlefield. Plastic beakers crackled under his heavy feet. 'Ah, Jacinta!' He looked hopelessly around him. 'Can I offer you a drink?'

I shook my head and then he shook his.

'They're downstairs. Hilda's making tea. Listen,' he took my arm, 'before you go, you did very well, with the reading. A credit to the Conqueror. He'd be proud of you.'

Would he? No one, least of all me, would ever know for sure.

The other survivors were female. Just as Muslim women, in the privacy of their homes, feel free to drop their head coverings, so the majority of the women in Mrs Duggan's drawing room had put on their spectacles. I sat on the chesterfield beside Eyebrows Sheila, who was feeding her baby. She noticed that I'd been crying, and so did Mrs Duggan, but, as they were sure I wouldn't mind them telling me, they were glad about that. Such tears were long overdue.

Then the Deli Manager from our local Sainsbury's, a Dietrich blonde with thin scarlet lips and frames to match, told the Jacket Lady how well she was looking since she'd been on the egg and orange diet. The Jacket Lady stood up so that we could all verify this, patted her planed stomach and said that it probably wouldn't last. Ma was agreeing with her but, probably because I had joined them, Mrs Duggan would not allow this kind of digression.

'Ah yes. What does last? What's worth lasting for now?' We were told, in great detail, how happy Eugene was with his Maker. 'Even if he didn't manage a whole repentance, his sins were only small.'

'Right you are! A weekend in purgatory at the very most, that's what I'd say.' That was our across-the-street neighbour, who had been on that No. 29 bus and was now getting the full benefit of Mr Byrne's measures.

Just then Mrs Bugler appeared, with Amelia in tow. As she led her to the orphaned piano stool across from Mrs Duggan's bay niche, the Jacket Lady and Deli Manager removed their glasses. In the silence, Mrs Duggan, myself and Ma, were thinking technically: she wasn't welcome, but she had been invited.

'Oh hallo,' Ma ventured, just as soon as Mrs Bugler was out of the room. 'Ophelia, isn't it?'

'Amelia,' said Mrs Duggan, as graciously as the spider to the fly. 'This is Amelia, everybody, one of Eugene's newest friends. We were only saying, how he'd have had a weekend in purgatory at the very most. He was a decent man, with such nice manners.'

Ma rolled her eyes and I saw them readjusting to catch a look of possible solidarity from Xanthe, who had stationed herself by the window. Reaching over to finger the hem of Amelia's black dress, the Jacket Lady offered admiration.

'Now I'll bet that wasn't secondhand.'

'No,' Amelia said shyly, 'but I have had it for yonks.'

'That's the thing with black,' said the Deli Manager, 'it's so adaptable.'

'Oh yes,' said Ma, 'black's great for funerals, and Halloween, and . . .' The cavalry in the shape of Mrs Bugler with the accoutrements for tea had arrived.

'Now I'll put the milk down here Dymphna, if you don't mind.'

'Lovely Hilda, that's lovely. We were just saying how lovely Eugene's manners always were. He was full of etiquette.'

That was okay by Eyebrows Sheila and the Jacket Lady, both of whom managed watery smiles, but my mother was a more seasoned heckler than any of them.

'Etiquette! Little ethics, that's just about the size of it, of him. He stole books, for gawd's sake. He was a wet kisser and a . . . I won't say.' Mrs Duggan nodded in appreciation of this restraint.

'Well, I'll miss him, anyway,' said the Jacket Lady. 'He was, oh I don't know, just sort of there, and you could take him anywhere.'

'Yeah,' the Deli Manager agreed. 'He's been to every wedding in my family for the past ten years.'

'That's right,' said Eyebrows Sheila, 'he wouldn't let you down in company and it was so sweet, the way he ate everything. He couldn't get enough of my ratatouille.'

'He got more than enough to eat in this house.' Mrs Duggan was fighting to control her indignation. 'And whatever he ate, wherever, Eugene had no trouble keeping his figure. Marvellous it was, the appetite he had.'

'For food,' said Ma, pointedly. Then, holding herself back from the brink of another vulgar recollection, she laughed. 'He was a regular rag and bone man, so he was, but he could always handle food, if some woman was fool enough to waste it on him.'

Eyebrows Sheila decided to look affronted by this but it was Amelia, the only woman in the room who hadn't wasted food on Eugene Morphy, who squeaked up in his defence.

'This is so negative! You're so old and bitter. I really think . . .' she sniffed into her hair, 'I really think, we shouldn't be talking like this until we've sorted out our feelings about Eugene.' Tearfully, she took one of the Jacket Lady's cigarettes.

'Huh, I don't know about you, wouldn't like to say, but I've got no trouble sorting out my feelings,' Ma stopped for a study of Amelia's shiny black slingback shoes, 'and I'm not that old, thank you very much.'

'But you never cared for him.' Physically, this accusation was directed at Xanthe, into whose rigid hand Mrs Bugler had just fixed a cup of tea. 'You just took him for granted. He was so beautiful and gentle . . . and I really loved him.'

The silence that followed was one of anger, irritation or

241

embarrassment, depending on who you were. From the embarrassed corner, Eyebrows Sheila made a stab at consensus. 'Oh Xanth' took him for granted all right,' she said cautiously, 'got him to sit still for hours on end. But, if you ask me, he liked it. It's what he was put on earth for.'

With the merest flicker of her armoured eyelids, Xanthe was prepared to agree: 'Yes, Sheila. He was a good model.'

'Oh! You're all so cold. I loved him. I was looking after him.'

Amelia's voice and cigarette were wobbling. As the Jacket Lady searched for an ashtray for her, my mother started to clap. 'And that's all he needed, another Mary Magdalene. Listen sweetheart, God's gift to women was on the bargain rail when you picked him up.'

'Now that's enough Maria,' said Mrs Duggan sharply. 'If you can't speak respectfully of the dead you can at least think of Jacinta here. Whatever else he was, Eugene was her father.'

'Oh, that's all right, Mrs Duggan, really. He gave a bit of himself to everyone here. I mean he was free, and like all free things, he didn't belong to anyone in particular.'

I'd taken the limelight. Amelia stopped sniffing. Mrs Duggan stopped stirring her tea. The Jacket Lady stopped cleaning her spectacles. Eyebrows Sheila probably stopped lactating. 'That's right,' she said, 'you must express your feelings.'

'I'm sorry, but I don't have very complicated feelings, or at least I'm not sure they're appropriate.' The newish baby was de-latched and now he was having a stare at me. 'I mean, until recently I thought of Eugene as a romantic accident to my mother when she was young and impressionable.'

'Young and impressionable,' Ma sang out, 'you're telling me.'

'Gosh!' Eyebrows Sheila was inspecting Ma. 'That's very mature of you, Jacinta, I'm sure, but there's your genes to think of. You have his genes, no matter what.'

242

'Of course,' I said, 'but it's all a bit academic really, isn't it, how the genes work. They're like vitamins . . .'

'Are they?'

'Yeah. You can gobble vitamins 'til the cows come home but you can't be sure that you're absorbing them efficiently.'

'Can't you?' In dismay Eyebrows Sheila was glancing round the room, but no one there knew enough about vitamins, genetics, my mother, or Jack Fennessy, to contradict me. The Jacket Lady, who worked in the library, was wondering about the etymological connections between 'genes' and 'genius' and 'generous' when we had a useful diversion.

The most obvious candidate for suttee was Mrs Duggan, shin-deep in flowers despite Mrs Bugler's efficiency. But it was Amelia who grabbed that rôle with the help of the cigarette so inexpertly manipulated that it made contact with the frizz of her hair. We watched as a little flame shot up, and was clawed out. The Deli Manager took prompt but drastic action. She seized a tablecloth, flung it over Amelia's head and bundled her out into the hall as if she were a sex offender leaving the Old Bailey. We were left with the smell of singed hair.

'Ah the poor child,' said Mrs Duggan, half-heartedly. Then Eyebrows Sheila started wrapping her baby and the sozzled neighbour said she had to be going. To see them off, Mrs Duggan rose from her seat. We got one more account of Eugene Morphy's status in heaven.

Whatever they had been during his time on earth, his sexual options up there were decidedly male. By now he was enjoying the company of Socrates and Hannibal as well as JFK, Martin Luther King and Buddy Holly. I was willing to imagine them, propping up the back bar of the Holy Ghost's Hostelry, but the pedantic Jacket Lady wasn't. With her glasses back on her nose, she had the nerve to query the eligibility of pagans like Socrates and Hannibal for heavenly rewards. Mrs Duggan was quick to point out that Socrates, Hannibal and the rest of them would have been covered by baptism of desire, but Ma wouldn't be convinced. Irresponsibly, she reminded Mrs Duggan of the thumbs-up gesture, of the possibility that Eugene had died of his own volition. 'And that's a mortal sin, isn't it?'

I desperately wanted to avoid another round of the assassination/suicide debate but, as I realised too late, asking how Hannibal met his end wasn't the best way of going about it.

'Yes, yes,' Mrs Bugler trumpeted, 'what did happen to him?'

'When his enemies were closing in, when the Roman agents were creeping up round his lonely country villa, he called for a cup of deadly poison.' Mrs Duggan waved her own teacup, as though it had been Hannibal's last, and then sat down again.

'Perhaps that was it. We were closing in, weren't we, in a way, with the birthday party?' That was the Jacket Lady again. Luckily, she was on her feet, boxing herself into a brocade bolero, and before she could do any more damage, Ma ushered her out.

'That's it, then,' she said, hobbling back to us without her shoes, 'my feet are killing me.'

By now, though Xanthe was still being a tree by the window, Mrs Bugler had allowed herself to sink into the chesterfield. 'I must say Jacinta, how very very touched I was by your reading. Charming, wasn't it?' She turned to the others.

'Encore and amen! That's my girl for you. She's got it in her all right. She was always picked for the school plays, weren't you, Jacinta?' I wasn't. We never had plays at school. But at my mother's knee I'd learnt the art of improvisation, so I smiled modestly. 'An' whatisname, your friend, Xanth',' Xanthe shifted herself agreeably, 'Eric. He was telling me, only today, how good she is at recitation.'

'Recitation?' Mrs Duggan was puzzled. 'What did you recite for him, Jacinta?'

'Nothing Mrs Duggan. He was just being nice about how I answered his telephone, that's all.'

But Mrs Bugler was getting Ma's drift, which is what mattered. 'Dymphna! My little book, is it behind you?'

Obligingly, Mrs Duggan got up and out from behind the flowers in order to reach for the large and leatherbound volume which had been acting as a door-stop. It was a scrapbook about the making of Jack Fennessy's *Patrick* from a walk-on floosie's point of view. Mrs Duggan heaved it out into the middle of the floor and everyone except Xanthe craned over it.

Mrs Duggan's house was plastered with framed stills of Eugene as Saint Patrick, and she had a biscuit tin full of newspaper clippings, so the only new material before us was fake bearskin. Confronted by one pin-up after another, of a gorgeous flame-haired Hilda in a furry halterneck bikini, Mrs Duggan decided to linger over a photograph of four children on horseback.

'Now there's horseflesh for you,' she exclaimed, 'just look at the cut of them!'

The riders were junior Fennessys. Mrs Bugler was ever so fond of young people, but of all the young people she knew, none could compare with Jack's severely gifted children. Bertrand was a tip-top philologist at Yale and Brigitte was a psycho-therapist of such repute that her child prodigy clients had to have their appointments made at birth. Greta was 'in ceramics', doing dinner plates for clumsy socialites, and the youngest, dear darling Malachy, he was a hermit in Iceland, living on lentils as he honed the thirtieth draft of his screenplay about the life of Saint Brigid.

Mrs Duggan, for one, didn't want to hear about the rest. She got us back to what was between the riders' legs.

'Lovely lovely animals! Didn't he have a great eye for them?'

'Lovely lovely legs,' Ma had walloped through the album

245

until we were looking down on another pagan Hilda. 'He had an eye for them an' all.'

'Oh yes indeed,' Mrs Bugler was rubbing the silver brooch on her lapel. It was a Celtic cross.

'That's nice Hilda, isn't it Maria, tasteful.'

'Do you think so? It's only of sentimental value. Jack gave it to me, as a petite chose, a souvenir of . . .' she squirmed coyly, 'our work together.'

'Aah!' Ma was adoring the little brooch. 'He was very generous like that, wasn't he?'

'Now I mustn't be disloyal. After all, Eugene was, really, rather exploited.'

'A natural martyr, through and through . . .' Mrs Duggan was off again, but Ma's silence was a diversion. From under her blouse she'd produced a golden chain and dangling out of it there was a gold Celtic cross.

'I've never seen that before?'

'Oh, haven't you Jacinta? Well, I'm not sentimental, or religious neither,' she smirked over at Mrs Bugler, 'but, as I was rooting round, before coming over, I found it and, I don't know, for old times' sake I put it on.'

'And where did you get it Maria?' Hoping for a closer inspection, Mrs Duggan leaned forward, but the cross was no longer on show. Ma had it in her fist.

'Where do you think Dymphna?'

While Mrs Duggan was thinking, Mrs Bugler grabbed the ball: 'Jack must have known you awfully well,' she said, staring from Ma to me, and then back again, 'you must have been such good friends.'

Ma shrugged. The butter in her mouth was melting fast. 'For all the good it did me, or anyone. I'm always telling Jacinta here to mind out for randy Americans.'

'Maria!' Mrs Duggan was making another lunge for the cross when the voice inside Xanthe said: 'It is time for me to go.' Then, as portentously as any statue come to life, she moved across the room to take the cross off my unresisting

246

mother and toss it into my lap. 'Jacinta should have it.'

'Ah now there's an idea.' A happy Mrs Duggan settled back into her chair. 'It'll go nicely with the ear-rings.' She knew the odds. The cross left to Maria when Jack dumped her would complement the ear-rings dumped by Hilda after her disappointing night with Eugene. These nasty receipts were mine to keep and play with, the stake for a nice, each-way double bet.

SAINT MARANA AND SAINT CYRA

arana and Cyra, two women of Beraea, of noble birth, left their homes, found a little roofless hovel near the city, walled up the door with stones, plastered it over with clay, and left only a narrow slit for a window, through which they might receive food. They only spoke to those who came to see them once a year, at Pentecost. Not content with the squalor and solitude of their hut, they loaded themselves with masses of iron which bent them double.

Theodoret, who narrates this, was wont to look through the chink at the revolting sight of the ghastly women walled in, a mass of filth, crushed double with great rings and chains of iron. Thus they spent forty-two years, and then a yearning came on them to come forth and visit Jerusalem. The little door was accordingly broken open, and they crawled forth, visited the holy city, and crawled back again. Then they went

249

off to visit the church of Saint Thecla in Isauria. When they died is not known. They were, probably, alive still when Theodoret wrote.

13

Mrs Duggan got great wear out of the black linen coat. She wore it to Bertie Bugler's funeral and she had it on again when she came with me to collect Eugene's ashes. Of venues to consider, we had a list as long as Ma's arm. It began at the Hill of Tara and finished at the local job centre. The choice was mine and at first I thought of ducking it by distributing the ashes in no particular place. Like the relics of Saint Bartholomew, they could be sent out to all his friends, in economical little sachets, so many milligrams for so many pints, or hot dinners. But, in the end, it was easiest to do the decent thing, and that meant the canal, a Seine for Eugene Morphy's Napoleon.

We put the plastic urn in the shopping trolley and walked as far as the Camden Road, where we were met by Ma and Mr Byrne. From the bridge we could see Amelia's bench, 'in memory of Eugene Morphy who so loved this spot'. Xanthe was already sitting, bolt upright, at one end of it. Ma and Mrs Duggan sat at the other end while I got the urn out of the trolley. It was then that Hector and a panting Hilda Bugler, clothed in the canary yellow that marked her liberation from the nether realm, caught up with us. They stood beside Mr Byrne.

Everyone got a fistful of ashes to fling at the stagnant, slow-moving water. But after that there was still an embarrassing quantity left. I decanted this residue straight from the tub. The ashes floated like scum on the canal surface. Insouciant pigeons flocked overhead, ready to try anything, but the coots on the far side kept a tactful distance.

251

The others weren't sure about it. Mrs Duggan was afraid it was illegal. She thought you were supposed to get permission to dump ashes in public places. At least Ma's scepticism was silent. Only Xanthe appeared to approve. As I replaced the empty urn in the trolley she began to clap and then Ma, who always had an instinct for tidy finishes, joined in. Mrs Bugler was frantic because Hector had parked the BMW on a double yellow line.

November saw the return of Cortes. A Mexican boy held his hand. His gold-embroidered leather jerkin was too small for him and his beard was wispy and grey. With the boy leading, they ambled down a dirt track. At its end, the local peasants were gathered and in the distance, on the main road, there was a stirring of dust. First came the emperor's baggage train, mules laden down with pewter plates and spices. Next, flanked by scurrying foot soldiers, came the junior, peripheral members of the royal household. Then, after a contingent of cavalry, the emperor's gilded coach was in view. Cortes removed his cap and sank to his knees. The emperor gazed benignly at the humble folk and one of his retainers flung small silver coins at the children. But when his eye caught sight of the prostrate Cortes, the coach curtain was abruptly drawn.

The peasants glanced at one another uneasily. Slowly, slowly, Cortes raised his head. The boy was in tears. Standing tall, Cortes patted him on the head and, then, reaching into his jerkin pocket, he rewarded him with a Miller's Ingot. The haunting pipe music faded and a voice, not Eugene's, spoke: 'Miller's Chocolate Ingots, one of life's little consolations.'

'There you are, Dymphna, what did I tell you?' said Ma, massaging one of the suede boots that Mr Byrne had paid for. 'Did you see that pate? He always said he'd die before he'd lose all of his hair. No wonder he liked the baldy coots better than the ordinary ducks.' But Mrs Duggan was fast asleep.